"What do you want?" Holly asked

It was on the tip of his tongue to blurt out, "You." But he knew that wasn't what he wanted. He needed to think with his head, not his hormones.

"I'm not here to cause trouble," he said.

"Then why come back?" Holly asked, toying with her silverware. Ty wondered if his presence made her nervous. It should—he had a score to settle.

"I inherited a ranch. Time to buckle down and build something for the future," he said.

"Sell it and buy another one back in Texas," she shot back.

"Now, why would I want to do that?" He leaned in, his eyes never leaving hers. "I'm not going to be run off," he said, his voice as hard as the thoughts that filtered through his mind. He had no interest in Holly Bennett's suggestion. He had no interest in Holly Bennett.

And he couldn't let himself forget it.

Dear Reader,

Ever think about your first love? The kind you thought would last forever, but ended for some reason or another? What if you met that special person a decade later and all the old longing rose— but he'd married and moved on?

For most people, life takes a fairly straight path— school, marriage, family. But for some, obstacles or detours spring up and alter the course planned from childhood. Given a choice years later, which road will they now choose?

The Last Cowboy Hero returns to the town he grew up in a decade after an accident that changed his life. He's no longer the teenager who left town bitter at the turn of events. Coming home to Turnbow, Wyoming, rights some old wrongs, and has Ty making concessions he never expected to make.

I love Wyoming. To me it's the epitome of the Old West. Cowboys still work the ranges and live the code of the west. Communities are close, with folks watching out for one another, sharing in the good times and the bad. The land demands the best of the people who live there. And they demand the best of themselves.

Come join Ty and Holly as they uncover old betrayals and discover new truths. Life's journey is always interesting.

Sincerely,

Barbara

THE LAST
COWBOY HERO
Barbara McMahon

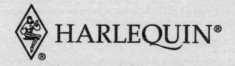

TORONTO • NEW YORK • LONDON
AMSTERDAM • PARIS • SYDNEY • HAMBURG
STOCKHOLM • ATHENS • TOKYO • MILAN • MADRID
PRAGUE • WARSAW • BUDAPEST • AUCKLAND

ISBN-13: 978-0-373-71406-3
ISBN-10:   0-373-71406-8

THE LAST COWBOY HERO

This edition published by arrangement with Harlequin Books S.A.

® and TM are trademarks of the publisher. Trademarks indicated with ® are registered in the United States Patent and Trademark Office, the Canadian Trade Marks Office and in other countries.

www.eHarlequin.com

Printed in U.S.A.

ABOUT THE AUTHOR

Barbara McMahon thinks writing is the best job going. After more than sixty books, she still loves the start of each new manuscript, and is always sad to see the story end—until she starts up the next one. Living in a rural area of Northern California, she writes every weekday morning, taking breaks only to play ball with her two dogs, or to add wood to the fire in the winter months when the snow piles up outside.

Her books have sold in fifty countries, in twenty-two languages. She is a two-time RITA® Award finalist, and her books have won a National Reader's Choice Award, Holt Medallion, Golden Quill, *Romantic Times BOOKreviews* Reviewer's Choice Award and numerous others. But what really brightens her day is an unexpected letter from a reader saying she (or he) liked one of her books.

Books by Barbara McMahon

HARLEQUIN SUPERROMANCE

1179—THE RANCHER'S BRIDE
1235—THE FIRST DAY
1318—THE GIRL WHO CAME BACK*
1335—LIES THAT BIND*
1353—TRUTH BE TOLD*

*The House on Poppin Hill

To my aunts, Barbara McCabe
and Elizabeth Gilland. I love you both!

PROLOGUE

September, ten years ago

HOLLY FOLDED ANOTHER shirt and put it in her suitcase. She sank onto the edge of the bed, listless and tired. She should be excited about heading off to college, but the depression that had clouded her summer hadn't lifted. The doctor had told her it would pass, given time.

But time wasn't something that she embraced. She felt adrift. She knew her father wanted only the best for her, but she hated his constant harping on how foolish she'd been to fall for a "no-good cowboy's son who had only one thing on his mind."

At first she'd defended Ty. But as the weeks dragged by and Ty hadn't called, hadn't come to see her, she'd had to admit her father might be right. Maybe Tyler Alverez had been after her only for sex. Once their excitingly illicit affair was exposed, he'd never contacted her again.

So much for his saying he loved her. Would he really ever have married her? She'd believed him when they'd discussed it. Three months ago she'd been looking forward to college with the freedom from parental pressure. Remembering their plans now did no good.

She and Ty had both been accepted at the University

of Wyoming. But she was going to a different college instead. Ty had won a scholarship to the university; she was going to Colorado. Her father had insisted.

So there would be no studying together. No planning a wedding. No setting up their own ranch.

Ty was out of her life.

Despite her best efforts tears spilled. Her hand went instinctively to her stomach as the same aching loss she'd had all summer overcame her. She'd never even felt the baby move. But she'd known it was there, growing beneath her heart.

They'd been so scared when they'd discovered she was pregnant. Ty had promised to marry her as soon as school was out no matter what her father said. Since she'd turned eighteen last May, she could make decisions like that for herself.

Only—by the end of graduation night, a drunk driver had ended all their dreams.

She brushed away the tears and went to get another shirt. In the morning her father would drive her to Denver and a new chapter in her life would begin. She tried to be enthusiastic for his sake, but she would just as soon stay in bed and never have to go out again.

A few minutes later a commotion downstairs interrupted her thoughts. Her aunt Betty had been staying with them this summer. She could handle anything.

Then Holly heard *his* voice. Her heart stopped for an instant. He'd ignored her all summer and *now* had the nerve to show up? She ran out from her room to the top of the stairs to face Ty.

TY STOOD AT THE FRONT DOOR staring down the determined woman who refused to let him enter.

"Get going, boy. Ryan gave me strict instructions. You are not to contact Holly," she said, blocking entry into the house.

"Yeah, I get that." His frustration had been building day by day. He'd been trying to talk to Holly ever since the accident. Her father had made sure he hadn't made contact. She had not been allowed visitors in the hospital. Once home, phone calls had been intercepted—Holly was never available. He'd sent two letters, but the lack of response made him doubt they'd ever been delivered. He'd came by more than once to see her on the ranch, but the vigilant cowboys who worked for Ryan Bennett hadn't let him get ten feet inside the boundaries. He'd looked for her in town, but in three months she had not shown up once.

Even friends had hesitated to act as go-betweens.

Today had been the first real chance he'd had to see her, and he could feel the seconds ticking down until someone realized how far he'd gotten. He half expected Ryan Bennett to drive up and order him off the ranch at gunpoint.

"I just want to talk to her for five minutes," he said. If he had to, he figured he could lift this woman out of his way to get into the house.

Her father was gone—Ty had seen him leave. And the cowboys who did Ryan Bennett's bidding were otherwise occupied so they couldn't gang up on him again. His ribs still ached from the beating two of them gave him when Ryan meted out punishment because Ty had gotten his daughter pregnant. His nose would never be the same.

None of that mattered. He had to see Holly.

"What do you want?" Her voice came from the top of the stairs.

There she stood, glaring down at him. For a moment he didn't register how cold she sounded.

"Holly," he said, his throat nearly closing. She looked so beautiful. Tired and thinner than when he'd last seen her all dressed up for their graduation night dance. But she was still the prettiest girl he'd ever known.

"Get out," she said. Bitter anger laced her words.

"What?" Her father had told him she didn't want to see him, but Ty hadn't believed him, because of the bad blood between her father and his. But Ty loved Holly and she loved him. He'd spent all summer torn up with guilt and regrets. He needed to talk to her.

"You heard me, get off this ranch and don't ever come back."

He stared at her, unable to take it in. He thought she'd want to see him as much as he wanted to see her. Had her father been telling the truth?

"I need to talk to you," he said. He could feel the pressure of the little ring box against his thigh. Nothing had gone the way they'd planned. Time was running out. He had to leave for school in a couple of days. "Just talk."

"It's all been said, Ty."

So she had known. And blamed him, obviously, for what happened.

A slow anger simmered. He'd risked his safety to see her today. As he had several times over the past weeks. She was no longer interested in him. His dad had told him she'd been playing with fire but would never really want a long-range commitment with him. He should've known when he'd wanted to tell everyone they were dating this past year, but she'd insisted on secrecy.

His father had been right. He was nothing to Holly

Bennett. The only daughter of the largest rancher in the county had been playing games and now was moving on. He'd heard she was heading to Colorado for college, not UW as they'd planned. As he'd thought they'd planned.

"Run along," the woman said gently. "Before Ryan gets home."

He met her eyes, seeing tender regret. He hated learning Holly didn't want him—but it was all the more difficult to see the compassion in a stranger's gaze. He didn't need any pity.

"Shit, what a waste of a year," he growled and turned, heading for his horse. He took the small, velvet-covered box from his pocket and opened it. The diamond sparkled in the sunshine. He'd spent every dime he had and then some on the ring. As he stared at it, the scents of a ranch provided a familiar background: horse, cattle, hay. The cloudless sky was a huge blue dome over western Wyoming. Ty wondered if he'd always associate a beautiful day with the black heart of the girl he'd loved. He clenched the box in his fist for a moment, then hurled it as far as he could.

CHAPTER ONE

May, present day

"I LOVE WYOMING," Sara Montgomery said as Holly turned the pickup truck into the long sloping driveway that led to the Montgomerys' house. "I don't know why Montana gets the big-sky tag. Look at the sky here, it's glorious."

The sun was setting in the west, flinging a kaleidoscope of colors overhead. A gentle breeze carried the fresh smell of grass and cattle as it wafted onward.

Holly smiled and shook her head. "You say that all the time. You've been here for years now. Hasn't the novelty worn off yet?"

"Do you know of a better place?" Sara asked.

"Nope." Not that she'd been to that many places. Colorado. A trip to San Francisco, and one to Chicago. But she loved her home and couldn't imagine settling down anywhere else. "But I hear Kentucky's pretty."

"Oh, it is. But closed in, with trees everywhere and neat plots of fenced land, not rolling open hills where when you reach the summit you can see forever."

"Or at least to the next range of mountains. Not quite forever."

"I'm being poetic."

"Oh." Holly wasn't the poetic type. She was practical and down to earth. She'd once been romantic, but life had shown her a different side.

They rode in silence until they saw the ranch house. Then Sara turned slightly and looked at her.

"Things any better on the home front?" she asked.

"You wait until now to ask?" Holly said. "We had all of dinner."

"Yes, but I didn't want to put us off our food."

"It's not that bad."

"Hank not bothering you anymore?"

"I can handle that," Holly said, with only a hint of doubt in her tone. Hank worried her. But she didn't believe he'd actually cross the line. Ever since her father had had his stroke and been away, Hank had been making moves. Holly was not interested, but the man had a hide thick as a steer's and wouldn't be discouraged. "Dad's lack of progress worries me more."

"Your father has to be so frustrated being confined to that hospital room," Sara said. "He was involved in so much."

Holly nodded. "He wants to be instantly okay, but his doctor says it will take time. Dad's never been much on patience and he's more impatient now than ever. What scares me is what if he doesn't get back to normal."

Sara didn't know the full extent of her father's difficulties, Holly had tried to ignore his temper, because he'd always been her biggest supporter. And Holly wanted to be the same for him, despite the arguments they seemed to have every time they were together.

"He could have put you in total charge of the ranch," Sara said loyally.

Holly couldn't argue that point. It was a bone of contention between her and her father. He tried to run everything in absentia, so each time she visited the rehab center, he made sure he countermanded at least one of her orders—just to show he was still in charge. She'd begun reporting one stupid decision each day so that most of her real orders stood. She wondered when he'd catch on.

She wished he was back on the ranch. She missed him so much. It had been just the two of them since her mother died when she was four. She couldn't imagine staying on the ranch if he never returned.

Holly pulled the truck to a stop in front of Sara's long single-story house—a new wood-shingled dwelling built only five years ago. It was completely different from the old two-story house that had been in Holly's family for three generations. She liked the modern lines and the bright blue shutters Sara and her brother, John Montgomery, had put on the house.

"Come in for coffee. The night's still young," Sara invited. "You're not going to bed for hours, no matter how early you get up in the morning."

Holly nodded. "I'll stay for a while. But decaf, otherwise I won't get any sleep."

The two women had spent a girls' night out enjoying a meal they didn't cook and conversation that good friends shared. Trying to get together with the demands of their respective ranches wasn't easy.

With mugs of coffee laced with cream, they headed for the front porch. The mild May evening was too nice to spend inside. Holly sank onto one of the wicker rockers as Sara sat next to her. The brother and sister had bought the ranch years ago, breaking away from a family concern in Kentucky when they'd found what they considered the perfect cattle ranch in Turnbow, Wyoming.

Sara and Holly had become friends in short order. Several times over the past few years Holly had wished she could form the same close attachment with Sara's brother, John. How cool it would be to marry into their family. She'd have a ready-made sister and strong family ties.

As much as she liked John, however, she didn't trust her own instincts about men. Holly shook her head and forced her thoughts away from the past and focused on what Sara was saying.

"We're going to one of the cattle sales in Denver next month after all the branding," Sara said, sipping the hot coffee. "Want to go?"

"I'd love to go, but who knows when my dad will be released."

"I thought he was doing better."

"Better is relative. The doctor says he's improving, but I don't see great strides. He still can't walk without the walker and his left side is almost useless." Her father resented being in the rehab facility trying to regain use of his left arm and leg. Every day she visited, he insisted he could continue to improve at the ranch. His doctor vetoed that idea and Holly stood by the doctor's orders.

"But he will return home one day, right?" Sara asked tentatively.

"So the doctor says. If he doesn't have another stroke. And I'll be glad to have him back. I'm supposed to be taking care of things, but without him giving me actual power, it's a pain. I've been a part of the ranch my entire life. You'd think he'd trust me to know what to do in its best interest."

Holly suspected his lack of confidence stemmed from her poor judgment about Tyler Alverez when she'd been in high school. Her dad faulted her decisions then and he still questioned them now.

"How's the training going?" Sara asked.

"On hold. I don't have time to do anything with horses or even work in my garden. I double-check everything to make sure the ranch is taken care of, and then try to keep up with the paperwork. At least the computer upgrade Dad bought last year makes that easier."

"Are you still going to be able to help with branding this year?"

"Of course. I've penciled in our men starting in a week. First your place and then Fallons'. We're third on the rotation this year. Wilkens follows us."

"We lucked out being number one this time. I can't wait," Sara said.

"The first few days are okay, but by the time we hit the Mallo place, I'll be so sick of the stink of burning flesh I'll feel like throwing up," Holly said. Cattle ranching wasn't her passion. She envied Sara's enthusiasm for the routines. She'd lost her enthusiasm long ago. Except for the horses she trained.

"But we have all those cowboys strutting around, eating, bragging, telling tall tales," Sara said. Even after five years of ranching, she loved the mystique of cowboys.

Holly laughed. One day her friend would likely find a cowboy she'd fall for and find out once and for all that the mystique didn't last. Holly knew cowboys were simply men like any other men. Some strong and true, others liars and cheats. However, she wasn't any good at spotting which was which.

The night grew darker; the stars sprinkled the sky. It was after nine. Before long she had to head for home. Tomorrow she'd tackle the logistics of covering the work at the ranch while the majority of her cowboys helped neighbors with their branding. Once her father was back, if she never saw another steer in her life, except to use in training, she wouldn't miss them.

The mournful sound of a harmonica drifted on the night air. Holly caught her breath, her heart racing. "Across the Wide Missouri." The last time she'd heard that she had been an enthralled teenager, listening to a boy play it for her. Tyler had loved that harmonica of his, often serenading her when they spent the evenings on distant fields of one ranch or another.

She hadn't thought about those days in a long time. She'd been so young, so free, so happy. She hated that she'd also been so gullible.

"Who's that?" she asked, pushing away the memories of ten years ago.

"Our new neighbor. The guy who inherited the old Wilson ranch, which borders ours on the south. Moved up from Texas. He came over for dinner the other night. He and John hit it off when they first met and he offered to help with the branding until his own stock arrives. John said we can use all the men we can get."

"I knew someone once who played that song," Holly said slowly.

"Want to walk over and listen?" Sara asked. "On nights like this, the cowboys sit around a campfire outside the bunkhouse, drinking beer and swapping stories.

Now I guess they're listening to music as well. It's sort of a sad song, isn't it?"

Rounding the ranch house a moment later, the two women strolled toward the bunkhouse some distance away. The low flames of the campfire silhouetted the men lounging around. The haunting notes of the harmonica seemed to fill the night.

When she was close enough to recognize the musician, Holly faltered. *Ty.* What was he doing here?

He hadn't seen them. As he continued playing, the others weren't talking, just listening. She felt her heart pounding. For a moment she was a love-struck teenager again, longing to see the boy of her dreams. Then resentment flared. This was her home—he had no business returning to Turnbow. What had Sara said, he inherited the Wilson ranch? How? The Wilsons were no relation to Ty.

She wanted to turn and flee, yet her feet were leaden. She could only stare at the man the boy she'd loved so foolishly had become. It was hard to see clearly in the flickering firelight, but he looked bigger, harder. His hat was pulled down, obscuring his eyes. His hands cupped the harmonica and moved as the different notes sounded. His shoulders were broad and the denim-clad legs stretched out toward the fire, crossed casually, looked muscular. He'd been taller than six feet when they'd been teenagers. Had he grown any more? He'd certainly filled out.

The song wound down and Sara clapped. "That was terrific, play another."

Ty smiled, then caught sight of Holly. Time seemed suspended as the smile slowly faded. Then he deliberately knocked the harmonica against his leg and shook his head. "No more tonight. I'm headed home."

Despite protests from a couple of the men, he rose and turned without another word, heading into the bunkhouse.

Holly watched him stride into the building, unable to believe her eyes. Tyler Alverez, back in Turnbow.

She stared at the bunkhouse door, still in shock.

"Hi, Holly," John called from the group. "Come sit a spell."

She dragged her gaze from the door and found John near the fire. Smiling, she tried to cover her rampaging emotions. "Another time maybe. I need to get going myself." She was stunned to see Ty again after all this time. She didn't want him here. This was her home. He had no right to disrupt her life now. Yet a part of her yearned to talk to him, find out if he had any regrets for what he'd done to her ten years earlier. Clear the air and tell him— what? That he'd changed her forever? That she was not married and not likely to ever trust anyone who claimed to love her? That he'd ruined her for other men? She needed privacy to untangle her thoughts and feelings.

"I'll call you," she said to Sara, then turned and walked to her truck on numb legs. She couldn't focus on anything but Ty's return.

The old ache rose. Then the idea of her father finding out almost made her cringe. He had not liked Ty before; she had no reason to suspect his opinion of him would have mellowed in the interim. He'd want to defend his little girl. Holly almost smiled at the thought. She was twenty-eight years old, no longer her daddy's little girl. Still, he'd come to her defense in a heartbeat. She would have saved herself a lot of heartache if she'd listened to her dad all those years ago when he'd told her to stay away from cowboys.

And how had Ty inherited the Wilson ranch?

HOLLY ARRIVED HOME AND ENTERED the dark house without even thinking about anything other than what she was going to do about Tyler Alverez. Without her father and aunt there to act as buffers, she'd have to deal with him herself. How often would they run into each other? If he really was staying, there'd be the cattlemen's association meetings and church and maybe the occasional meeting at the feed barn. Beyond that, she could stay out of his way.

A knock at the still open door startled her. She flipped on the kitchen light and turned.

Hank Palmer stood in the opening. Holly shivered.

"What is it?" she asked, refusing to show her nervousness. Give him an inch and who knew what he'd do.

He leaned against the door, his Stetson tilted rakishly over his brow. On someone she liked, she might find it sexy; on Hank it made her want to slap his smarmy face and send him packing. If he didn't watch himself, that's exactly what she'd do. She was on a short fuse tonight.

"Saw you come in. Thought you might like some company," he drawled, letting his gaze run down the length of her. "The night's young yet."

She glanced at the clock. It was after ten. She was shaken by her encounter with Ty. There was no way she wanted a confrontation with Hank tonight. But if he forced the issue, she'd rise to it.

"It's late. I have things to do before heading for bed." She wished she'd shut the door before he showed up. Had he been sitting in the dark of the porch? How'd he get inside so fast?

"Come on, have a nightcap before bed." The look he gave her made her skin crawl.

"No."

He stared at her. "Just no?"

"Absolutely no." No matter how much she wanted to step closer, push him out and slam the door in his face, Holly refused to move an inch. She always left some space between them, not enough for comfort, but it would have to do. Sheer willpower kept her eyes steady on his. If he took a step farther inside, she'd raise hell.

After a long moment, Hank gave a half smile. "Another time, then," he said as he stepped out into the dark. She strained to listen for his footsteps, finally hearing him move across the gravel at the bottom of the porch. Calmly, belying her churning nerves, she walked to the door and closed it, clicking the lock before she felt safe.

TYLER SAT ON THE BED opposite the one his son slept on. He'd have to get Billy up and get on home. But for a moment, he couldn't move. He'd seen Holly. Not as he'd pictured their first meeting. But at least she hadn't made a scene.

He'd known he'd run into her sometime. He thought it would be in town, in the daylight with lots of people around. He'd nod, she'd probably be polite—she always had been—and the first bridge would be crossed.

Instead, he'd seen her in the moonlight, the flickering flame of the fire causing shadows that made her all the more alluring and mysterious. His heart had lurched and he'd thought he'd end up a babbling idiot. Leaving had been the wise choice. He should hate her and her father. But the desire that had shot through him at the sight of her made him question his sanity. She'd made her position clear years ago.

Thoughts of that senior year of high school crowded

in his mind. How would things have played out if that drunk hadn't smashed into the car and killed their baby? His father had been convinced Holly was just stringing him along. Ty wasn't as sure. He thought she loved him. But it was a long time ago and the facts couldn't be changed. She'd wanted nothing to do with him after the accident. He had finally accepted it and moved on.

Was coming back a mistake?

He studied Billy, sleeping so peacefully. The boy hadn't a thought in his head except the excitement of moving to Wyoming and how soon his pony would be shipped up from Texas. Ty felt a love so powerful it almost overwhelmed him. His son. His link to the future. If things had been different, he would have another child—one who'd be almost ten now. Had that baby been a boy or a girl? He'd never known.

"Hey, Ty, you okay?" John stood in the doorway, backlit by the light from the common room.

"Yeah, just holding off picking him up in case I wake him." It was a stupid excuse, Ty knew. Once asleep, Billy never stirred until he was ready.

"You could leave him here. Maria is going to watch him anyway, she'll get him up in the morning."

"I'll take him home. There've been enough changes in his life without having him wake up without me around. We'll be back over around seven. I appreciate your letting Maria watch him here."

"Hey, she has her own two, what's one more," John said.

Maria Dennis was the wife of one of the cowboys who worked for John. She was happy to earn a bit of extra cash by watching Billy. Until Ty got going, money would be tight. He couldn't afford live-in help. But he'd been managing Billy on his own since his wife died two years ago. He wanted his son nearby. It wasn't a hardship to drive over to the Montgomery place twice a day to drop him off and pick him up. Besides, most nights lately John had insisted he stay for dinner. He appreciated the company and the friendship that was growing between the two of them.

He'd seen one or two men in town that he knew from high school, but he hadn't wanted to spend a lot of time talking about years gone by. John didn't know his past and offered friendship with no preconceived ideas.

Someday, he'd tell him the story of Holly Bennett.

Once Ty had Billy safely buckled in the truck, he headed for home.

When his father had died six months ago, Ty had been stunned to discover he'd put a down payment on the old Wilson ranch back when they'd still been living in Turnbow. Apparently Jose Alverez had made payments all through the years they'd been in Texas without telling Ty. But at the reading of his father's will, Ty learned not only had he instigated purchase, he'd had the foresight to get mortgage insurance. The loan had been paid in full upon his death and Tyler Alverez was the sole owner of a 1650-acre ranch outside of Turnbow, Wyoming.

Granted the place had been vacant for more than a dozen years. There was a lot to be done, but with the help of his cousins from Texas, where Ty and his father had gone after that first year of college, he was going to stock it with cattle and build up his business as a top cutting horse trainer. He had a list of clients as long as his arm who would give good recommendations. Maybe he should have stayed in Texas, but the thought of owning a ranch free and clear had been too tempting.

Ty turned into the rutted drive of his new property. The number of tasks to be done before he'd start making money was formidable. His uncle Tomas was staking him until he showed a profit. He'd prioritized things—first, get the house in order. Then the barn. He had two studs in Texas he planned to bring up. Then he had to see about getting some clients. His reputation of impressive wins in cutting horse events had spread and already one of the ranchers from town had asked if he'd take on a green horse that showed a lot of cow sense. Ty needed more than one client, but it was a start.

He could hardly wait to get back in the saddle. The move had been accomplished, except for their stock. Once he had the barn fixed up, he'd see about getting his horses and the small herd promised. His uncle had volunteered to pasture a couple of hundred head at Ty's ranch, and let Ty keep the calves born the first few years. He needed more than one way to make money. The cattle market was volatile, but a fallback in case the training lagged.

Ty was determined to make this ranch the best in the state in honor of his father—no matter who he had to butt heads with. He expected problems from the Bennetts, but he would deal with them as they arose. He was no longer the teenage boy sleeping with Ryan Bennett's precious daughter. He was range tough and savvy now. Bennett would find a different man from the eighteen-year-old boy he'd buffaloed.

He pulled to a stop in front of the ranch house. The wide porch was the best feature of the place, he thought as he lifted his sleeping son from the truck. He could picture himself and his boy sitting on it summer evenings after dinner, talking over the day's events. Right now Billy wanted to help in every way. Ty just hoped Billy would be a better son when he hit his teens than he'd been.

But the past couldn't be changed. He had the present and future to think about.

And right in the forefront was what was he going to do about Holly Bennett? Could he see her around and not lose his head again?

CHAPTER TWO

HOLLY ROSE EARLY after a restless night. She'd dreamed of Ty. They'd been by the river, making love beneath the cottonwoods—just as they'd done so often the spring of their senior year. She shook off the clutches of the dream and prepared for another day of doing chores around the ranch when all she wanted to do was take one of her horses out for a ride or hide in her garden retreat and forget the problems she had to face.

If she could do anything she wanted, she'd fire Hank and hire a really accomplished manager. Instead, she had to get things caught up before they started branding which would set them back several weeks. A necessary part of the business, but time-consuming and disruptive to normal routines. Maybe she could talk her father into giving her the okay to take on another man for the duration.

She grabbed a cup of coffee and went into the office. Studying the map of the ranch, she wondered if she should have the men drive the cattle closer to the homestead for branding.

Her gaze was drawn to the narrow point where the old Wilson ranch adjoined theirs. It couldn't be for more than a quarter of a mile at the river. A favorite place she and Ty had sought when they'd wanted to spend time together with no one knowing. That summer between their junior and senior year, they'd snuck away many afternoons to swim in the river and talk of the future. He'd played that harmonica for her, usually fast songs that made her wonder how he could form the notes. Sometimes the sad refrain of "Across the Wide Missouri."

She stepped away from the map. She had more important things to do than reminisce about a time she'd spent years trying to forget. And the person who had made a complete fool of her.

Holly checked the calendar. She'd written down the dates she was expected to send cowboys to neighbors. As far as she knew, the Wilson ranch had no cattle. But next year? Did Ty think he could return to Turnbow and smoothly become a part of the community like John and Sara Montgomery had?

Once her father heard the news, he'd go ballistic. Could she somehow warn his friends not to mention it until he recovered more fully?

She almost laughed at the idea. That would only prod them to be the first to tell Ryan Bennett that the son of that cowboy Jose Alverez was back in town. Might as well let the news unfold however it happened.

Gathering up the tally books, she headed for the barn. With any luck, she'd catch at least one of the men and pass on their new directives. She'd have to arrange work schedules to cover the necessary chores and still be able to send three or four to help at the branding.

Donny Dobson was in the barn currying his horse. Intent on his work, he nodded as Holly came in. Donny was at least sixty years old. He'd worked the ranch since before Holly was born. He was quiet and kept to himself, but she knew he'd help in any way he could when the chips were down.

"Did I miss the rest of the guys?" she asked, coming up beside Donny and watching him as he brushed the gelding.

"Thom and Randy headed for the far fence line. Jerry's in the bunkhouse making a list of provisions. Don't know where Hank is."

"When you're saddled up, can you take these tally books out to the others and all of you start a count? I want an estimate on how many calves need branding. Our turn's coming up in a couple of weeks or less. Maybe we should start moving the herd closer to where we'll muster and brand."

He glanced over at her. "Did you hear about the new owner showing up at the Wilson ranch?" he asked.

She nodded. "Know anything?"

"Jerry heard about it from one of his friends when he went into town last night. Just that it's occupied again. No cattle running yet, but a small herd due up from Texas."

She debated telling him who it was, but decided against it. She didn't want to have to explain to anyone. And if she told Donny, he'd tell the others and one of them was bound to mention it to her father when they visited. Donny would know in an instant the ramifications of Ty's return. Donny, Thom and Randy had been at the ranch ten years ago. They had undoubtedly heard her father ranting against Ty.

"I'm catching up on paperwork today," she said, handing him the leather-bound tally books. "Tell Jerry to go ahead and get the provisions. I'm not going into town."

Holly usually did the grocery shopping for the ranch as it was an opportunity to visit Turnbow, but today she didn't want to take any chances of running into anyone she knew.

"You going to see Ryan later?" he asked.

"Sure," she said. She tried to visit her father every day. It took away from much needed time working her horses, but she hated thinking of him being alone and was glad to spend a half hour or so with him to help break up the monotony and exercise regime of the rehab center. It was hard to see him incapacitated. She couldn't believe the strong man who had tossed her in the air as a child, who had taught her how to ride her first horse, and had nursed her through chicken pox at age ten, was so frail now. She hoped the doctors were right in their prediction he'd make a full recovery.

"See if he's interested in Helton's bull. I heard he's selling him," Donny said.

"Right." It would never occur to Donny to ask her. To let her make the decision. She returned to the house, wondering what would happen if her father never became well enough to run the ranch.

By ten-thirty, Holly was tired of being inside, tired of juggling the bills that seemed higher than ever. The ranch was still in the black, but they skated closer to the edge every month. She needed to sell some of the calves if she wanted to stay ahead of the expenses. Her father's rehab wasn't fully covered by insurance and was draining the reserves he'd so carefully built up over the years.

Already things were changing, with cowboys growing cocky and McNab trying to get her to sell. He had wanted some of the land over by the north boundary for years. Her father had always refused to consider selling any of the ranch. Now with him out of commission, the neighbor was offering to help Holly out by giving her top dollar for a few hundred acres. She refused as she knew her father would, but the money was tempting.

The old truck wasn't working. Who knew what it needed in repairs. The harvester needed new blades before the fall hay was ready and she didn't want to know what else was lurking that'd cost a small fortune.

Beef prices had been down the last couple of years. Ranching was becoming an iffy way to make a living. Did Ty have enough money behind him to make a go of it? She frowned. It was none of her business.

AFTER LUNCH, HOLLY HEADED for the rehab center on the far side of town. It was small, an adjunct to the county hospital, but the care was top-notch and it was much better than having her father in Cheyenne or Laramie. This way he still felt he was involved even when the day-to-day responsibility rested with Holly.

"You're late," Ryan Bennett said when she entered his room. He sat in a wheelchair near the window, which overlooked the grounds. Lilacs were beginning to blossom on the large shrubs near the window, their fragrance drifting in on the breeze. She glanced at the manicured lawn, wishing he had more to see besides green grass. At least she'd brought a bouquet to brighten his room. At home the English country garden she nurtured so faithfully was starting to blossom. She needed to make time to care for the different beds, eliminate weeds, give every plant a dose of fertilizer and check the irrigation. Maybe she'd carve out a few minutes to do some stopgap weeding when she got home. Her father loved the flowers. Other summers they often sat in the garden after dinner. Would they this summer?

"Hello to you, too," she said, bending to give him a kiss on his cheek. "How are you today?"

"Still in this damn blasted chair," he growled.

"Dad, it takes time, you've heard the doctor. But you are going to get better. Some people here aren't so lucky."

"The doctor's too young to know what he's talking about. It seems like I have been stuck here forever."

"Then call in another specialist," she said, taking the flowers to the small sink and refilling the sturdy vase. She placed it on the bedside table and sat in the visitor's chair. They'd had this discussion more times than she could count. It seemed to be a part of the daily routine.

"Thanks for the flowers. They're the only bright spot in this room."

"It's a nice place, Dad. Concentrate on getting better, not the decor."

"What's going on at the ranch?" he asked.

Holly began relating the plans for branding at the local ranches. She knew he liked to visit with his cronies and discuss everything under the sun at this time of year. They usually sat on their horses, to one side of the activity, and watched as the younger men caught, castrated and branded the calves. Sometimes they bet on which cowboy would get the most calves, or who could rope them with the fewest misses. It had to be hard to be cooped up inside and left out of it all this year.

"Those Montgomerys don't know what they're up to," he said when she mentioned they were first up on the rotation.

"They're learning. They have a good number of calves. That bull John got last year throws true. It takes time—and better beef prices to build fast."

"You could do worse than to hook up with John Montgomery," her father said.

Holly sighed and shook her head. "It's not going to happen, so forget it."

"Donny was in here last night. Says we're missing some cattle."

"Now how would he know that? And why not tell me?" Holly bristled. Darn, why wouldn't the men report anything to her?

"Still my ranch," Ryan said.

"I know you own it, Dad, but I'm doing my best to keep it going while you're here." She had to work to hide her frustration. Some days she wondered why she bothered trying. Her dad was of the school that believed men ruled the world.

"Women can't run a place full of men," he said predictably.

"Fine, then appoint a manager and let *him* run it." Holly was getting tired of this. If he didn't trust her, let him find someone he did so she could go back to doing what she loved.

"No one would look after it like you. You're family. It'll all be yours one day," Ryan said gruffly.

"Not for a long time, I hope." She watched him closely. He was beginning to look better.

"You need to get working on making me a grandfather."

"Dad, let's not have that discussion again."

"Hell, Holly, you find a good man and settle down. I can't believe you let that no-good cowboy ruin your life ten years ago."

"It's hardly ruined. I like my life. Or I do when you're home." What would he say if she told him Ty was back?

"You're no closer to getting married than you were when you graduated college."

"Being married isn't the be-all and end-all," she retorted. "Besides, there aren't a whole lot of eligible men around Turnbow."

Ryan sat back for a moment, then looked at her. "If you don't want John Montgomery, Hank Palmer's got his eye on you."

"No way."

"Loosen up, girl. When a man's interested in you, it doesn't hurt to check him out. You aren't getting any younger."

"Hank Palmer goes after anything in a skirt."

"Getting hitched would put a stop to that," Ryan said.

"I doubt it. But it doesn't matter. I can't stand the man."

"Give him a chance."

"Forget that. There will never be a spark of attraction from me for Hank. I promise if the right man comes along, I'll jump on board so fast your head will spin."

"And if not?"

"Then when I die the great state of Wyoming will get a wonderful ranch."

"Don't even joke about it, Holly. I didn't spend my life building this ranch to see it go to the state. I want grandchildren!" Ryan pounded the arm of his wheelchair.

"Donny asked me to tell you Helton's selling his bull," she said to change the subject.

HOLLY WAS GLAD TO ESCAPE the rehab center when her visit with her father ended. He'd been more critical than usual and she was growing tired of his tirades. She wanted her father back to the way he used to be.

He told her to buy the Helton's bull. When she argued money was getting tight, he almost yelled at her about running the ranch into the ground and what damn-fool things was she doing now? It was so unlike the man she'd known all her life. One effect of the stroke. But knowing that didn't always help when emotions ran high.

She'd been calm and quiet, and finally he reluctantly admitted that his medical care could cost more than expected, but once the price of beef rose, they'd be back in fat city. In the meantime, he wanted that bull.

Holly agreed to call Helton and see what he was asking, but she refused to make a commitment to buy, no matter what her father said.

She had to drive down Main Street to get home from the center. It was after six. Acting on impulse, she stopped near the diner. She never ate with the men on the ranch. Her father had put his foot down about that years ago when she'd first started becoming a woman.

Cooking for one wasn't that much fun. Tonight she'd treat herself to dinner out. After that visit with her father, it was richly deserved. A quick meal at the diner couldn't be compared to last night's at the Rustler's Roost, the town's finest restaurant. Still, it was a meal she didn't have to prepare.

Glancing around to see if she saw any friends, she slipped into a booth. She wasn't close to anyone these days except Sara but knew most of the people in the town, having lived in Turnbow all her life except the years she was away at school. Since taking over running the ranch, her social life had declined all around. It felt good to be out.

She waved to Ted Robertson and his wife Sally. Exchanged called hellos with Bonnie Stewart, who was trying to feed her toddler and enjoy her own meal at the same time. For a moment Holly watched her. It wasn't easy being a single mom in a western town, but for a second she envied Bonnie and her little girl. Holly was twenty-eight years old and had no prospects for marriage. Would she ever be a mother?

Once her order had been placed, she opened one of the horse magazines she'd had in the ranch truck. It was hard to get enough time in a day to read, might as well take advantage of this down time.

"I'LL BE DAMNED." TY slowed the truck. He'd come to town to get a part for the pump which had given out this afternoon and arrived at the hardware store just before it closed. Now he was on his way to pick up Billy and see about dinner.

But Holly caught his eye as she headed toward the diner. Her hair was longer than he remembered, caught back in a single braid which swung as she walked. The Stetson she wore shadowed her eyes, but he knew she wasn't looking around. If she spotted him, it would have shown.

Acting on impulse, he pulled into the next vacant parking space. He flipped open his cell phone and called Maria. After making sure Billy could stay there for dinner, he snapped it shut and got out of the truck.

This was a damn-fool stunt, he thought as he headed for the diner. But maybe catching her unawares would give him some answers. Or at least let it go on record that he was back to stay and wouldn't take any grief from the Bennetts or their men.

The diner hadn't changed since he'd last eaten a meal there shortly before heading for Laramie ten years ago. Stepping into the past, he looked around, surprised to see Holly in a booth by herself. He'd have thought she'd be meeting a friend.

All the better. He headed toward her and slipped on to the opposite bench before she looked up from her magazine.

She didn't say anything, just stared at him.

For a moment, Ty forgot what he wanted to say. She looked beautiful sitting there, her hair, streaked with sunshine, pulled back from her face, her blue eyes luminescent in the artificial light. The surge of awareness wasn't what he expected. He had to force himself to remember why he should hate this woman. He'd been too long without any physical contact since Connie died, that was all. And he'd never be able to deny Holly appealed to him as no woman ever had.

"What do you want?" Holly asked, breaking the silence.

It was on the tip of his tongue to blurt out, "You." But he knew that wasn't what he wanted. He needed to think with his head, not his hormones.

"Can't an old friend stop by to say howdy?" he asked, anger flaring at the memory of that last summer. What kind of friendship had that been?

"How did you get the Wilson Ranch?" she asked.

"The Alverez Ranch now. My father bought it. I'm registering it as the T-Bar-J."

"He bought it on a cowboy's salary?" she scoffed.

He smiled coldly. Ryan Bennett had always belittled his father. He should have expected the same of his daughter. "Think only the privileged can own property, Holly?"

"I'm just surprised, that's all."

"I'm not here to cause trouble," he said.

"Then why come back?" Holly asked, toying with her silverware. Ty wondered if his presence made her nervous. It should—he had a score to settle.

"I inherited a ranch. Time to buckle down and build something for the future," he said.

"Sell it and find another one back in Texas," she said.

"Now why would I want to do that?" He leaned back, his eyes never leaving hers. "My father bought this place, I'm going to make a success of it for him," Ty said, his voice as hard as the thoughts that filtered through his mind. "So I'm going on record, I'm not putting up with any bullshit from neighboring ranchers. I'm not going to be run off. I'm not going to be driven from the land my father never got to work. Tell your old man."

Holly's eyes widened. "No one is trying to run you off. But you can't expect the town to welcome you back with open arms, either."

"The town or the Bennetts? Just because you don't want me around doesn't mean the rest of the town feels that way. I have friends here. Always have. And I'm not leaving. Got that?"

She stared at him, silence stretching between them until the waitress came with a plate for Holly. "Oh, I didn't know anyone was joining you. What can I get you?" she asked, smiling at Ty.

"He's not staying," Holly said.

Watching her lips move brought back memories of what it had been like to kiss her. What it would be like to kiss her again. Scowling at the wayward thought, he rose.

"Just so we're clear," he said, conscious of the looks from the other customers. Had they expected a scene? He'd bet tongues would wag as a result of their meeting, even though the volume of their voices had never escalated.

"Goodbye, Ty," she said, pulling her plate closer and dropping her gaze to the hamburger and fries that filled the platter.

He strode from the diner, calling himself every kind of idiot for speaking to her. He should have left things alone.

Kissing her would have backfired. He wanted that too much to risk it. He certainly never expected that instant attraction.

Hadn't he learned anything about Ryan Bennett and his daughter? His father had warned him when he'd been in high school and he'd ignored the fatherly advice to his own detriment. If he had learned anything since, it was to stay away from danger—and that was Holly all wrapped up in a feminine packet that didn't quit.

He got into his truck and headed for the Montgomery place. He'd pick up Billy and get home with enough daylight left to fix the pump. Next time he was tempted to speak with her, he'd remember why he shouldn't.

HOLLY TOOK A BITE, BUT the hamburger tasted like cardboard. She dipped a French fry into ketchup and glanced around. Several people quickly averted their gaze, but it was obvious that her conversation with Ty had made her the center of attention in the diner tonight. And the worst part was she hadn't a clue what he'd been talking about. She'd been too busy cataloguing the changes she saw to ask him to clarify.

He was harder than she remembered, filled out and muscular. His eyes that had once intrigued her were intense and angry. What did *he* have to be so mad about?

He'd used her and dumped her. Yet there was no mistaking the anger; it had radiated from him.

Despite everything, there'd been a flare of awareness. She still felt the pull of attraction. If they'd just met, if they didn't have a past, she knew she would have handled things differently.

She pushed away the still full plate. She couldn't eat. She couldn't think. There was enough time before nightfall to ride Bunting, her favorite mare, or work in her garden as she'd planned. She'd put her other responsibilities on hold and claim a part of the day for herself.

Once she reached home, Holly headed straight for the corral. She made a modest living training horses for stock work. She had a feel for the ones that would train well and the ones better suited to other purposes. Her father let her stay rent-free in exchange for cooking their meals. Since his stroke though, she'd stopped training other people's horses, not enough hours in the day. But she still had her own to practice with. Too antsy to work in the garden, she decided she'd ride out to a nearby pasture and put Bunting through her paces.

Once on the mare, Holly headed for the back section where she knew a portion of the herd grazed. Sitting easy in the saddle, she picked out the cows and calves she wanted to separate and went to work. Or rather, Bunting went to work. Holly was pleased with how savvy the horse was about cows. When a mama cow would break, Bunting was right there between her and her calf. Some ranches had chutes and herded all the cows in a corral and then prodded the calves through the chutes for shots, castration and branding. Holly was glad most of the ranches around Turnbow handled it the old-fashioned way, culling the calf away from its mother using horses.

She could understand what Sara found fascinating in following a tradition handed down over generations.

After a good workout, Holly was ready to take it easy. She turned Bunting toward the river on the Wilson ranch boundary. She should start thinking of it as the Alverez ranch. Could Ty really make a go of it? It was hard enough to make ends meet with the history of the Rocking B. How much harder would it be to start up in today's economy?

The evening was warm with a light breeze blowing from the west. As she rode, she thought she'd have to check the tally against the last count and make sure they weren't missing any head, then ask Donny why he thought some were missing and why he hadn't told her. Sometimes steers wandered into the most bizarre places—rocky gullies offering little to graze on. They seemed to gravitate to the out of the way places just to make it hard on cowboys when rounding them up.

The river was wide and slow. Even in spring the snow melt never seemed to cause much velocity. It was so shallow at one point, Holly rode her horse through with no trouble. Only a few yards away was the barbed-wire fence separating her father's land from that now owned by Tyler Alverez. The fence actually bisected the river, giving both ranches access to the water.

Gazing at the rolling hills, she saw nothing but endless grass and sagebrush, rocks and scrawny trees. Ty's house was too far away to see from this vantage point. She started to turn back when she noticed that the fence a few yards away was not fastened to the post. She dismounted and walked over. The five strands of barbed wiring that should have been attached to the post instead bushed against it, cut. The men were to check the fence periodically. Had they missed this? They carried enough wire on routine patrols to mend this small breach. Had it been cut recently?

Like since Ty took over the property?

Holly mounted the mare and urged her back to the homestead. She'd make sure that fence was mended first thing in the morning.

During the ride, she replayed Ty's words that evening. She didn't know why he'd think her father would try to get him out of town, except for Ty having gotten his only child pregnant a decade ago. But so many years had passed and Ryan Bennett had bigger things to worry about these days.

After releasing her horse into the corral, Holly headed for the bunkhouse to speak to one of the men about repairing the fence. She didn't want any cattle drifting onto Ty's land. Holly stepped into the common room. The TV was on and three of the men lounged on the chairs surrounding the television. Hank spotted her first.

He rose and strutted over as if thinking she'd suddenly decided she had to have him. Why couldn't any of the other men have come to see what she wanted?

"Looking for me?" he asked.

"The fence is cut near the Wilson boundary," she said. "I need someone to go fix it first thing in the morning."

"Ain't Wilson's spread anymore. Someone else is living there," Hank said.

Holly knew Hank didn't know about her and Ty— he'd only been in Turnbow for three years—unless one of the others had told him once they'd learned Ty was the new owner of the neighboring ranch.

"All the more reason to have the fence repaired," she said. "Please make it a priority."

"Right. Tomorrow. Come and have a seat. You never visit."

"I have work to do. Let me know when the job is done."

Donny rose and came over. "Problem?"

Hank looked at him and shook his head. "Some fence near the river is down. I'll fix it tomorrow."

"Cut," Holly said.

Donny and Hank both looked at her.

"Sure about that?" Donny asked.

"All five strands, cut near enough the post to not be noticeable from a distance. But clear sheer marks, not broken for other reasons."

"Why would anyone cut that fence?" Donny asked.

"Check with the tally books," Hank said. "Maybe your new neighbor is rustling."

Holly shook her head. "Unlikely. There aren't any cattle on that range. If some show up, we'd know. I'll double-check the tally, though."

"We didn't do all the sections," Donny said, going to get the small notebooks. He handed them to Holly. "Still a mess of cattle near the butte we didn't count today."

"Have someone count tomorrow. I want a firm estimate of calves for the branding."

"Will do," Donny said. He looked at Hank, then back to Holly. "Good night, Holly," he said, not moving.

"Good night, and thanks." She turned and walked briskly to the house. Donny would keep Hank occupied until she got inside. He seemed to have picked up on the unwanted attention from the cowboy. She wished her father was as protective of her where Hank was concerned.

Holly quickly showered, put on her nightshirt and pulled on some sweatpants to wear until she went to bed. Going into the office, she booted up the computer and began to enter the tally into the spreadsheet she used to keep an estimate. The only way they'd have a completely accurate count would be to bring every head of cattle down off the range and hold them somewhere until they were counted. But allowing for a small percentage to be in the gullies and canyons, she could still get a handle on how many calves would be branded.

Finished with her task, she turned off the computer, noticing for the first time the flashing light on the answering machine.

It was Sara, inviting her to a pre-branding barbecue at their ranch Saturday night.

The Montgomerys had become known for throwing a party on the slightest pretense. A holdover from their upbringing in Kentucky, she figured. And they'd had one on Derby Day just two weeks ago. And they'd held a big feast on the first day of spring, even though snow was on the ground and everyone had to huddle in the barn to keep warm.

She picked up the phone and dialed.

"Holly, so glad you called back," Sara said when she recognized her voice.

"Another barbecue?"

"Good idea, don't you think? And it'll give us a chance to introduce our new neighbor to everyone. You didn't really get to meet him the other night."

"I didn't realize it was Ty Alverez who moved into the Wilson place. Ty lived here before," Holly said. She was having second thoughts about attending.

"I heard that but I didn't know you two knew each

other. Anyway, we're inviting all the ranches. The weather's supposed to be good through next week, so we want to take advantage of it."

"And get ready for branding."

"Yep. Hey, bring the cowboys from your ranch, too. Who knows, maybe we'll get lucky."

Holly grimaced, thinking of Hank. If Sara thought *that* would be lucky, she had rocks in her head.

"I'll pass along the invitation."

"Can you come early and help me with the food? What do you think about Rocky Mountain oysters as a theme?"

"Yuck." Holly had never acquired a taste for the delicacy. She preferred other cuts of beef.

Sara laughed. "Maybe we'll save that for the after branding party."

"Another party so close?"

"Sure, why not?! Anyway, come early on Saturday."

"Okay."

She had to attend. To not show up would cause comment. The last thing Holly wanted was more gossip running rampant through Turnbow. She'd been the subject of enough of that ten years ago.

CHAPTER THREE

SATURDAY MORNING TY HUNG UP the phone and turned to see Billy watching him as he ate his cereal.

"Is Uncle Felipe coming to visit?"

"He and Uncle Pete are bringing up the first of the cattle and our horses." The rest of the herd his uncle was stocking his ranch with would come up in the weeks that followed. Felipe and Pete were his cousins, but Billy knew them as uncles.

"Yippee! I want Ace here so I can ride him." Billy bounced in his chair.

"They'll be here midweek."

"When is that?"

"Four sleeps from now," Ty said, hoping to give the boy some idea of time. To a four-year-old, anything longer than two minutes seemed a lifetime away.

"I wish he was here now," Billy said.

"Yeah, well, he'll be here soon enough. You'll have to ride him a lot when he gets here since no one has ridden him since we left Texas."

"And that was a loonnngg time ago," Billy said, taking another bite. He looked at Ty again, his dark eyes so like Connie's. "And I get to go branding, right?"

"Right. But you'll ride with me, not on Ace."

Billy nodded happily, content with his father's promise.

Ty hoped he was doing the right thing. He wanted his son to grow up knowing all about ranching. He'd wait until the last day at one of the spreads, and then bring Billy. They'd ridden together last fall in Texas when his uncle had been gathering steers for market. The boy had loved it.

It was hard to know, however, how much was too much. Not for the first time, Ty felt the full responsibility of raising his son as a weight that would best be shared. If Connie had lived, he could discuss with her the advantages and disadvantages of taking a small child to the branding.

And talk about whether to enroll him in kindergarten this year or next. His birthday was in September. He felt Billy would do better to wait another year before starting school, but maybe socialization should start now. Hell, how did parents ever manage? He'd ask Maria and Rob Dennis; maybe they could offer some feedback.

"Today is the party," Billy said.

"That's right. When we finish our chores, we'll come in and take a bath, then get dressed."

"Duded up," Billy said solemnly.

Ty laughed. "Where did you hear that?"

"From Brandon. He said his mom and dad get duded up for Sara Mongummery's parties."

"I guess everyone will get duded up. We want to look nice, right?"

Billy nodded. "When will Ace be here?"

"By Wednesday. Finish your breakfast so you can come help with the chores."

"Can we get a dog? Brandon has one. And if it has puppies I could have one just like it."

"We'll see." Having a dog certainly wouldn't make

anything easier. But if it made Billy happy, he'd consider it.

Although Ty had managed to get the pump repaired, it had taken time away from the other work he needed to finish in time for his cousins' arrival. The reroofing had been postponed until after branding. Ty just hoped it didn't rain before they got to it. The corral rails had been replaced, the posts still as sound as the day Wilson had put them in the ground. If nothing else, his horses had a safe place to stay. He wanted the barn ready if possible. Though with the summer approaching, they'd be fine in the corral. It was the winter rains and snow he wanted to provide protection from.

Hay was being delivered Tuesday. John Montgomery had offered a horse so Ty could check the fencing on the perimeter before turning loose the cattle coming up from Texas. He planned to do that tomorrow. He'd take Billy with him. And a picnic lunch. Billy liked those and Ty liked the time together, just the two of them.

Today, he'd get the tack room in order. Then head for Montgomery's. He was over there so often, his truck could probably drive itself there.

Ty almost didn't recognize the place when he drove up to the Montgomerys' home late that afternoon. There were pickups, SUVs and cars parked everywhere. Only a narrow lane was left open for travel. He headed to the barn, hoping to find space there. Vehicles of all sizes lined every inch of space. He turned and headed for the bunkhouse. There were a few spots left open and he pulled into one and parked.

"Wow, look at all the people," Billy said, gazing out the window.

Sara had transformed the backyard into a party area, hanging lanterns on the trees and planting wrought-iron poles to hold more lights. Several huge tables were crammed with food and a large barbecue grill was already smoking. The aroma was tantalizing. Ty knew this could be a watershed for him. If everyone was okay with him being in Turnbow, he'd make a go of the ranch. If for some reason sides were taken, he'd be hard-pressed to fight the Bennetts' influence.

"Ready, cowboy?" he asked Billy.

"I don't know all those people, Daddy," Billy replied, his eyes wide as he took in the crowd.

"Me, either. But we'll hunt up Brandon and you two can hang out together. And we'll meet lots of those people. That way we'll know everyone in town soon."

"Okay."

The men far outnumbered the women present. Figured, with so many ranch hands in the area. John had told Ty everyone was welcome. It made for a huge gathering. Ty couldn't help wondering how the Montgomerys could afford it. Not that it was his worry. He'd budgeted his own finances so carefully, there wouldn't be room for extravagances for a while—until he was pulling in enough training jobs to start making money.

Ty carried Billy into the thick of things. He didn't want him getting lost before they found Maria's son. There were a number of children playing near one of the food tables, he hoped they'd find Brandon there.

"Are we duded up, Daddy?" Billy asked, his arms around Ty's neck.

"Look around. See anyone looking finer than we do?" Ty felt a wave of tenderness wash through him as Billy carefully scanned the others. His black hat matched Ty's as did the shiny boots and fresh pair of jeans. Did all little boys want to be just like their dads when they grew up? Ty just hoped he never let his son down. His father had been there for him; he wanted to always be there for Billy.

Ty's progress was interrupted more than once as long ago acquaintances recognized him and exchanged greetings. Some had heard he had the Wilson ranch and talked briefly about stopping by to see him, offering any help he needed. Others admitted surprise to have heard he'd returned.

Not one seemed the slightest bit unfriendly.

"There's Brandon!" Billy called excitedly. He squirmed to be let down and once on his feet, took off in a run toward his friend. Ty kept an eye on him until he was in the midst of several boys, laughing and playing.

Maria Dennis came over. "I'm watching the kids until six and then another mother volunteered to take over. We'll watch Billy as well."

"I appreciate that. Didn't mean to have you babysit today."

"Hey, a mom's job is never done. But at six I'll be free to have a grand time. You'll find Rob and John over by the smoke."

"Thanks, Maria."

He grabbed a beer from one of the large iced barrels and headed for the grill.

HOLLY WATCHED THE GATHERING from the sink in the kitchen. The large window gave a wide view of the backyard. As the afternoon progressed, more and more people arrived until there were almost too many to count.

She recognized neighbors and friends. But the one she was watching for hadn't shown up. Was he coming?

"Looking for someone special or just looking?" Sara asked, joining her. Her teasing grin on any other day would have Holly making a sassy comeback. But her nerves were stretched taut and she wasn't in the mood to tease.

"Just looking."

Sara studied the crowd a moment. "Well, that one's hot," she said, pointing.

Holly followed the line and swallowed hard when she recognized Ty. He moved with easy grace toward John Montgomery, who was manning the large grill.

"I like the way that cowboy moves," Sara murmured in her soft southern drawl as she gazed out the window. "There's something about a cowboy, code of the west and all."

"Unless they're liars and break your heart," Holly said, her eyes still on Ty. Even with all the heartache he'd left behind, he was a dazzling man. Tall with wide shoulders tapering to narrow hips and long legs, he was a poster-perfect male model for the legendary cowboy. His dark hat was pushed back so she could easily see his face. The bronze skin bore testimony to his many hours in the sun.

Seeing John and Rob Dennis greet him, Holly knew he'd already found his feet in town. Of course, no one else knew all the details. None knew the hopes and dreams that had been shattered with his lies and betrayal.

"Here, take these out to John," Sara said a moment later, handing Holly a huge tray of raw steaks. "Find out what he wants next. He's started the hamburgers for the kids and the ribs and chicken. Ask if he wants more chicken or if this will do for now."

"I... Isn't there someone else?" Holly did not want to deliver anything to John with Ty standing only a few feet away.

Sara turned to look at the other women making salads. There were several volunteers working to get the mammoth meal underway. Holly would seem to be shirking her share. How could she not do what Sara asked?

"Never mind, I've got it." She lifted the tray and headed out, feeling like she was walking through a quagmire, her feet leaden. As she walked toward the grill, she spoke to those who spoke to her, but couldn't remember a word she said. All she focused on was Ty, socializing so casually with some of the other ranchers, talking and laughing with a camaraderie that was not extended to her. Of course she was just a temporary rancher until her dad recovered, and female to boot, but still it was annoying.

John looked up and grinned when he saw her.

"Just in time. Now we can get the serious cooking going."

She smiled back and tried to ignore Ty.

"You didn't get to meet Ty when you were here the other night," John said, putting the platter on the table next to the grill.

"I know Ty," Holly said, conscious of the lag in the conversation. Each man near her was watching. Could they sense her tension?

"Hope your dad's doing better," Carl Warren said. He'd been ranching to the west of town as long as her father had.

"He's improving," she said, longing to escape, unable to move an inch.

"Give him our regards," Bert Simmons said. Another family who had been in Wyoming for generations.

"Will do."

She looked at Ty. He took a sip of his beer and stared back, his face devoid of expression.

"I hope you're settling in," she said politely. She refused to give way to her inclination to ask him to leave her alone. Not that he was doing anything but standing there, yet her entire body was reacting to him. She wanted to run her fingertips along that crease by the side of his mouth to test its depth. See how hard those lips were that had once kissed her with such passion. Or push him away, all the way back to Texas if that's where he had come from.

"More and more every day," he said.

"Hear you'll have some livestock this week," Carl said.

"Coming in on Wednesday. Two semis worth. It'll be a start."

"Cattle?" she asked, startled. What had she thought? That he'd run an empty ranch?

"Cattle and horses."

"Hey, Holly, Ty'll give you a run for your money. He's training stock horses, too. Won a few prizes for cutting events," Bert said.

She forced a smile. "How nice. I hope there's enough work to go around."

"Daddy, Daddy." A little boy came running straight at the group. Holly frowned, not recognizing him. Bert's kids were older.

Ty turned and scooped up the child as soon he was close.

"Hey, pardner, what's up?" he said.

"Maria said I could spend the night with Brandon if it's okay with you. I had to ask first. Can I? She's gonna make pancakes for breakfast."

The men laughed.

"Who can resist pancakes?" John asked.

For a shocked moment Holly couldn't even breathe. *Ty had a son.* The pain that hit was sharp and piercing.

The little boy clung to his father's neck, chattering away. His black hat matched Ty's, as did the rest of his outfit. Holly guessed he was about five years old.

"No one told me you were married," she said, unable to take her eyes off the child.

He looked at her, his expression changing from the love he showed for the boy to the hard glare she'd seen at the diner. Glancing around, he stepped away from the group, leaned closer and spoke softly so no one could hear,

"Did you expect me to lust after you forever? Get real, Holly. Your father may think you're too good for a cowboy's son, but most men like women who are honest and loyal and look beyond stereotypes to the real person. I got the message that last summer. And moved on. As I'm sure you did as well."

He turned away and carried the little boy back to where Maria Dennis hovered over a group of children.

Conversations swirled around her, but Holly heard only the echo of Ty's voice. She turned and headed back to the house, the scathing words ringing in her ear. The way he talked made it sound as if she'd hurt him instead of the other way around. But the thing that struck the hardest was that he'd moved on.

And she hadn't. Despite her best attempts, she had not felt able to trust anyone. She'd built her life so it was full and satisfying—and lonely. But it was better than another heartbreak.

He'd married, started a family. She felt tears welling. When she entered the house, she headed straight through the house to the hallway bathroom. She had to be alone for a moment.

Closing the door, she leaned against it, the ache threatening to overwhelm her.

"Holly, are you all right?" Sara knocked on the door a moment later.

"Yes. I'll be out in a minute."

"Take your time. You just had this odd look on your face when you came in."

"I'm fine."

She moved to the sink and ran cold water, splashing it on her face.

"Suck it up, Holly. Life is what it is. He wasn't for you back then, and he's definitely not for you now."

She wondered if she could stand to meet his wife today. Maybe she should tell Sara she was feeling ill and leave. It was a coward's way, but she'd sustained enough of a shock for one day. There would be plenty of people around who knew of their past to make it uncomfortable. Ty must have warned his wife. If not, she was in for a shock herself.

Holly dried her face and pinched her cheeks to get some color in them. Taking a deep breath, she opened the door and headed for the kitchen, her excuse ready.

When she entered the kitchen, she looked for Sara.

"Holly, just the person I need. Come here and taste my potato salad. Tilly says it needs more mustard, but I think it's perfect." Elise Paddington called her over. The two ladies had been rivals in cooking events at the

county fair for many years. Holly didn't want to come
between them. Tilly Larson was the town librarian and
always culling recipes from cookbooks. Elise had been
married for thirty-seven years to the same man and de-
clared practical experience was far more valuable than
cookbooks. Everyone in town knew better than to take
sides.

"I think I'm coming down with a cold. Can't seem
to taste anything," she said quickly.

Sara laughed from across the room and gave her a
thumbs-up. Holly was warmed by her friend's
support. She wouldn't leave. She planned to live in
Turnbow the rest of her life—might as well keep on
as she meant to go on. She had done nothing wrong.
Only something dumb. She wasn't the first woman to
fall for the wrong man. The key was not to let it ruin
her future.

She asked to help and was assigned cutting the corn
bread into squares as it came from the oven. Sara came
over at one point.

"I saw you talking with Turnbow's newest heart-
throb," she said.

"They went to school together," Tilly said. "Ty was
a wild boy back then. But with all that went on, it's no
wonder." Tilly looked at Holly.

She held her breath. Was Tilly going to bring up
that last year?

"When life gets you down, it's often best to go back
home," Tilly said.

"It'll be good to have the Wilson ranch inhabited
again. No telling what the teenagers in town have been
up to there over the years," Elise said.

"Life seems to be treating Ty just fine," Holly said in

response to Tilly's comment. "He's married, has a cute little boy and now owns a ranch."

"Oh, Holly, his wife died a couple of years ago and his father just a few months ago. Plus he was thrown by a rogue horse last fall and hurt his back. He can still work, but from what I understand there's some pain that won't ever go away," Sara said. "Maybe things are looking up for him now that he's inherited the ranch. I hope so. I like him."

"Holly likes him," Elise said. "They were sweethearts in high school."

"That was a long time ago and people change," Holly said shortly. How many people had known back then? Her father hadn't. Not until the car crash. Of course the gossip had run rampant after that, despite her having tried to keep their relationship a secret. "I'll take this stack of cornbread out and be back to cut more."

She should have run when she'd had the chance.

BY THE TIME THE BARBECUE was winding down and Holly felt she could leave without causing comment, darkness had fallen. The festive lanterns around the yard gave enough illumination that people could see each other. Beyond their light, however, it was black as pitch.

Holly walked to her truck, tired of pretending to enjoy herself when all she had wanted was to go home hours ago. Her face ached from the phony smiles. She wished she could get into bed, pull the covers over her head and sleep until everything went back to normal.

"Heading home?" Hank sidled up and fell into step next to her. She wanted to tell him to get lost, but knew it would only egg him on.

"It's late. I want to check the horses and make sure Randy handled everything. He could have come, too," she said, moving away from him.

"We drew straws. I'll follow you home."

"I know the way."

"Sure, but just to make sure you get home safe. What if you have a flat tire or something?" Hank asked reasonably.

It irritated her that he sounded so solicitous. She knew what he wanted. And she had no intention of dating one of her father's cowboys.

It had nothing to do with Hank being a ranch hand or working for her dad. It had to do with the way he made her feel. He could be the president of the town bank, or of the United States, and she'd feel the same. She did not like Hank.

"I can manage. Good night." Thankfully she'd reached her pickup truck.

"You and I could stop off in town for a nightcap. Talk about the branding and who's going to work what spread," he suggested, leaning a hand against the door of her truck to prevent her from opening it. She stepped back, wishing he'd leave her alone.

"Not tonight. I've had my limit and don't want to drink any more and drive. Besides, how I decide who goes to which ranch isn't up for discussion. Good night, Hank." If he wasn't holding the door closed, she thought, maybe she'd reach for the rifle in the gun rack in the back window. Not to use, but to show him she wasn't going to be pushed around.

"Hey, your father isn't going to live forever. You're going to need a man around when he's gone. A woman can't run a spread like the Rocking B for long. You'll need someone who knows what to do," Hank moved closer, almost wedging her between the truck and his body.

"This woman knows what to do and how to do it when the time comes." Holly didn't like being reminded of her father's mortality. Was that what the other men on the ranch thought, too? That her dad wasn't coming back and she needed help to manage the place? She knew McNab thought so. He'd called two days ago with another offer. "Back off."

"I like a challenge," he said.

Holly turned her face to avoid his mouth and shoved him with all her strength, glad for the solid support of the truck behind her. "Get away from me." Maybe she did need to reach for the rifle.

He laughed just before he was spun around.

"The lady said get away," Ty said evenly. He didn't even look at Holly.

"This is a private matter," Hank said, automatically going on the defensive.

"Not when a man's forcing himself on a woman."

The two men faced each other, tension rising. Holly was afraid they'd come to blows. Then laughter drifted by as a couple walked to their car, obviously still enjoying themselves from the party. Hank gave a shrug, glanced at Holly and left without a word.

"I could have managed," she blurted out, hating to think Ty had seen her in such a vulnerable position. Pride was all she had when a man had used her.

"I'm sure." He nodded and moved away, soon lost from view in the night's darkness.

More shaken than she wanted to admit, and secretly glad Ty had intervened, Holly got into the truck and locked the doors. With luck, she'd beat Hank home, get into the house and lock that as well. Funny, until her father had had his stroke and gone to the hospital, they'd never locked the door to the ranch house.

If she didn't think it would needlessly worry her father, she'd tell him of the trouble she was having with Hank. But she didn't want him to feel like he couldn't help when needed. She'd keep this to herself. But something had to change. She couldn't continue to fend off Hank..

TY GOT INTO HIS TRUCK and slammed the door. "What the hell did you think you were doing," he growled as he started the engine. "What did you expect—that she'd throw herself into your arms and say she made a mistake ten years ago?"

The roar of the truck caused him to take a breath, to calm down. He'd seen red when he'd come across that big cowboy pawing Holly. She'd been resisting, but didn't have the strength to keep him away.

He backed out of his space and started down the driveway, following another truck. The car holding the couple who had unknowingly interrupted the standoff pulled in behind him. Another group was walking toward their cars. The exodus from the party had begun. As he headed down the long Montgomery drive, it took him a moment to realize he was following Holly's truck.

When they reached the highway, Holly turned left. Ty followed, but only for a mile. Then he turned right, toward home. Holly had made sure he knew she wanted nothing to do with him. Let her get herself home under her own steam. And if that half-drunk cowboy tailed her, Ty was sure she could take care of herself. Hadn't she made that clear?

It felt odd to be going home without Billy. He knew his son and Brandon had gone to bed around nine, later than they normally stayed up. He'd checked on them before he left the party. Maria assured him they had both fallen asleep quickly. And she was looking forward to having Billy in the morning when Brandon got up.

Thinking of his son reminded him of Holly's expression when Billy had run up to him earlier. If he didn't know better, he would have thought it was pain he saw in her eyes. Impossible.

Unless she was thinking about the baby they'd made. She hadn't married. He'd learned that tonight. He hadn't asked around about her. Their paths diverged years ago and what she was doing now didn't matter a damn. If she wanted children, she could marry and have a bunch. But some of the comments had clued him in. She still lived on the family ranch. Old man Bennett had had a stroke not too long ago. He was expected to recover, but for now was in a convalescent home where Holly visited him every day.

Ty couldn't work up any sympathy for the man. Anger at the way he'd treated his dad and him that last summer in Turnbow would always be there. Holly's father thought he was right in everything, just because he owned one of the biggest ranches in the area. Well, Ty was back and planning to stay. If he butted heads with Ryan Bennett, so be it. The old man would soon find out Ty Alverez wasn't taking grief from anyone for any reason.

The rutted drive was difficult to navigate in the darkness. A bad jolt interrupted his brooding on the Bennetts and focused his attention on driving. He had to do something about this stretch of road. He knew his cousins would have a fit when they brought the big rigs in on Wednesday.

On a particularly bad lurch, he swore. He'd call around first thing next week to see if someone could recommend an outfit with a grader. That led to mentally reviewing the other things he had to do, and then to wondering when he was going to find the time to still help out at the Montgomerys' branding. And another one or two spreads if he was asked. He wanted to start off right in Turnbow. Here neighbors had always helped neighbors.

The run-down condition of the house didn't show as much in the night. Once the headlights had swept over it, Ty pulled in nearby and parked. If things went as he hoped, sometime in the summer, he'd throw a house-painting party and call in some favors. All the more reason to help out wherever he could at this time of year. No one person could manage everything on a ranch.

THE NEXT MORNING TY ROSE early. He grabbed a quick bite to eat and headed for the barn. Without Billy to slow him down, he'd get a lot done. John Montgomery had lent him a fine gelding. He planned to ride the perimeter fence today to make sure there were no breaks. He'd make a start, then pick up Billy. He'd told his son he could ride with him today and he was careful to always keep his promises. He wanted his son to know a man stood by his word. His own father had taught him that.

It felt good to be back in the saddle. He headed

down the drive, opened the gate near the cattle rails and let himself into the enclosed part of the ranch. Slowly he rode the horse along the fence, visually checking for worn areas, damaged supports and breaks. It was mindless work, as long as he kept an eye on the barbed wiring. Suddenly he became aware things weren't quite right. For a moment, he couldn't figure out what—then he saw the cow patties. Ones that couldn't be more than a month old. No one had leased the land from his father. There shouldn't have been any trace of cattle for the past twelve years.

Moving on, he scanned the section. No sign of any animals, except for the droppings. Who'd been running cattle on his land? Had they moved them off when they heard he was coming?

He crested a small rise and stopped. Ahead of him lay the river that meandered in and out of several properties. This was the short junction of his land with the Bennetts. The barbed wire stretched across the water at an angle, as the river left the Rocking B and cut across his before moving on to Hudgins' land. Ty nudged the horse forward and headed for the water. This was where he'd planned to have a picnic with Billy. His son would love it and as long as Ty was around to watch him, he could play in the shallow depths.

A horse stood in the shade of the cottonwoods that lined the opposite banks. Looking closer, Ty spotted a figure near one of the posts.

He continued slowly, wondering what the odds were of someone else checking fencing on a Sunday. Most hands had the day off, except for chores that couldn't be neglected. Scanning the land on the far side, he didn't see any cattle. Yet it seemed obvious someone was repairing the fence. Had it worn through? Or was this where the cattle came from? Had Bennett used his pasture land for his own cattle and was now trying to cover up?

He stopped near the water's edge when he recognized Holly. She looked at him.

"Problems?" he asked.

"You tell me," she retorted, pulling with all her strength to make the wire taut. She looped it around the post, then hammered in a heavy duty brad to keep the wire from recoiling. "It was cut."

"There are cattle droppings on my land. You running cattle there?"

"No." She looked around. "Nothing here to show any have been through recently. We haven't been using this section since the snow melted. You see any cattle?"

"Didn't see anything but month old cow patties. Can't help but wonder who's been using my land."

"No one. Or maybe Hudgins or McNab—someone who thought it was empty. It's been vacant for years," she said.

"Still belonged to someone. Anyone checking at the recorder's office would find out who," he said.

"Our cattle aren't on your land," she said firmly.

"Think so?"

She glared at him. "If you find any with our brand, let me know and I'll transfer ownership."

He settled back in the saddle and watched her work. Her offer was a pretty good indication she didn't know of any cattle. No way would a Bennett give up any.

She resumed work. "I don't need help. You can move along." She had one strand attached, the other four still hung loose.

"I'm giving the horse a rest," he said, knowing she didn't like him being there. Too bad, he was on his own land. The satisfaction ran deep.

"Go find some shade." She tugged, and the second wire sprang loose, snapping and narrowly missing her face. He backed his horse out of range of any possible mishaps.

"Don't you have some place else to be?" she asked a couple of minutes later, still struggling with the wire.

"I'm riding fence. I have stock coming on Wednesday. I'll just make sure you do a good enough job here first. Don't want my stock mingling with yours."

"I know what I'm doing."

Ty knew his presence was frustrating. All the more reason to stay. It was time Holly realized the past was truly over. He'd moved on. There was nothing left of the boy who had so adored the girl she'd been. Now he was a neighbor concerned only with running his ranch.

But waiting around just to annoy her was pointless. He gathered his reins in preparation to leave when she spoke again.

"Okay, I could use some help. My fingers are aching from pulling so hard. One of the men was supposed to see to this. I came out this morning to give my horse some practice time and thought I'd stop by to make sure the job was done. Good thing I did." She hadn't looked at him since that first glance.

Ty dismounted easily, dropping the reins to the ground. The horse would stay. He grabbed pliers and leather gloves from his saddlebags and walked over to the post. Vaulting over the fence, he landed hard. Pain shot through his back. He covered a groan and tried to stand up without dropping to his knees. He still wasn't fully healed from the fall last October. But he'd be hog-tied before he let Holly know anything was wrong. He put on his gloves, stalling to let the worst of the pain recede.

"I'll connect a strand to cover the break, when I'm done, I'll pull and you hammer," he said.

Stringing fence always went easier when there were two working together. He twisted the connection in place, pulled and waited while she hammered the brad to cover it. He then twisted it into the other side, which was still connected to the post.

He glanced around, remembering this had been a favorite spot of theirs that year. He'd cut through the deserted Wilson ranch and Holly would meet him beneath the trees. A gate would have been handy back then, he thought wryly.

He glanced at her as she worked. For a moment he could almost forget the past ten years. If he'd let himself, he could imagine that they were still two kids crazy about each other. He'd pull her into his arms and kiss her until neither could remember their names.

Disgusted with his thoughts, he focused on the work at hand. He was a realist. The likelihood of him ever kissing Holly again was so remote it was laughable.

"Any more sections cut?" he asked as he began on the bottom wire.

"Not that I've seen. I'm having Donny ride the perimeter tomorrow. Only Donny."

Ty recognized the name of a man who had worked the Rocking B when he'd been sneaking around with Holly.

"Someone you trust." He nodded.

"I'm going to fire Hank's ass," she said bitterly. "It's bad enough to have him coming on to me like last night, but this is pure insubordination." She looked at him, her eyes unhappy. "Thanks for your help."

"My fence, too."

He didn't want any gratitude from Holly Bennett.

CHAPTER FOUR

HOLLY STOOD THERE, feeling tired and discouraged and exquisitely aware of a man she should avoid at all costs. Yet she didn't want to walk away. The fence was repaired. They had nothing to say to each other. How dumb could a woman be? Ty had gotten on with his life years ago. His being her new neighbor didn't change anything.

Ty stepped on the second strand, using the post to vault over to his side. He put away his gear, picked up the reins and easily mounted his horse. Tipping the brim of his hat, he turned and began riding along the common fence.

Did he really suspect she'd been behind the sabotage?

She gathered her tools and headed for her own horse, who was half dozing in the shade. Ty was almost out of sight and had never looked back. It didn't matter. The past was dead. She had a cowhand to fire, a new wrangler to locate and work to do.

It didn't take Holly long to reach the barn. She unsaddled her horse and turned him loose in the corral after a brief rub. Then she checked to make sure the water trough was full. They had an automatic-fill mechanism, but old habits ingrained into her by her father were hard to ignore. Never depend on a mechanical device, he'd said, checking every time he passed the trough. She'd learned all she knew about horses and ranching from her dad. She missed him.

Still angry over Hank's blowing off the repair job, Holly walked into the bunk house, hoping he wouldn't make a huge stink, but knowing he was not going to be happy with her decision.

Donny was reading the Sunday paper. There was some country music playing softly.

"Hank around?" Holly asked.

"He and Jerry went to town. Should be back this afternoon," Donny said, glancing up. "Something wrong?"

"I told him to repair that section of fence between our place and Wilson's. When I checked this morning, it still wasn't done."

"No cattle running in that section. None on the Wilsons' spread," Donny commented.

"There will be soon. And if I decide to move ours for the fresh grass, I don't want to worry about their getting out. When I give an order, I expect it to be obeyed."

Donny said nothing for a moment, then nodded. "You're the boss."

"Glad someone recognizes that," Holly murmured as she turned and headed outside. She scanned the area. Several dusty pickup trucks baked in the sun, but Hank's wasn't one of them.

The shade near the house looked inviting. Nothing moved except the horses in the corral. The heat was building. She'd give anything to just take off and find a cool spot on the river to go swimming. Other than the place she'd been that morning. Too many memories.

What she'd really like to do was get away from the

ranch altogether. Forego for a day all the responsibilities foisted on her by her father's illness.

But it wasn't gonna happen. She headed for the
house. Until Hank showed up, she had paperwork she
could do. She'd cut his final check while she was at it.
And then she'd treat herself to some time in her garden.

TY CONTINUED ALONG THE COMMON fence between his
spread and Bennett's, following the contour of the land.
Who had cut it near the river and why? Had old man
Bennett grazed on his land, thinking no one would
know? It had been vacant so long, Ty wouldn't put it past
him. He was arrogant enough to think he could run his
cattle anywhere.

When Ty got to the boundary post that marked the
change of neighbors, he turned toward home. Past time
to pick up Billy if they wanted to have a picnic today.

He arrived at the Montgomery ranch just before
lunchtime. Billy ran out to meet him when he stopped
the truck in front of the Dennis house. He talked a mile
a minute telling his dad all he'd done with his friend
Brandon.

"I appreciate your watching him last night," Ty said
to Maria when she followed on Billy's heels.

"He and Brandon are great together. They keep each
other occupied. Rob showed them how to rope this
morning. Billy will be asking for a lariat, I bet. Brandon
has already whined for one."

"Can I, Daddy?" the little boy asked, jumping up and
down with excitement. "Then I can really help at the
branding."

"We'll see. Let's go. The day's wasting away and
we've got things to do."

"We're going riding, right?" Billy asked as soon as he was buckled into the car seat.

"Right. I want you to see our ranch. Maybe we'll go swimming. It's getting plenty hot." Holly would no longer be at the river. Today was about Billy, not vague regrets about the past.

BY THE TIME HOLLY WAS fed up with paperwork, she heard the truck coming into the compound. Grabbing the check she'd written for Hank, she went outside. She hated doing this, but she would not put up with his deliberately ignoring her orders. How could she run the ranch if the hired help refused to follow her directions? She decided she wouldn't tell her father until it was a done deal. She knew he hated not being in control, but there was no question she was right in this instance.

Hank and Jerry were laughing at something as they ambled toward the bunkhouse.

"Hank, I need to speak to you," she called, stopping at the edge of the shade. She watched as he smirked and made some comment to Jerry before heading her way.

"Sure thing, sweets. What can I give you?"

"It's what I'm giving you," she said. Holding out the envelope, she waited until he took it before speaking again. "This is your final check. As of today, you are no longer working for the Rocking B."

"What the hell are you talking about?" he asked, his expression turning mean.

"I told you to repair the fence along the river where it had been cut. I checked it today and found it hadn't been done. I won't have men working for me who don't follow orders."

"Hell, we don't have any cattle running in that section. The Wilson spread doesn't have any livestock. No harm done. I was going to get to it."

He held out the envelope, but Holly refused to touch it.

"Pack your things and clear out," she said. "I want you gone tomorrow."

"You didn't hire me, you can't fire me," he said, stepping closer.

She held her ground, looking at him with all the determination at her disposal. "I'm running the Rocking B now and I say you're fired. Maybe at your next job you'll remember when you're told to do something, it's best to do it."

"Bitch! We'll see about this."

"Goodbye, Hank." Head held high, she walked to the house, half afraid he'd tackle her from behind or something. But when she turned to close the door, she saw he had already gone back to the bunkhouse. Her knees were trembling and her lunch threatened to reappear. Swallowing hard, she took a deep breath. She should have gotten rid of the man when he'd first tried to foist his attention on her.

She decided to spend some time in her garden. It looked sad and neglected. Quickly she found her tools and began weeding, loosening the soil and setting a soaker hose in places that were too dry. The soothing activity brought calmness and for the first time in a long while, Holly gave herself to the work and blocked out all the troubling aspects of life these days.

When she was finally satisfied with the state of her garden, it was almost dark. She needed a shower and dinner. It was too late to visit her father today. She rarely missed seeing him, but had needed this time for herself. Calling wasn't as good as a visit, but it would have to do tonight. She was too tired to drive all the way across town to see him.

"Where are you?" her father asked when she phoned.

"I got busy in the garden and time slipped away. I'm wiped out. After a quick shower, I'm just going to eat a light dinner and go to bed. We start branding tomorrow at the Montgomerys' place."

"You could have come to see your father. That garden takes up too much time if you ask me."

Well, I didn't, she wanted to say, but held her tongue. She hadn't touched the flower beds in weeks. She kept reminding herself his entire life had been turned upside down and he was anxious to get home and back to normal.

"Coming in tomorrow?" Ryan asked.

"I'm not sure. If the branding is as hectic as other years, I'll be too tired."

"Let the men do the work."

"Is that what you did?" she countered.

"No, but I'm a man. Women do fine fixing the meals."

Sara would roll her eyes at his comment. Holly loved her father, but she wished he'd move into the twenty-first century and start believing women were more than ornaments and cooks. "Daddy, that's too chauvinistic, even for you. Check with the doctor. Maybe you can get a ride in a jeep or something for one of the days, to see your friends and watch the action."

"I have people stopping by to see me. Going to the brandings wouldn't be the same in a damn-fool jeep when I should be on a horse."

"Still, it would get you out for a while," she coaxed.

"I'll see what the doc says about that," he agreed reluctantly. "Maybe I'll ride a gentle horse."

Holly almost laughed at the thought. She could just imagine that confrontation. Nevertheless, her money would be on her dad.

"You do that and see what it gets you," she teased. "I'll see who has the slowest horse in town."

"Think I can't handle myself?"

"You can handle anything you choose, Dad. Just get well and hurry back home. I miss you."

"Don't go getting mushy on me, girl," he warned.

She laughed. "Fat chance. I'll call tomorrow when I can."

Holly replaced the receiver and shook her head. "Coward," she said. She hadn't told him about firing Hank. She needed to post the job opening at the feed store and talk to some of the men from the other ranches to see if there was a competent cowboy needing work.

Time enough to deal with that tomorrow. She'd have to get up early to make sure the chores were done before setting out for the Montgomery ranch.

As she drifted to sleep, she hoped Hank didn't cause any more trouble.

IT WAS EARLY WHEN TY DROPPED Billy at Maria's and headed for the area by John Montgomery's barn. On Wednesday, he'd have to take off to be home when his cousins arrived, but today and tomorrow, he was part of the activity on the Montgomery ranch.

Familiar work, branding. He saddled the horse John let him use, while listening to the conversations that swirled around him. Some of the older men were complaining about the early hour, the younger ones were making bets on who could flank and brand the most calves. One or two were bragging about rodeo events. Ty listened, but didn't join in. He'd done his fair share of bragging when he and his father had joined the cousins in Texas. And he had a good number of trophies from rodeos packed in one of the boxes still to be opened. He was here to blend in, not show off his successes.

He heard another large horse trailer pull in and glanced over. Holly. He watched as she hopped down from the truck and went to the back. Two men got out the other side and went to help her. Soon, three horses, already tacked up, were out of the trailer and tied to the rail fence. The group returned to the trailer to back out two more horses. These they turned loose in the corral. Many of the ranchers had brought extra horses to spell the ones that got tired or injured.

Ty concentrated on tightening the cinch, all the while keeping an eye on her.

Her hair was in a single braid down her back again. Ten years ago, he remembered it flowing around her shoulders, remembered grabbing a handful and wrapping it around his hand, savoring the satiny texture. Her hat was pulled low to keep off the sun, but he could tell her dark tan came from years of sunshine. He tried to drag his mind away from the woman who barely gave him the time of day.

Holly seemed friendly with the others. Everyone called a greeting, which she freely returned.

John rode into the center of the yard and gave an ear-piercing whistle. "Listen up." The talk died down. "For the last week my men have been moving the herd into the section closest to the house. Some of the cows aren't happy with that, so they're cantankerous. I want Carl and Norris to start up the fires and heat the branding irons. Pick some men to help you. The men from the Rocking B, join with Warren's men and start on the west side, culling the calves and keeping them separated until we get them fixed. Tyler, you ride with them. Men from Fallon's spread and Wilkens', take the east side and funnel them in through the low ravine. That'll make it easier to control, as we found out last year. My men, bring in stragglers and help at the fires. Any questions?"

Sara rode up. "And don't forget, dinner here tonight and bedding for anyone who wants to stay."

Ty mounted and sat, watching Holly as she absorbed John's directions. Would she ride with him or find a reason to be elsewhere?

"Rocking B's here," she called, throwing a look of challenge in his direction. He urged his horse forward, pulling in behind Randy.

The cowboy turned to offer a greeting, the words dying when he recognized Ty.

"Didn't know you were back," Randy said, his eyes narrowing as he took in Ty's rig and horse. "Ryan know you're here?"

"How do I know what he knows," Ty responded. "Didn't Holly tell you, I own the old Wilson spread. I'm back for good."

"Holy shit," Randy said. He leaned over the far side of his horse and spat out a stream of tobacco juice. Sitting upright, he glanced at Holly. "There'll be hell to pay."

"It's a whole new game from ten years ago," Ty said. "This time you aren't dealing with some teenage kid."

"Ready to ride?" Holly rode in front of them, glancing from one man to the other as if sensing the hostility. "Is there a problem?"

Randy shook his head, facing front and gathering his reins. Holly looked at Ty.

"Nothing I can't handle this time 'round," he said, settling his hat lower.

Holly started off and Randy rode up beside her.

"Known he was back for long?" he asked.

"A few days," she said, her head held high. She didn't want to gossip with one of the ranch hands.

"Your father know?"

"I don't think so."

"He didn't like the guy when you two were kids. He isn't going to be happy to hear he's back."

"It's not as if we're taking up where we left off," she bit out. No danger there.

"Maybe not, but Ryan's going to have a conniption when he learns Jose Alverez's kid owns the adjacent ranch. Where's his old man?"

"Ty's? I understand he died recently. When he bought the ranch he took out mortgage insurance." So Sara had told her. Ty owned the property free and clear, which was more than her father could say about the Rocking B. One of the wealthiest men in the county, Ryan Bennett was still more land rich than cash rich.

The day got off to a slow start as different cowboys worked with men and women they hadn't before. Some of the younger ones started by showing off. The older, more seasoned men ignored their antics or called them on it.

Holly knew the drill. She'd been working the range since she'd been a girl. She kept an eye on her men and on Ty. She couldn't help looking his way when he rode near. He and the horse worked well as a team. Not as flawlessly as she suspected he would work with his own mount, but he handled John's gelding like the pro he was.

As the day progressed, it grew steadily hotter. The sun beat down mercilessly and the heat from the milling cattle rose enveloping riders and horses. As the hours passed, the ground became churned into dust. Holly pulled a bandana over her nose and mouth, squinting against the flying dirt. By noon, she wished she could fall face down in a cool swimming pool—using scuba gear so she wouldn't even have to move to breathe.

She rode up to the chuck wagon when it arrived, hoping for a tall glass of something cold. Sara was already flirting with a couple of cowboys. The southerner looked as cool as a mint julep. Holly, hot and dusty, hated standing next to Sara. The comparison wouldn't be good.

Not that she cared what anyone thought, she told herself. These were neighbors she'd known for years—or randy cowboys whom she had no interest in.

Except for one.

Ty was talking to John and Ben Hudgins as he held the reins of the borrowed horse. His hat was pushed back, and she smiled at the grime on his face, the lower portion clean where his bandana had been, his eyes looking like a dark brown mask.

Ben Hudgins turned to watch Holly as she dismounted. He was a neighbor who shared the river with Ty and the Bennetts. He had asked her out a couple of times. He still followed her with his gaze whenever they were in the same place. Holly wished he'd find someone else to focus his attention on.

"You look like a raccoon," Sara said, sidling up to

her and offering a cold, wet washrag. "Take a few layers of dust off."

Ty glanced at that moment. Self-conscious, Holly took the rag and held it against her face. It felt heavenly. After a moment, she dragged it down. Seeing the dirt that had coated her skin, she turned her back on the men and wiped again.

Sara laughed. "Now you look like a sideways-striped zebra. Come with me. We need more than a couple of swipes to get you prettied up again."

"Don't bother, I'll just get dirty after lunch."

"Honey chil', we don't want the men to see you like this. Trust me," Sara said, teasing her.

Holly wouldn't make a scene, but even with a clean face, her clothes would still be dusty and damp with perspiration, and no one was in the mood for flirting anyway—except Sara.

She washed her face and got a mug of iced tea. Taking her plate, she piled it high with sandwiches and chips and found a spot on one of the logs dragged over for the meal. Cattle milled around only a few hundred yards away. The bawling of the calves had subsided. The lowing of the mothers frantic about the babies separated from them was a constant background noise. Several of the men continued to work. They'd rotate in for lunch when those now eating went back.

She'd been present at more of these than she wanted to acknowledge. Only this one was different. She was acutely aware of Ty Alverez wherever he was. She tried to ignore the flare of interest that could not be squelched. What had he been doing these last years? What had his wife been like? What was it like to have her die so young? How would he make a go of ranching when he wasn't wanted?

Though from the way the other men treated him, Holly suspected it was only the Bennetts who didn't want him around. There was small comfort in the fact no one seemed to remember or care about their relationship a decade ago.

"I'm not going out this afternoon," Sara said, sitting beside Holly. "When the chuck wagon heads back, I'm going with it. Want to come with me?" She sipped her iced tea and watched the scene with avid eyes.

"Nope. I have to do my fair share. Everyone will be out at our place in a week or so. Don't want lollygaggers there, so I can't do it here."

"And I'm half owner of this spread. But I'm still not going to break my neck trying to prove I'm as good as any cowboy here. I'm who I am."

Holly stared at her. "Does that seem like what I'm doing? Trying to be as good as any cowboy here?"

"I was watching you today and it sure seemed like it to me. What are you trying to prove? Or who are you trying to impress?"

Holly didn't answer. But her gaze involuntarily moved to Ty. Was she trying to show him she didn't need a man? That she'd gotten over him long ago? If so, she was afraid she'd missed the mark. She'd never caught him looking her way once, except when she was washing her face. Great timing.

As if in direct contradiction, Ty glanced up at that moment, his gaze locking with hers. For a long moment they stared at each other. He broke first, turning back to the conversation he was having, giving no clue to his thoughts. Holly felt her heart speed up. Just looking at him caused a reaction she wanted to ignore. Turning to Sara, she met her friend's knowing eyes.

"I have to leave early today, so I'll work a couple of more hours. I need to post a job opening. I fired Hank yesterday."

"Good for you. I'll let John know. He'll put out feelers for you. Hopefully you get someone good."

"I wish I could inspire the men to work for me like they do for my dad," she said, watching Randy ride in. None of them were as insolent as Hank had been, but none of them gave their all to their jobs lately.

The afternoon passed swiftly. Holly watched the time. The feed store closed at six and she wanted to get into town before then to post the notice. She'd swing by to see her dad and get something to eat from the drive-through at the local burger place. She was too tired to bother with cooking when she got home.

REACHING THE STORE WELL before closing, she was surprised to see Ty's truck parked in front.

Entering the large barnlike building, she went to the bulletin board near the cash register. All sorts of notices were posted, from a car wash by the 4-H group, to a dance being held in a neighboring town in a couple of weeks.

"Tomorrow, around ten," Josh Pedarson was talking to Ty. Holly took the folded paper from her pocket and tacked it to the board.

"I can be there if you need me to be," Ty said. "I've been working on the branding at Montgomery's place, but John knows I can't make it every day."

"Naw, we'll load it in the barn where you said. You don't have to be there 'less you want to be. Got the rig out back all loaded up if you want to check it. Good red oat hay."

"Sounds fine to me." Ty noticed Holly just as Hank sauntered out from between the rows of liniments and food supplements.

"What have we here?" Hank asked, walking up to Holly and making a big deal of reading the job wanted notice she'd just tacked up. He reached up and tore it off, crumpling it into a ball.

"Don't need that. I'll be heading back to the ranch now," Hank said.

"You were fired," she said evenly, conscious of Josh and Ty turning to watch.

"Not this time. Talked to your old man. I'm back on the payroll."

Hank's smirk made Holly want to slap him. "I'm in charge."

"Better check on that, missy, before you throw your weight around. Ryan said he hired me, he'll do any firing that needs to be done." Hank stepped closer. "You need me at the ranch. He recognizes the fact, and you need to realize that as well. Ranching's no business for a woman."

Holly could feel her anger escalate another notch. How dare her father second-guess her on this call. There would be no living with Hank if that decision stood. She turned and almost ran into Ty.

"Need any help?" he asked, his gaze on Hank.

"Not from you," she said, pushing past him and heading for her truck. She would settle this with her father once and for all.

Her anger had not abated by the time she reached the convalescent home. It was still early—dinner wouldn't be served for another forty-five minutes. She stormed into the building and down the hall to her father's room. Knocking on the door, she took a deep breath, hoping she wouldn't become totally unglued by his behavior.

"Come on in," Ryan called.

He sat in a wheelchair near the window.

"What do you mean by countering my decision?" Holly said, not moving from the doorway. She was so furious she could pick up his bed and throw it!

"Don't you be messing with the ranch hands, Holly," Ryan said, frowning as he looked at her. "I have a good group of men who work well together. You remember that. You're only filling in until I'm up and around again. Deal with them!"

"No way. Hank was insolent, ignored my request to repair fencing and he's constantly harassing me. I'm not putting up with it."

"He said you overreacted to things. Maybe I should hire a man who would know how to ramrod the outfit."

"*I* know how. And one way is to make sure I have the clout to back up my demands. You've cut the legs out from under me. Hank won't ever do anything I say from now on, knowing you're backing him. Dad, he's not working. And if he doesn't stop pushing himself on me, I'll have him charged with sexual harassment."

"Calm down," Ryan said.

"I am not calming down until this is resolved. Either you back me on this, or I quit. I'll find another place to live and go back to training horses, which is what I really want to do. Let the ranch rot for all I care."

"Holly, come in and shut the door. I don't want everybody in the place to hear you," he said.

"But you didn't mind if the entire town learns you rescinded my firing Hank."

"What do you mean?"

"He was in the feed store when I posted the job opening. He took it down and practically threw it into my face as he gloated that you overruled me."

"It's my ranch. I have the final say."

Holly stared at her father for a long moment. It had been the two of them for as long as she could remember. He'd been the one to teach her to ride, help her with math and comfort her when she lost the baby. He'd been her mainstay all her life. Yet he wasn't backing her on an important matter like this. Couldn't he see that she was a responsible adult, capable of making sound decisions?

"Impasse, Dad," she said. "It is your ranch. You are not capable of running it. If you won't back me, I won't even try."

"Ridiculous. Hank's okay. He'll buckle down and do what's needed. You just keep an eye on things. Let the men do more."

She stared at him. She was twenty-eight years old. Yet her father treated her like a little girl. Other women had moved away from home, started their own businesses, built careers, made a life. She'd been content for far too long to settle at the ranch, training horses as it suited her, working in her garden.

"It's not too late for me," she murmured softly.

"What's that?" Ryan asked, looking at her sharply.

"Here's the deal. Either I get full control of the Rocking B until you're back at the helm, or I'm out of here."

"Stop talking nonsense."

"It's not nonsense. That's the deal. You have until tomorrow to let me know your decision. Think about it. I'm deadly serious."

She spun on her heel and walked away, the anger not abated at all. How dare her father back one of the hired hands over his own daughter!

CHAPTER FIVE

As SHE'D PLANNED, HOLLY headed for the burger place. She was still fuming, but after all the work she'd done that day she knew better than to skip supper. Turning into the parking lot, she was dismayed to find a sawhorse blocking the drive-through lane with an out-of-order sign posted on it. She slapped her palm against the steering wheel. Damn, the perfect ending to a horrible day.

Whipping her truck into a vacant slot, she got out and brushed herself off the best she could. She'd gotten rid of the worst of the dust before going to see her father. But after talking with Hank, she hadn't cared much what she'd looked like. Now she was hoping to get in, eat and leave without having to talk to anyone.

It seemed most of the seats were taken. Obviously others who had hoped for the drive-through had ended up coming inside. Her eye was caught by a cute little boy, bouncing in one of the booths. Recognition dawned. It was Ty's son. She looked at the back of the cowboy hat opposite the boy. Ty undoubtedly.

After ordering her burger, fries and drink, she waited by the counter. When the order was up, she took the bag. She'd eat in the truck and decide what to do next about the situation with her father.

"Holly?" Suddenly, Ty stood beside her, two drink cups in hand for refills.

"What?"

"Whoa, just saying hello," he said.

"Stay out of my way, Alverez. None of this would be happening if not for you."

"What are you talking about?" he asked. One or two people at a nearby table looked up.

"The past has a way of catching up." She was clutching at straws. Ty had nothing to do with Hank or her father.

"Join us," he said, sliding the cups across the counter so the boy behind it could refill them.

"Don't push your luck. I have nothing to say to you."

"Your silence that last summer said it all, I expect," he replied, his expression turning stony.

"You're a fine one to talk. How many others have you loved and left?"

His gaze narrowed. "Recasting history?"

"What?"

"You're the one who pretended I didn't exist."

"What are you talking about?" she asked. She was too fired up and tired to be playing games.

He picked up his full cups. "I can't leave Billy alone for long," he said and headed back to the booth.

Holly hesitated only a moment, then followed him over.

"Scoot over, son, we have someone joining us," Ty said. He sat next to Billy and pulled his food to that side of the table.

Holly slid in opposite the two. She couldn't help staring at the little boy. "Hi," she said. He looked a lot like Ty—dark hair, dark eyes, a dimple in his left cheek.

She swallowed hard and surveyed the man himself. His face was more chiseled than when he'd been a boy. His eyes more watchful and wary.

"For the record, I think Hank should have been fired and banished from the county," Ty said. "If for no other reason than how he behaved at Montgomerys' the other night."

"He's the one who was supposed to repair the fence you and I fixed yesterday. I could ignore the heavy-handed flirting, but not insubordination."

"You've seen your father?"

She nodded, unwrapping her hamburger and taking a bite. Her nerves were jangled. Adrenaline depletion from her anger? Or something to do with the disturbing man sitting across the table from her?

She chewed, swallowed hard, then took a sip of the iced tea.

"I love French fries," Billy said, rubbing one in a pool of ketchup and then eating it with a blissful expression.

"I do, too," she said, taking a couple from her pile. As they simultaneously ate their fries, she felt envious of the little boy. Life had been so easy back when she'd been five. Why couldn't it remain like that forever?

On the other hand, maybe that was what her father was trying to do—keep her five forever. The thought brought a fresh flare of fury.

"If looks could burn, you'd incinerate that hamburger," Ty said easily.

"What did you mean about recasting history?" she asked, trying to distract herself from the churning feelings surrounding her father, the ranch and this man.

He leaned forward a little, talking softly so no one could overhear. "I mean after the car crash I tried everything to see you, talk to you. I was blocked at every turn. And now you're acting like I was at fault. I didn't drive carelessly, Holly. It was Stu Sterner. If he hadn't died in the crash, he'd have been sent up for driving drunk and without a license. I never saw him coming."

She stared at him. "What are you talking about? I was in the hospital only for a week, then home the rest of the summer. You could have visited at any time."

He shook his head. "I couldn't get through until that day in September, when you told me to get off the ranch and never come back."

Was she missing something? "You could have called."

"Daddy, there's Brandon. Can I go see him?" Billy asked excitedly, pointing toward the door.

Ty looked that way and saw Rob Dennis enter with his son. When he saw Ty he nodded, then his gaze moved to Holly.

"You can go say hello, but come right back," Ty said, scooting out of the booth so Billy could get out. The little boy practically ran to his friend.

Ty slipped back into the booth and glanced around. No one was paying them any attention. He turned to Holly.

"I did call, but I never got through to you. Your aunt or father always answered the phone."

"Unlikely. My father knew how much I wanted to talk to you. It took him forever to convince me that you'd gotten what you wanted from me, and now that there was no baby, you were relieved to be free of any obligation. We're not living in the dark ages. You could have reached me if you'd tried."

Ty leaned back, scowling. "I'm not feeding you a line, Holly. I tried almost every day from the day I was released from the hospital until that day in September. You didn't know that?"

"You were in the hospital, too?" She hadn't known *that*.

"Twice that summer. Once courtesy of Stu, once from your father."

"What?"

"He wasn't too happy about me knocking up his daughter. Made damn sure I knew it from the beating he and his hands gave me. So maybe he owed me for that. But not the rest."

"You're making that up. He knew I wanted to talk to you," she repeated.

"Maybe he knew it, but he was boss on that ranch and what he said went. Still does, looks like. Think about it, Holly. We were crazy about each other. Do you really think I wouldn't have come to see you if I could have? Wouldn't have tried to find out how you were doing? You were carrying our baby! We lost that child. But I never thought we'd lose each other."

"Dad wouldn't have kept us apart," Holly said. She pushed her fries away. She was quickly losing her appetite.

"Of course he would. And he did. You know there was bad blood between him and my father. He'd have moved heaven and earth to make sure we didn't get back together."

"None of that's true. If you're trying to assuage your guilt over dumping me after I lost the baby, you have a sick way of going about it." She scooted out of the booth, and then leaned over the table and glared at him. "I waited all summer for you to contact me. Your halfhearted attempt the last day I was in town didn't cut it. By then I was so over you I never wanted to see you again," she lied.

Straightening, she turned and almost stomped out of the café. Her anger carried her to the truck, and halfway out of town before reactions began to set in. She couldn't believe she'd let Ty get to her like that. In front of everyone in the café.

Had he convinced himself over the years that her father had kept them apart? Like some modern-day Romeo and Juliet? It certainly gave him a better role than he'd played in reality.

She turned into the ranch sometime later. She'd taken a stand against her father. Either he supported her, or she'd make good on her promise and leave. As she approached the house, however, doubts surfaced. Where would she go? She had no money—most of what she'd put away from training horses had been used up keeping the ranch in the black since her father had had his stroke.

She had no marketable skills beyond working with horses—and maybe cattle. She pulled to a stop in front of the dark ranch house. She had about twelve hours until she'd learn her father's decision. At that time her entire life could change. Could she get hired on somewhere as a ranch hand? There weren't a lot of female cowboys. Logistically it caused problems in bunk houses, and on the range. But it was the only thing she knew.

No use borrowing trouble before it came, she decided, shutting off the engine and getting out of the truck.

She heard loud music from the bunk house. She imagined Hank strutting around, even more cocky now that he'd been reinstated. The thought angered her almost as much as Ty's accusations.

Half an hour later, Holly had showered and put on shorts and a loose top. Her hair was still damp, but it would dry before bedtime. She went to the office and logged onto the Internet to search for job postings. Most listings were for summer work at dude ranches. She scrolled through several. Few wrangler jobs still needed to be filled—most of the ranchers were looking for cooks or housekeepers.

As she studied the ads, she realized lots of city people fantasized about working on ranches. Maybe they could supplement their normal income with a few guests who would pay to stay on the ranch and work, just until they had all the medical bills paid.

She could imagine her father's face at the mention of that idea.

A pang hit her. She might not even get the opportunity to make the suggestion.

Feeling restless, she pushed away from the desk and rose. Could she stick to her guns? Could she leave all she'd ever known if her father wouldn't back her?

Had he been behind her ten years ago? The question popped into her mind.

Could there be a hint of truth in Ty's story?

Holly refused to believe it. Her dad might be hard to deal with sometimes, but he loved her—she'd never doubted that. He wouldn't have kept Ty from contacting her. He'd told her over and over Ty was no good, and his strongest argument had been that Ty had not tried to reach her that summer.

TY TUCKED HIS SON INTO his bed and pulled the covers up. Wyoming nights grew cool at this elevation—even in May.

"Why didn't that lady eat all her dinner?" his son asked.

"She was upset," Ty said, sitting on the edge of the bed to ease his back. The work that day had been hard on the still healing injury. "You ate all your dinner, which was good."

"I got ice cream. Maybe she would have eaten hers if she knew she'd get ice cream."

"I think Holly would need more than ice cream to sweeten her up," Ty said, thinking of her indignant attitude. Bennetts still had to have things their way.

"Tomorrow does Ace come?" Billy asked.

"No, tomorrow we get the hay. Then everything will be ready when Ace arrives the next day."

"And we see Uncle Felipe and Uncle Pete?" Billy asked, naming Ty's cousins.

"Right you are. So get to sleep, then we have one more day until Ace is here."

"And then I can take him to the branding."

"Whoa, not so fast. We'll go one day, but you'll ride with me. It's too dangerous for Ace."

"Okay." Billy smiled at his father and Ty felt the tug of his heart. He loved this little boy with an intensity that constantly surprised him.

"Good night, pardner," he said gruffly as he rose.

Ty grabbed a beer from the refrigerator and headed for the room he was making into an office. His computer was set up on a table and rudimentary files stacked on the floor nearby. There were several boxes yet unpacked. He'd get proper cabinets one of these days, but that wasn't high on his list.

He booted up and opened the financial program he used. Once again he began to review his forecast. So far he'd kept expenses at a minimum. The hay would eat a chunk of the money he had saved. But things still looked good.

His thoughts drifted to dinner. She hadn't appreciated what he'd told her, but he doubted she'd given it two thoughts after she'd left. After all, she didn't believe a word of it.

Which, when he thought about it, was interesting. Her version of that summer was completely different.

He wished he could convene a meeting with Ryan, his sister who'd been visiting and Holly and force some truths.

Ty walked out to the front porch, listening to the silent night.

Tomorrow he'd see Holly again. Ty remembered how she'd worked today, as hard as any man there. Her horse was good. John said she trained him herself. They'd both loved working with horses.

He had to get Holly out of his head. There was enough to be done around this place to keep him busy for years. Focus—that's what he needed. Thinking about a girl who was no longer part of his world was a waste of time.

HOLLY ROSE EARLY AND WAS ready to leave for town before six. She knew the convalescent home would not appreciate such an early arrival, so she made herself a large breakfast to make up for missing most of her meal last night. She was about to pour the last of the coffee when Donny knocked on the door and entered the kitchen.

"Morning," he said, holding his hat in one hand.

"Good morning. Want some coffee? It's still hot."

"No, thanks, Holly. Hank showed up last night. He said Ryan had hired him back."

She nodded. "I'm talking to Dad about it this morning."

"So does he work or not?"

"Not."

Donny turned his hat in his hand. "That windmill up on the section near the timber is broke. Spotted it late yesterday. There's no water. The cattle have about finished what was in the holding tanks. We need to move them before it gets too hot today."

"Did the pump give out?"

"Looks like someone deliberately broke the shaft. I called in for a replacement as soon as I got back yesterday, but it'll take a week or more to get the part."

Holly put down her cup. Hank immediately came to mind as the saboteur. He had been furious about her firing him, but would he have taken revenge for the termination? Sure, he had left angry. But when would he have had a chance to ride out to the windmill and damage it?

"Anyone else know about it?" she asked.

"Yeah, we all do. I think we better move that part of the herd to the river until the pump is fixed. Plenty of fresh grass and water there and we won't have to move them again for a few weeks," Donny said.

"Was it Hank?" she asked.

"I don't know who it was. But I doubt it. He's been here for years. He doesn't like taking orders from a woman, but that doesn't make him go crazy and wreck his employer's property."

"The fence near the river was cut. If I hadn't repaired it, when we move the cattle, they could have drifted into the Wilson ranch."

"So, we would have rounded them up once we found out."

"It's not a vacant ranch any longer."

"Yeah. Your old man probably had a fit when he heard Alverez is back."

Holly didn't respond. She knew her father wasn't yet aware Tyler was back. He would have had plenty to say if he had.

"Take Randy and Jerry and move the cattle."

"Randy and Thom have already taken off for Montgomery's place. That leaves me, Jerry and Hank."

"Not Hank. Have him muck out the stalls."

Donny took a deep breath and then shrugged. "Whatever you say, boss."

He put his hat on and left.

"Boss for how long?" Holly wondered aloud.

She cleaned up the dishes, called Sara to let her know she wouldn't make it to the branding today and left the house. She wanted to check the windmill herself, and make sure the fence repairs had held.

They routinely rotated the cattle between different sections to give the areas time for grass to regrow. It was a dry summer when they couldn't feed their stock by range alone. As she rode toward the river, she hoped this one didn't prove so. The cost of hay continued to rise. If they had to supplement the range feed, it would shoot the budget to hell.

After checking the fence, she'd headed for the pump Donny told her was broken. The shaft had been hit numerous times, was knocked out of alignment and looked unable to be repaired. She tried to judge when it had happened. There was little water in the tanks, but it had been hot lately and cattle could have drunk more in recent weeks than normal.

There was no denying they needed to be moved. By the time Donny and Jerry showed up, she had already started circling the herd in preparation to transfer them to the new section where water would be plentiful.

"Hank went to Montgomery's," Donny said when he drew near.

Holly nodded in acknowledgment, concentrating on the job at hand. The man was not going to get the satisfaction of hearing about her making a scene.

"You riled Hank up good, Holly," Jerry said, riding up next to her. "He came in last night cock of the walk. Says what you need is a good man. Hell, what does he think the rest of us are, chopped liver?"

"He didn't mean it like that," Donny said.

"Hey, I know he's had his eye on her since he arrived. Now that Ryan's out of the picture, he figures he can step in and get the inside track," Jerry said.

"There is no inside track and Hank Palmer is the last man I'd consider if there were," Holly said. "Let's move these critters."

She had to call the sheriff about the damage to the pump, and then see her father.

AS SHE PULLED INTO THE parking lot at the convalescent hospital, she wondered just what Hank had thought he'd get from her with her father away. She'd never been more than moderately polite with him. His actions lately, however, *were* bordering on harassment as she'd told her father. Maybe the threat of calling the law in would make him back off.

Wiping her hands on her jeans, she prepared for the inevitable confrontation. Her heart was racing. She needed her father's support. She didn't want to leave. But she wasn't going to continue with things as they were.

She headed down the hall and knocked on the half-opened door.

He was sitting at the window again, looking out as

he normally did. She wished he didn't still need the wheelchair.

"Hi," she said, hoping against hope that he'd changed his mind and planned to give her full authority at the ranch.

"What the hell is Ty Alverez doing back? And when were you planning to tell me? You aren't shacking up with him again, are you?" he asked her, his face scarlet.

Holly was dumbfounded by his accusation.

"What are you talking about?" she asked. "How dare you say such a thing to me." She stormed into the room and closed the door, leaning against it and staring at her father. He'd been such a bulwark when she'd been grieving that summer. Now this. She couldn't believe he'd just said those crude words.

"You knew Alverez was back. Why not tell me?"

"Maybe because I suspected a reaction like this? Only, truth to tell, I never did. But I didn't want you getting upset. Who told you?" she asked.

"Doesn't matter. The fact is *you* didn't. Is his old man back, too?" Ryan clenched his hands into fists and pounded on the wheelchair. "I won't have them sashaying back into town like they owned the place. I got rid of them once, I'll do it again."

"Jose Alverez is dead. And I don't think you can chase Ty off so easily." She paused, thinking. "When did you get rid of them before? That summer after I graduated from high school? Ty said he tried to talk to me and you kept him away."

"I don't want you seeing him. He's nothing but trouble, and probably can't wait to stir it up again."

"He owns the old Wilson ranch," she blurted out.

"What?"

Holly pushed away from the door and crossed to the chair near her father. Sitting on the edge, she took off her hat and brushed back the loose hair that framed her face. Taking a deep breath, she tried to figure out a way to ask her father more about what Ty had told her. For the first time, she wondered about that summer. She was already surprised to learn her dad felt he'd run the Alverezes out of town ten years ago.

"So, what really happened?" she asked.

He eyed her warily. "What do you mean?"

"Not everyone claims to have run people out of town. Sounds like an old western where the marshal chases the bad guys out."

Ryan didn't answer, just turned to scowl out the window.

Holly didn't know whether to repeat Ty's accusations, or wait for her father to respond. She studied her father for a long moment. He was getting old. His hair was thinner and almost completely iron-gray. The limited mobility he had on his left side may or may not improve as physical therapy tried to teach his mind to reuse his leg and arm. His speech had been affected for a few months, but it was back to normal.

Getting so angry couldn't be good for him. What if he suffered another stroke? One that killed him this time.

Holly wanted to reach out and hold on, not lose the only parent she knew. Not have the world be a place where her father no longer existed.

She sighed. "I didn't come here to talk about Ty Alverez. The last thing he'd do is take up with me again. He made his feelings perfectly clear that summer. Guess you called it right back then, huh, Dad?"

He glanced at her. "Stay away from him," he said.

"Hard to do. He's working the Montgomery branding. And as far as I know, he plans to make the circuit like the rest of us."

"Then you stay away. Tell him he's not wanted when they brand our cattle."

"Don't you think that will cause more problems than solve?" she asked.

"Send Hank and the other men."

"Which brings me to my reason for being here. I don't want Hank on the ranch. If my firing him won't stand, then you need to find yourself a new manager. I'm not going to keep butting my head against your rules and regulations when you aren't there to see how things are."

"Things are the way I want them. I hire the men, I'll fire them."

Holly stared at her father. He didn't trust her to take care of the ranch she'd lived on all her life. She didn't want to believe it.

"He's insubordinate, lazy and careless. If he gets away with it, the others will start slacking off. We're down one with you gone. If I can hire one or two others, we can keep up with things," she said. "But if I don't have complete authority, I'm not staying." Please, Dad, show me you trust me. Give me full authority, she prayed.

"Don't talk to me like that, missy. You'll do what I say."

Holly gave a short burst of laughter. "You're kidding, right? I'm fully grown. Twenty-eight years old. I don't do what my father tells me anymore."

Ryan pounded the arm of the chair again.

"It's that blasted Ty Alverez. Did he put you up to

this? Damn it, I told his old man to stay the hell away from Turnbow, we didn't want him here."

"Why not?"

"Never you mind." Ryan looked away. "You were too gaga over that boy to have any sense."

Holly couldn't argue that she'd been so in love with Ty that nothing else had mattered. Which was what made it so damaging when she'd had to accept the truth. And over the years, it seemed easier to guard her heart rather than become involved with anyone. Regrets for lost opportunities grew. Not every man was like Ty. She should have tried harder to find a mate, someone she could depend upon, count on. Someone to share every aspect of her life.

Someone who had the power to shatter her heart like Ty had.

She shook her head. She wasn't brave enough to risk that again.

"He's probably back for revenge," Ryan murmured.

"What would he want revenge for?" she asked in astonishment.

Ryan ignored her question. "Check with the records office, see if that property really belongs to him. Wouldn't put it past him to horn in and cause trouble without a leg to stand on."

"Come on, that's too far-fetched to be believed. It's too easily checked."

"So check it."

"I'm not here to talk about Ty. I'm here to get power of attorney to run the ranch as I see fit, or leave."

Ryan stared at her. "Leave then. It's my ranch and I say what goes."

She nodded once, rose and headed for the door.

"Holly!"

She turned. "What?"

"If you leave, don't come back."

She knew he'd suffered a great deal from the stroke. And his personality had changed slightly as a result. But even he wouldn't turn his back forever on his only child, would he?

"One question. Did you keep Ty from contacting me that summer?"

Ryan scowled again. "What brought that up? Is he putting ideas into your head? He did wrong by you. He's lucky I didn't have him up on charges."

"Did you keep him from contacting me?"

"If he had wanted to get in touch with you, he would have," Ryan said, turning back to gaze out the window.

Holly left the building, not satisfied with his answer. If she had had more time, had been able to work up to it in her own way, maybe she'd have received a more explicit response. Yet, if he had shielded her that summer, wasn't it because he hadn't wanted her hurt anymore?

Not for the first time she wished that drunk driver had never been born.

She had to accept partial fault for what happened. Her emotions had been so ragged. Depressed, she'd listlessly gone along with suggestions from her father and Aunt Betty. In retrospect, she should have sought out Ty herself and confronted him earlier than that day in September. Even then, she gave him no chance to talk, just ordered him away.

Would it have made a difference?

Or would he still have moved away, married, had that adorable little boy and left her behind?

Starting the truck, Holly ignored the prick in her heart. The way things were going, she would never have any of those things.

Now she had to find a place to live, to work and to take her horses. All before the men at the ranch found out the true state of affairs.

CHAPTER SIX

WHEN SHE REACHED THE RANCH, Holly went straight to the barn and saddled her horse. One last ride around the place before she gave some last-minute instructions to Donny. Then she'd pack up and leave. She felt numb. Deep down she'd thought her father would come through for her. He always had in the past.

Randy, Hank and Thom were at Montgomery's. She needed to talk to Sara. See if she could stay with her a few days until she found a job. They wouldn't mind boarding her horses, either, she thought. Trying to remember the exact amount in her savings account, she knew the few thousand dollars there wouldn't last long.

But she wasn't ready to get just any old job. And she wasn't sure she wanted to stay in Turnbow now. How humiliating for the entire community to know her own father hadn't trusted her to run the ranch while he was sick. Yet all her friends were here. Everything she knew and loved.

She rode to the river. The men had finished moving the herd to that section. Once satisfied everything was okay there, she'd be ready to go. The sheriff hadn't found anything to point to who caused the sabotage at the ranch. She suspected Hank, but just because she didn't like him didn't make him guilty, the sheriff said. Whoever had damaged the pump and cut the fence had left no clues.

When Holly reached the river, she was shocked to find the fence had been cut again—this time in dozens of places! Cattle had drifted across the shallow water onto Ty's land. How many, she wasn't sure. She had to get them back before he accused her of running them deliberately on his range.

Who was sabotaging the ranch? She hoped this incident would provide the sheriff with enough evidence to stop the perpetrator.

"THANKS, MAN. I APPRECIATE your bringing up the stock," Ty told his cousin Pete. Born Pedro, he'd taken the Anglo version of his name in school. Made things easier, he'd told his father. Pete always chose the easiest way. Not that he wasn't a hard worker— he was one of the mainstays of the ranch in Texas— but if there were two ways to do something, he'd find the simpler.

The horses had been unloaded and were now milling in their new corral. The barn still needed work, but the corral fencing was strong.

The second big rig had carried fifty head of cattle, mostly Texas longhorns. They'd been turned loose in the field nearest the homestead. Ty had spent the last couple of evenings riding the fences and cross fences. This section had feed, water and shade. They'd be on their own until he was ready to begin training again after the neighbors had finished branding and his time was his own.

"Hey, Felipe and I wanted to see what you have. It's not as large as the home ranch," Pete said, looking at the house, the barn and the other buildings, which would obviously have to be torn down and rebuilt.

"Don't compare it yet. I'm just starting out. Check back in a few years," Ty said. He knew the place needed work; his cousin didn't have to tell him that.

"You'll want some help around here. Whenever I get wanderlust, I'll head for this place and put in a few days."

"And you let me know when you need me in Texas. Billy and I will come in an instant," Ty said.

"So, you going to show me around your spread before we get lunch?" Pete asked, closing the trucks' loading ramps and making sure everything was set for the return trip. Their ranch in Texas supplied rodeo stock, so the big rigs were in constant use. Ty knew they had to get back right away.

"It's not that small. I'll show you a couple of vantage points before we eat. Saddle up," Ty said. He looked forward to sharing his plans with his cousin. With hard work and determination, he knew he could make the ranch pay. Especially supplemented by his training of cutting horses.

The two men bantered back and forth as they rode away from the house. Billy was entranced with his pony and Filipe had volunteered to stay and watch the boy.

"Got a steady supply of water?" Pete asked as they walked the horses. Several of the steers fell in behind them.

"Access to a shallow river along one boundary. It's a pretty spot. I've taken Billy there to play. When cattle aren't around, he can go swimming."

"Fatten the cattle up on your range, breed them and

keep the calves, that was Dad's deal," Pete said. "You and Uncle Jose made a difference to us when times got tough a few years back. We pay our debts."

"No debts in families," Ty said. "You know we were glad to be there."

Pete studied the layout of the land as they rode, commenting on various aspects.

"You lucked out," he said at one point, taking his hat off to wipe his forehead.

"No luck involved. My father knew what he was doing," Ty said. "I wish he could have been here with me, though. This was his dream." Ty knew how much it must have meant to his father to have been paying the mortgage on the ranch for so many years. Even if he didn't have his own agenda, Ty would make a go of it for his father's sake. But he wished his father could have savored the triumph when it came.

When they crested a small rise, both men pulled in their reins in surprise.

"You running lots more head than I expected," Pete said, surveying the cattle grazing on the land in front of them.

"They aren't mine," Ty said, startled. "But I have an idea who they belong to. Come on." Ty urged his horse forward and rode through the animals to the stretch of border shared with the Bennetts. As he drew near the river, he spotted Holly, She was riding around several head, driving them back toward Bennett land.

Ty spurred his horse and quickly covered the distance.

"Just what the hell are you doing?" he asked.

She stopped and glared at him. "You wouldn't know

who cut our fence, now would you? I gave you the benefit of the doubt the first time, but less than two days later, it's cut to bits and there's a sizeable number of our cattle on your range. What I said about you keeping any you found held for last time, not today."

"I'm not after your cattle. What are you trying to pull, get me arrested for rustling or something? Damn good thing I have a witness?"

Pete rode up to hear the last.

"Can't be rustling if she's herding them on your property," Pete said. He looked at Holly and then glanced around. "Reckon there's more than fifty head here."

"I am trying to round them up to put them back on my land," Holly said between gritted teeth.

"So you say," Ty said. "Wouldn't be the first time a Bennett made something up."

"Bennett?" Pete said. "Any relation to Ryan Bennett?"

Holly turned to him.

Ty answered, "Holly's his daughter."

Pete's eyes moved sharply to his cousin, then back to Holly. He shrugged and turned his gaze to the cattle. "I'll help move them back."

"We both will," Ty said. He didn't want to believe Holly would try such a stunt, but if encouraged by her father, who knew to what lengths they'd go to get him to leave town. Had that been the plan, push the cattle over and then call the sheriff?

"I did not cut the fence, or move the cattle over here," she said. "And I would certainly be the last person to accuse you of rustling."

Ty didn't want to believe it, but evidence was mounting. Had she been repairing the fence that first day, or had he caught her just after she'd cut it? How convenient that when he was supposed to be helping at the Montgomerys' place, the fence was again cut, this time with cattle moving on to his range. What other motivation could there be?

He stared at her for a long moment, then shook his head. "Doesn't matter, does it? Let's get them moved back."

The three of them worked together, rounding up the cattle, pushing them back across the shallow point in the river. The two men then effected makeshift repairs.

"You better get your own fencing up, and make it tight and strong," Pete said, as he stretched a line while Ty tightened it.

Holly dismounted and came to stand by them, watching, but not offering to help, he noticed. Why didn't she leave?

"Maybe Felipe and I should stay a little longer, help out until you get things sorted out," Pete said with a sideways glance at Holly.

"I'll find my own help. Your father would skin me alive if I kept you up here when you're needed at home."

"He might try," Pete said grinning.

"You looking for a hand?" Holly asked.

Ty nodded once, nailing the last of the wire to the post. He'd return tomorrow and restring the strands covering the entire river portion. And double-check to make sure no one caused more problems overnight. "I'm at the point where I'll need some help, and these cousins of mine think they're better off in Texas."

"Hey, I wouldn't mind trying a year in Wyoming, but you're right, that would leave Dad shorthanded."

"Thank you, both," Holly said formally. "I appreciate the help getting the cattle back on this side. I have a suspicion as to who cut the wire, but the sheriff wants proof before he does anything."

Ty hopped over to his side of the repaired fence, wincing at the pain that shot through his back. As he slowly mounted his horse, he glanced over at her. She looked tired—and sad. For a moment he felt a tug on his heart. But Holly made her position on him loud and clear long ago. He turned his horse around and spurred him back to the house.

Pete caught up quickly. They rode hard for half the distance, then Ty pulled his horse into a walk. He wasn't returning with a lathered mount.

"So tell me the tale of Holly Bennett," Pete said.

Ty hesitated. "I made a fool of myself over her when I was in high school. Her father set me straight."

"That was the girl?"

"Did my father tell yours?"

"Might have, I didn't pay attention to any names. That was a long time ago, cuz."

Yet it might have been only yesterday, Ty thought. He shied away from the memories that crowded whenever he was near her. His father had told him once a couple of years ago she still lived in Turnbow. As if testing the water to see Ty's reaction. He'd known moving back wasn't going to be easy, but he could handle this.

Ty put on a happy face until his cousins left. They'd driven the big stock trailers out of the yard by three, planning to make a couple of hundred miles south before stopping for the night.

"I wish they stayed," Billy said, still waving long after the dust settled and the trucks were gone from view.

"Me, too, son," Ty said. At least with his cousins he knew where he stood.

HOLLY WAS HALFWAY TO THE windmill when she realized she was stalling. If she was going to leave, she needed to just do it. Hadn't she decided she wanted to put some distance between her and her father's ranch?

Ty was hiring. She could get a job there.

The idea had come before she really thought about it. Dumb. Did she really want to be in such close proximity? Would he even consider hiring her? Probably not. He'd been pretty clear—he wanted nothing to do with her.

There was no call for her to do anything further on the ranch. It was time to stand by her word.

Once back at the house, she made quick work of packing her things. She called Sara to ask if she could stay with her for a few days. Thankfully her friend had asked no questions. She'd simply assured Holly she could stay as long as she wanted.

"Do you have someone to bring the trailer over. I'll need to transfer my horses." She had planned to leave the ranch trailer at the Montgomerys' until the branding was ended, not expecting to need it before.

Sara was silent for a moment. "This is more than staying here, isn't it?"

"I'll explain when I get there."

"I'll find someone to get it to your place as soon as I can," Sara said.

Holly loaded her boxes into the back of the blue pickup. It was hers—registered in her name and the joy of her life when she'd first bought it about eight years ago. A working truck took a lot of abuse. It was dinged, dented and scraped, but she still liked it and was glad for transportation.

She had moved to the tack room and was gathering up her gear when she heard the horse trailer drive up. Running outside, she glanced around. None of the men from the Rocking B had made an appearance all afternoon, for which she was profoundly grateful. She'd like to be gone before anyone even knew what was happening.

Sara hopped down from the passenger side of the fifth wheel. Lloyd Hanson, one of the older cowboys from the Montgomery ranch, climbed down from the driver's side.

"Need any help?" he asked, going round to the back to lower the ramps.

"We're taking the mare and gelding in the first two stalls," Holly said, hauling out one of her training saddles. She'd brought the horses in from the corral so they'd be easy to get. She opened the storage compartment of the trailer and tossed in the saddle. Going back for the rest of her tack, she was joined by Sara.

"This looks like a move to me," Sara said. She scooped up the bridles and reins. Holly handed her a caddy with brushes and picks. Her own arms loaded, they headed back to the truck.

"You're right. My father thinks I'm an idiot. He rehired Hank. Then told me to let him run his own ranch. So I'm doing that."

Sara stopped and stared at her. "He didn't. Holly, he can't run this place until he's better."

Holly kept on walking. "He'll have to figure that out for himself." She peered back over her shoulder. "You helping?"

Sara and Holly had the tack loaded by the time Lloyd had the two horses ready to go.

"I just have to get a couple of things from the office and I'll come over. You don't have to wait for me," Holly said, heading back to the house.

"Does anyone else know where you're going?" Sara asked.

"Nope. I plan to be long gone before the men know. Especially Hank. Blast him. I can't believe my own father wouldn't back me," she murmured.

With Lloyd and Sara gone, she ran back to the house. There were only a few papers she needed from the office: ownership papers for her horses and her truck. The statements for her bank account. She looked around. Nothing else she couldn't live without.

She drove down the long driveway, still feeling numb. Would her father have listened to reason if someone hadn't spilled the beans about Ty being back? Ty had turned her life upside down ten years ago. It seemed his presence was doing it again.

HER HORSES HAD ALREADY been unloaded by the time she pulled up near the Montgomery house. She parked behind the house and out of sight of the barn and the activity with the branding. Men were coming and going, horses being turned out for the night in the large corral, hay being tossed in.

Holly searched for Donny. She'd tell him. He was the most responsible of the men who worked for her father. Most likely, he'd be the one Ryan would put in charge. Not that it mattered to her anymore.

When Donny rode in, Randy and Hank were with him. She waited until they all dismounted and began to brush down their horses before walking over. She went up to Donny and ignored the other two. Randy stood between her and Hank, but she still heard his flirtatious greeting, which she ignored.

"I need to talk to you," she told the older man.

"Okay," he said hesitantly.

"Come with me." She turned and headed away from the others. Donny followed a moment later. He was dirty and tired. She wouldn't take long.

"I'm no longer taking care of the ranch," she said without preamble. "I don't know who Dad's going to have ramrod the place, but it won't be me."

He looked startled. "Now, Holly. That can't be. It's your ranch, too. Your father needs you."

"He rescinded Hank's termination. Undercut my authority. I'm not staying."

Donny studied her. "You're serious," he said at last.

"Yes. I've moved my things and my horses. I'm not going back."

He took off his hat and slapped it against his dusty pants, raising a cloud. "Don't seem right."

"As my father so clearly pointed out, it's his ranch, he can run it as he likes."

"Does he know how Hank's been pestering you?"

"He thinks I should go out with him, of all things." She shook her head. "You might want to go see Dad tonight. I think he'll want you in charge."

"I'm not a ranch manager, don't know accounting or anything like it. I'm a cowboy."

"You can handle the men. Dad will have to hire someone to handle the paperwork until he's back."

"I don't like this, Holly," Donny said in a low voice as he put his hat back on. "It's not right."

"Yeah, well, I'm not so happy about things right now myself. Know anyone looking for a wrangler? I can handle horses."

He shook his head, then looked over toward the corral. "Mighty sorry to hear this, Holly. We're going to miss you."

She swallowed hard, as the hurt at leaving flared unexpectedly.

"I'll keep in touch."

"I'll do what I can until your father's back." He touched the brim of his hat and turned to lead his horse to the corral.

Holly ignored the curious glances of the others and went into the house, warmed by Donny's comments.

FRIDAY MORNING, HOLLY WATCHED John and Sara and several of their ranch hands load up their trailers and head for the Fallon ranch. Their own branding had ended yesterday around midday. The visiting cowboys had returned to their respective ranches. Only the churned dust and echos of the bawling calves remained. The cattle had been split between two sections and moved back to graze until fall when they'd cull the herd, sell some and butcher a few to carry them over the winter.

She'd been invited to join them, but needed to send out some more resumes. She couldn't impose on the Montgomerys' hospitality indefinitely.

Her father had not tried to contact her. She'd avoided riding with the Rocking B's employees yesterday and pretty much stayed away from everyone who seemed as though he or she wanted to talk. She had no doubt the rumors had flown. Yet no one had said anything.

She felt like the odd man out. Once Fallon's branding was done, it would be the Rocking B's turn. The first one she'd ever missed.

After spending a couple of hours on the computer, Holly was getting antsy. She went outside. The ranch was almost silent. With most of the employees away, and only a few horses in the corral, there was little movement that she could see.

Then she heard the laughter of children. Smiling, Holly wandered around the house and saw several young kids running under a hose near one of the small cottages that housed the married employees. She went closer.

"Hey, Holly," Maria Dennis called. She was sitting in the shade near the house, watching the children play. "Come sit a spell. It's not bad in the shade."

Holly dragged one of the chairs over next to Maria and sat down. "Maybe I'd rather be under the hose."

"Looks like fun, doesn't it? I'm hoping to tire them all out so they'll take a long nap this afternoon. It's too hot to play in the middle of the day and with all the energy they have, I'm always trying to find ways to use it up."

"Wish we could bottle some of that."

"I agree."

Holly recognized Billy Alverez. "I see you're watching Ty's son."

"He dropped him off early this morning, then headed for the Fallons' place like the rest of them. I'm surprised you didn't go."

"Had some things to do this morning. I'll go tomorrow."

"How's your dad?"

"The last I saw, he was improving," Holly said carefully.

"Word's out that you aren't at the Rocking B anymore." Maria said hesitantly.

"No. And I'm hunting for work. Know of anything?"

"Not around here," she paused then asked, "Can you patch things up with your father?"

"Not unless he gives me full power to run the ranch until he returns."

"I thought you *were* running it."

"I thought so, too." She sighed. "It's time I move on. Most kids can't wait to get out of the family home and be on their own. I was dumb enough to stay instead of getting my own life."

"Rob was like that, anxious to get out on his own. But his father didn't own a large ranch. He'd have stayed if he had had that."

"Not if his father was as hardheaded as mine," Holly said dryly. She knew Rob Dennis. He wouldn't tolerate the limitations she'd put up with for a single day. More fool her.

Holly changed the subject, asking after Maria's boys. She loved talking about her children and how well Billy fit into their family dynamics.

"Ty is doing a great job raising him," Maria said. "Billy has lovely manners for such a young boy. And he sure is crazy about his dad."

Holly wished they'd continued the conversation about the Rocking B. It hurt to know Ty had had a child with another woman. That she'd died made it even worse. No one could compete with a ghost. Memories of any bad times faded and only happy ones remained.

Maria invited her to join them for lunch and Holly accepted. She'd have to get back to the computer later to see if there were any responses to her inquiries, but

she was losing hope of finding something fast. Most of
the summer jobs were already filled. And she did not
want to end up a cook for a ranch full of men.

Ty knocked on the screen door while they were eating, then entered when Maria called out.

"Daddy!" Billy hopped down and raced to his father.
Ty grinned, picked him up and tossed him into the air.
Catching him, he gave him a quick hug and set him
back on his feet. "Go back and finish your lunch." He
looked up and nodded to Maria and Holly.

Almost without thought, Holly jumped up. "Can I
see you for a minute, Ty?"

"About?"

"It's private," she said, glancing at the children.

"Sure."

She wiped suddenly damp palms on her jeans and led
Ty outside and over into the shade of the tree. She turned
to face Ty.

"I'm looking for work."

Ty stared at her. "What are you talking about?" he
asked.

She glanced away, embarrassed to have to ask this
man for anything, but she couldn't stay at Sara's
forever.

"I need a job. I have two horses trained for ranch work.
I'd need to board both, but that could be part of my pay."

"I'm not hiring you," Ty said.

She swung back to face him. "Why not? You ask
anyone, and they'll tell you I'm a good worker. And
you're looking—you said so yourself."

"Holly, this is crazy. What are you trying to pull?"

She drew a deep breath. "I can't stay here without a
job. I thought about moving away from Turnbow, but

for the time being, I need to be closer. I've looked at the postings on the Internet. Not much is still open. Most of the ranchers I know already have cowboys signed on. Some are seasonal, most are year-round. There are some dude ranches in the eastern part of the state still hiring, but not for jobs I want."

"You're serious?" Ty wrapped his mind around the thought—Holly working for him. Seeing her every day. Sharing chores, building his ranch. Just like they'd talked about a hundred times their last year of high school.

Only this totally was unlike what he'd envisioned then. He didn't trust her. He'd be a fool to risk the safety and potential of his ranch to his enemy's daughter.

"Did Ryan put you up to this?" he asked suspiciously. It'd be just like him, trying to find something he could use to his advantage.

"He'll probably have another stroke if he finds out I've signed on with you. But I'm serious, Ty. I need a job and a place to stay. With room for my horses. I've thought about it ever since we fixed the fence and you mentioned you'd be hiring. Please. I'd do my best working for you."

"I'll keep that in mind," he said. He had no intention of Holly Bennett moving onto his ranch. He could not live with seeing her sparkling eyes every day, hearing her laughter, longing to touch her and kiss her and know her every thought. That dream had ended long ago.

Still—he did need someone and so far the listing he'd posted at the feed store hadn't turned up anyone. The sooner he got started, the better off he'd be. But Holly Bennett?

"John told me this morning that you've left the Rocking B," he said slowly, mulling the idea over.

"That's right."

"I thought— Never mind what I thought."

He took off his hat and wiped his forehead with his arm. His shirt sleeves were rolled up, revealing muscular forearms. The muscles in his upper arms were clearly defined beneath the cotton. He was strong, fit and one hundred percent male.

Holly's concentration was fading. She steered it back. Now was not the time to nod off into some daydream.

"So?" she said.

Ty exhaled a deep breath. "So I do need help at the ranch. My horses have arrived—and some cattle. I've put notices in the paper and in a couple of horse magazines and have already had contact with three men wanting me to train their horses. I want to help the neighbors, get my setup going and not waste time each day running to and from this ranch to drop off and pick up Billy."

"If you're looking for a nanny—" she began to say, but was interrupted.

"I'm looking for general all-around help, including watching Billy from time to time. I want someone who knows horses and cattle."

"I thought you didn't trust me. You'd leave your son with me?"

Ty didn't answer at first, his eyes gazing steadily into hers. Holly was beginning to feel her heart race. Could she really work for this man? And not let the past spill over?

"There's an old saying, keep your friends close and your enemies closer."

"I'm not your enemy, Ty."

"Your father is," he said.

"So you're being totally daring in having me around, is that it?"

"I always liked a challenge," he said slowly. "Besides, as long as you are hiring out, maybe you should work for me. At least you know the land. But don't be getting too chummy with Billy. I don't see this job lasting long. I'm still looking for a full-time employee who will stay for years."

"And that just might be me. I bring two horses with me. I can help train horses, muck out stables, check the herd, ride fence…"

He raised his hand. "Can you cook?"

"I'm not hiring on to be a cook," she said. Was that all men thought women were good for?

"We'll take turns. I've been doing it all for the last two years. It'd be nice to alternate."

"Oh." Put like that, maybe she could take her turn.

"Let's be clear on a couple of things," Ty said. "First, your loyalty will have to belong to me as long as you work for me."

She nodded.

"Second, it's work only, Holly. I'm not looking to stir up old memories or try for a new relationship, got that?"

"I'm hardly likely to forget that lesson," she said.

His expression tightened.

"The pay's not much." He named a sum that was small, but she couldn't be too choosy, plus it included room and board, and board for her horses. Overall, things could have been worse. Much worse.

"Take it on the terms offered or I'll find someone else," he said.

"I'll take it. Starting now?"

"Sure, get your gear. We'll move you in today. I'll cook tonight, but tomorrow's your turn."

"Deal." She held out her hand. He looked at for a moment, then smiled wryly.

"Seems odd," he said, taking it in his and holding it longer than she expected.

Had she made a deal with the enemy as he seemed to think? Holly didn't even want to speculate on her father's reaction when he learned she was working for Ty Alverez.

CHAPTER SEVEN

HOLLY KNEW THE news would make the rounds within hours. Maria had not been asked to keep it quiet—why should she, they were doing nothing clandestine. She'd wished her luck when Holly and Ty had returned to pick up Billy. Ty said he'd get her horses later and they headed off, she following him in her still packed pickup truck.

When she saw the old homestead she had second thoughts. The place wasn't anything like the home she shared with her father. It needed paint, new posts on the overhanging porch and something to soften the austerity of the bare ground surrounding the house. Looking farther, she noticed the old barn, the recent repairs made to the large corral fence and the horses enclosed by it.

They were beautiful. She couldn't wait to watch Ty ride them. She'd spent more time than she should have watching him at the branding. Even riding one of John's horses, he'd made the animal look like an extension of himself, the two of them flawlessly working to cut the calves, keeping them separated from their mothers while moving them to the branding site. He knew how to coax the maximum from any horse. It was a gift.

He'd had it when they'd been younger and obviously he hadn't lost his touch.

Ty stopped in front of the house. He had Billy out of the truck before Holly pulled to a stop nearby. Where was the bunk house? Surely not that dilapidated building beyond the barn.

Billy ran to her truck, grinning at her. "Holly, want to come see my pony? He got here from Uncle Filipe and I can ride him all over the ranch. Want to see?" The little boy was dancing in excitement at the prospect of showing off his pony to a newcomer.

"I'd like that, but let me talk to your dad for a minute first," she said, getting out of her truck. Now that she was here, she was reconsidering the wisdom of accepting the job.

Ty was looking at the structure she'd noticed was falling apart. "The bunkhouse is in bad shape. I haven't had a chance to work on it. I put my spare time into fixing up the places for the horses."

"As long as it doesn't leak, it'll be fine."

He ran his hand behind his neck and looked at her. "That's the thing, I think it does. And there're mice everywhere."

She stared at him, already anticipating what he was going to say.

"We've got lots of spare rooms in the house, want one of those? There's one off the kitchen I thought my first employee could have. Not that you're the kitchen help, but it is separate from the rest of the house." When she didn't answer right away, he added, "I'm not going to come knocking on your door some night."

Damn, she almost said. Heat flooded her cheeks at the thought. As she moved to the back of the truck and

hauled out one of her boxes, she said, "That will work."
She had to focus on the situation at hand and not let any
wayward ideas creep in. For weeks, nothing had gone
the way she'd planned. Why not take what was offered
and forget everything else?

In less than an hour all her boxes were stacked in the
room that was to be hers. Ty had brought in fresh sheets
and bath towels. There was a half bath off the kitchen,
but the only full bath was in the back of the rambling
house near his room and Billy's.

"Not quite what you're used to," he said quietly after
giving her the towels.

"It's fine, Ty." Probably better than she might expect
at another ranch. She was no longer the pampered
daughter of the owner, but a regular hired employee. It
would take some getting used to.

"I'll let you get unpacked. Dinner's at six most
nights."

"First, I want to see Billy's pony. Does he really get
to ride all over the ranch?"

"As long as I'm with him. He's almost five, but too
young to be riding off on his own. But I want him to get
to know the place as soon as possible. I remember when
I was a kid champing at the bit to be allowed to do grown-
up things. Too bad kids don't realize how long they'll be
stuck doing grown-up things once they're adults."

She nodded, remembering how much easier things
had been when she'd been younger.

"Thanks for giving me this chance, Ty. I won't let
you down."

He shrugged. "We'll see, won't we?"

Holly knew he didn't trust her. Why had he hired her
on? To get back at her father? Her dad had said Ty wanted

revenge, but not why. That part didn't make sense to her. She should have pushed her father more for answers. Found out for certain what had happened that summer. Had he lied to her or had Ty?

AFTER DINNER, TY ASKED if she'd watch Billy while he went to get her horses from the Montgomery place.

"Ordinarily, he'd come with me, but with someone to watch him, it'll go faster if I go by myself."

"I can get them," she said, hating to be beholden to her new boss already.

"Easier if I go. I know this road. As soon as I can arrange it, I'm having this stretch graded. The potholes are big enough to eat a truck."

She nodded, looking at the little boy still eating his dinner. She didn't know the first thing about children. Still, he was only four—how hard could that be?

"He'll probably entertain himself, but if he gets antsy, there are lots of children's books in his room. Have him pick out one or two."

"We'll be fine," she said. "I'll clean up the kitchen since you cooked."

"Works for me." He got his hat from the rack on the wall and headed outside.

"I wanna go, Daddy," Billy scrambled down from the chair and ran for the door.

"Not this time, pardner. You stay with Holly and show her around the house. She hasn't seen it all yet. Be a good host, okay?"

"Okay." A forlorn little boy returned. He looked at Holly. "Want to see the house?"

"I'd like to," she said, smiling at him. She heard the truck in the drive. It was just the two of them. For a moment, panic flared. She hoped nothing happened before Ty returned.

Billy took her through the dining room to the front room of the ranch-style house. "This is the living room. We have a telebision, but it doesn't work here."

"No reception, I bet," she murmured.

"Daddy said he'd get it going before winter. We don't have much time to watch TV in the summer months, too much to do on the ranch, but we can watch videos."

Holly smiled, hearing Ty's remarks in his son's mouth. Her heart caught. Their child would have been quoting them, learning their values, following in their footsteps. The old ache rose unexpectedly. She thought she'd gotten over that long ago, but seeing Ty again, meeting his son, the old regrets and sadness came to life.

"We eat in the kitchen," Billy said, reversing his steps to the entrance of the dining room. "But we're getting a big table and lots of chairs so everyone can eat here. I like it when everyone eats at a big table. We did at Tia Sophia's house. That's where we lived after Mommy died. And there are lots of people eating and talking. Now it's just me and Daddy."

"I see," Holly said. Was Tia Sophia one of Jose Alverez's sisters? She didn't know what Ty had been doing over the past ten years, except the occasional times when she'd seen a PRCA rodeo magazine and noted he'd won events.

"The bathroom is here," Billy said, walking down the hall. He stopped by the door to the large room. It had a free-standing clawfoot tub. A shower curtain completely encircled it. The vanity looked to be from the 1950s and the toilet had a cracked tank. No water leaked however. The entire bathroom was much larger than hers at home.

"This is my room," Billy said, racing into the space. He had bunk beds along one wall and a shelf with lots of books and some toys. The rest of the toys seemed to be spread out over the floor. A chest of drawers stood next to the opened closet door.

"Very nice," Holly said, wondering where he put all the toys when not playing with them. There were horses and cowboys and superheroes and cars and trucks scattered everywhere.

"Here's a guest room, but we don't have any guests. Uncle Pete and Uncle Felipe didn't stay because there aren't any beds and Uncle Pete said he'd get a better night's sleep on a lumpy mattress at a motel than this floor," Billy said.

"Uncle Pete?"

"He brung the cattle and my pony. He's my favorite uncle. Except for Uncle Felipe."

"I see," Holly said, trying to figure out all the relationships. She'd thought the Pete she'd met was Ty's cousin.

"This is daddy's room. I come here sometimes if I wake up in the night and Daddy lets me sleep in his big bed. And we watch movies together."

The king-size bed dominated the room. The tall windows on either side had no curtains. Holly could see out to forever. She looked back at the bed, imagining Ty sleeping on it, a small boy curled up on the far side. To Billy it must seem humongous.

"Here's another guest room," he said, standing in front of another door. Holly turned reluctantly, knowing she had no business being in Ty's room, yet hating to leave. She could smell his special scent, recognized the jeans kicked into the corner. Wished she had the right to straighten the bedding, pick up the dirty clothes.

"That's all," Billy said.

"A fine house tour," she said. Now what? "Do you want to play with your toys until your dad gets home?"

"Sure." He headed back to his room and Holly went to the kitchen to clean up after dinner. She planned to pull her weight and not give Ty a single reason for regretting his decision to hire her.

Once finished, she checked on Billy playing in his room and then went to her room—leaving the door open—to unpack what she needed. She'd marked most of the boxes, so at one end of the room she stacked those she didn't need to open. Glancing around, she noticed how spacious the room was—almost a suite. Probably for the kitchen worker at one time, it was definitely bigger than any room in the average bunk house.

She made the bed, put clothes away in the dresser and checked on Billy every few minutes. She was surprised he could entertain himself so well.

When the truck sounded in the drive, Billy shot through the house to the back door. Holly came out of her room in time to grab hold of him before he ran outside.

"Wait a minute and I'll go with you. But you need to remember your father can't see everywhere from the driver's side. You could get hurt running out when he's not expecting you."

"Okay, but hurry. I want to see the horses."

She took his hand and they went out to follow the truck and horse trailer to the barn. Ty eased to a stop and in no time was coaxing Holly's mare out of the back.

Holly had made sure Billy was safely to one side before going for her gelding. They were her horses, bought and paid for with her own money and patiently trained through the years.

He nudged her shoulder, snorting softly against her. She patted his head before unsnapping the lead line. As he walked into the corral, she slapped him gently on the rump.

"Do you have to return the trailer to John's tonight?" she asked Ty, closing the gate behind her.

"Nope. He doesn't need it until morning, so I'll take it there first thing. He's taking some more of his horses to Fallon's place."

"You going there, too?"

He closed the ramp and locked it.

Billy came running from the corral fence, where he'd been watching. "We have more horses, Daddy?"

"Those are Holly's, not ours. She's going to keep them here for a while."

"Can I ride them?"

"What about Ace?"

"I ride Ace, but Holly has pretty horses. And one is not so big."

The mare was smaller than the other horses in the corral, Holly noted. But she was fast and true.

"One of these days," she told him.

"Okay." Billy smiled and opened his arms to his father. Ty swung him up. "Time for you to get a bath and into bed."

"I showed Holly the house. She liked my room best, didn't you, Holly?"

She nodded, feeling left out. Ty obviously adored his son. He gave him responsibilities commensurate with his age. And he treated him with respect. They were a family. She was the hired help.

"I'll see you tomorrow, then," she said as they went inside. She wanted to spend some time with her horses before going to bed. With no television or radio, there wasn't much to do. As soon as she could get to town, she was stopping in the library for a stack of books!

HOLLY WAITED UNTIL SHE HEARD Ty in the bedroom with Billy before heading for the main bathroom. It was still steamy from Billy's bath. She took a quick shower and then almost ran to her room. Gone was the luxury of an ensuite bath. She'd have to get used to sharing. They could easily work out a schedule, she knew. And if it became a problem, she could take her shower in the mornings.

Getting to sleep was harder than she expected. She was tired, yet keyed up from all that had happened. She reviewed her conversation, if one wanted to call it that, with her father. Nothing changed the fact that he refused to support her decisions.

THE NEXT MORNING HOLLY ROSE early, but before she was finished dressing she heard Ty and Billy in the kitchen. She pulled on her boots, made the bed and opened the door.

Billy sat at the table, a bowl of cereal in front of him. Ty stood at the stove cooking. The fragrant aroma of fresh-brewed coffee filled the room.

Billy looked at her when she walked in, his eyes wide. "Did you sleep over, Holly?"

Ty spoke from the stove. "She's working here now, pardner, remember? That includes room and board. The bunkhouse is in too bad a state for anyone to use. Until we get that fixed up, Holly has that room."

"Oh." Seemingly satisfied, he resumed eating.

Holly helped herself to coffee and went to stand next to Ty, not too close, but so Billy didn't hear.

"Is that going to cause a problem?"

"Not for me," he said, his gaze fixed on the eggs frying. A separate pan had country potatoes, onions and peppers simmering. Toast popped up from the four-slot toaster.

"Get those, will you."

"What's the plan for today?" she asked as she set to work.

"After we feed the horses, we'll get you acquainted with the ranch." He shot her a glance. "Unless you already know it?"

"No. I've only seen what I could from our side of the river."

"Someone was running cattle here."

"Try one of your other neighbors. We have plenty of land for the size of our herd."

"Free grazing while the owners were absent," he commented.

He scooped up mountainous servings of potatoes and eggs for him and Holly, smaller portions for Billy. The two of them joined Billy at the table.

"Think what you want, but we never had any trouble until recently," she said a few bites in.

"Meaning?" he asked.

"Just that things began to happen after Dad had his stroke."

"Like?"

"Like the fence being down and the windmill getting wrecked. We seemed to have lost some cattle and one of the trucks on the ranch doesn't work anymore."

"Anyone else having problems?" he asked.

"Not that I know about," she replied. She ate, knowing she needed fuel for the day, but there was no way she could eat all he put on her plate.

"Ask around," Ty suggested.

"Why?"

"Except for the fence, the rest could be routine hassles of ranching."

"Not the windmill. It was deliberately broken."

"Strangers around?"

"Not until you came," she replied.

"I'm hardly a stranger. I spent the first eighteen years of my life here."

"And then did you go to Texas?" she asked, no longer fighting the curiosity that burned so deep.

"No, I went to Laramie for my first year of college, just like I planned."

She ate in silence. Like *they* had planned, he meant. She'd spent her first and only year of college in Denver.

"Did you graduate?" she asked.

"No. Dropped out after the second year and went down to Texas. My dad's cousin needed help on the ranch."

"That's where you met your wife?" she asked.

"Connie's off-limits," he said. He shoved back his chair, still eating from the plate as he headed for the sink. Finishing the last bite just before he set it down, he wiped his mouth with a paper napkin and tossed it into the trash. "Daylight's burning. Billy, you finished?"

"Yes." He carried his plate over and Ty put it in the sink. He squirted some dishwashing liquid soap in and turned on the water.

Holly had finished all she was going to eat. Taking the last swallow of coffee, she rose.

"Stack the dishes, and leave them. Come to the barn

and I'll show you where everything is," Ty said, heading out the door.

She watched as he and Billy left. Obviously she'd hit a sore spot. He must have loved her—Connie—a lot to be so touchy this long after her death. Or was it just because of who'd asked?

They fed the horses, checked hooves, made sure the water trough was full. Ty showed her the tack room, the stalls that were ready for use and the ones still needing repair. The sweet-smelling hay was stacked rafter-high at the end wall. The place was old, not in perfect shape, but clean as a stable ever got.

They saddled up and took off for the range. Ty let Billy ride with him rather than take his pony. Holly followed right behind, studying the lay of the land as they rode. Before long she saw part of the small herd he said he'd brought up from Texas—longhorns. She had never worked with them.

She could hear Ty talking to his son as they rode. He was giving him information about the way water flowed on the land, why they had a well and how to spot brands on the flanks of the cattle.

Suddenly he drew in with an expletive. Holly rode up beside him.

"What is it?" she asked, searching.

"Here, take Billy." He handed off his son and then broke into a gallop.

She followed more slowly with the warmth of Billy held firmly against her chest.

Ty stopped and dismounted. From the closing distance, Holly could see one of the steers was tangled in barbed wire. Hadn't he swept the range before letting the cattle loose?

She slowed down to not spook the entangled animal. Stopping several feet away she watched as Ty carefully cut the wire, pulling it away. Blood oozed from various wounds, but nothing appeared life-threatening.

Billy was silent, watching.

Ty swore once as he dodged the animal's horns and tried to keep the wire away. Finally the steer was free and dashed away.

Ty then gathered up the wire, twisting it tightly into a figure eight.

She said nothing. What could she say but the obvious—he should have checked the long-vacant ranch land before turning loose his cattle.

He looked at her. "I've been over every inch of this range. This wasn't here last week."

He held it up for her to see. It glinted in the sunshine, fresh wire, not rusted or tarnished with age.

"So maybe others are experiencing the same sabotage the Rocking B is," she said slowly.

"Maybe. Now we check every inch of this section to make sure there aren't other bundles of trouble waiting. Then I'm heading for Fallon's place to talk to the other ranchers. If someone is causing mischief, he needs to be stopped!"

"The cuts were superficial?" she asked as he mounted.

"For the most part. I'll check on him again later, but I'm betting he'll be fine."

The search took more than two hours. The ranch was cross-fenced, so they didn't have to scour the entire acreage this morning, just the section where the cattle were grazing. No other problems were found.

After a hasty lunch, Ty drove them to Maria's to drop

off Billy before going to Fallon's ranch, taking two horses with them.

The work was in full force. They joined in and spent the next few hours culling calves, keeping them separated from their mothers, moving them to the branding area. For a short time Ty rotated with one of the cowboys notching ears, a messy job. After each notch, a bright orange tag was stapled on.

Timothy Fallon was not as organized as the Montgomerys had been. As the afternoon waned, it was necessary to ride farther and farther from the branding site to locate calves. Holly and one of the riders from the Montgomerys' place followed a trail into a thicket, finding several cows and their calves. They bunched the small herd and the cowboy pushed them ahead of him.

"I'll check for more," she called, riding farther along the gully. It grew silent as she rounded a bend and was cut off from the commotion of the branding. She listened and heard the sound of a calf bawling. Riding quickly, she soon found a half dozen more. She circled and got them moving toward the action just as Hank Palmer rode into view.

He reined in and looked at her, a sly smile on his face.

"Well, if it ain't the boss's daughter. What're you doing out here?"

"Working." Her horse moved to block a calf from bolting. She sat easily in the saddle, focused on the stock, ignoring Hank as much as she could.

"We miss you at the house. You coming home tonight?"

"I have a new job," she said, moving closer. "Are you going to help or not?"

"You're not my boss anymore, Holly. Leastways, that's what I heard."

"Get out of my way," she said. The gelding was well-trained; she hardly had to give it any commands for it to respond to the antics of the calves. As they darted this way and that, the horse met them at every instance, turning them back in the direction Holly wanted them to go.

When she drew level with Hank, he reached out and caught the reins on the left side of her horse.

"What's your hurry?" he asked.

"And what's your problem, Hank? Can't take no for an answer? I have no interest in you, not as a cowboy, not as a boyfriend, certainly not as anything more. I tried to be tactful but it didn't work, so I'll be as blunt as I know how. Leave me alone. I don't want to go out with you, work with you or have anything else to do with you," Holly said, anger spilling over until she thought she'd go crazy. How dare this man keep harassing her. How dare her father even suggest she consider Hank Palmer as a mate when she had loved Tyler Alverez her whole life.

The knowledge stunned her. She yanked the reins from Hank's hands, ignoring his bitter sneer, and kicked her horse. The animal surged forward, keeping the calves in sight and continuing to do what he was trained for. Seconds later, back in the open, Holly slowed to let the horse turn left to block the return of a calf.

She was almost shaking with fury.

Ty rode up on her right took one look at her and turned his horse to fall in beside her.

"You okay?"

"I am now," she muttered.

"Something happen?"

"Nothing I couldn't handle."

THE NEXT SEVERAL DAYS followed like the first. Holly was too tired at night to do anything after dinner but fall into her new bed and sleep. Up again early the next morning, they'd do chores around Ty's place, head to Montgomery's to drop off Billy and then on to branding. When they finished at Fallons, the entire company moved to the Rocking B. Holly didn't. She was not going there as a hired hand from another ranch.

There was plenty to do at Ty's place. She spent two days clearing out the bunkhouse, burning all the debris. Then she listed all that needed to be done to make it habitable. She took stock of food supplies and made lists of necessities.

Each night she'd listen to Ty talk to Billy about the day. The child didn't care; Holly knew Ty was filling her in without making her have to ask.

Soon the branding at her dad's place was finished and the next ranch was up.

EVEN SARA WAS DROOPING by the last afternoon at the Mallo spread. It had been a long three weeks, but almost all the calves on the neighboring ranches were branded and castrated.

"Still having that end-of-branding party?" Holly asked as she stopped in the only shade in miles to get a drink of icy lemonade Mrs. Mallo had for the riders. Sara was standing there looking cool as could be, though tired.

"Not today and not tomorrow. Maybe Saturday. When I get home today, I'm soaking in a tub until the water turns to ice. Then sleeping until Saturday. I never knew my bones could ache so much."

Holly laughed, drank the refreshing beverage and wiped her dirty face. "I like the part about sleeping for two days. But us working folks have to get up tomorrow and see what the bossman has in store."

"How's it going at Ty's?" Sara asked.

Holly shrugged. "Fine. Too early to tell, actually. We feed the stock morning and night and then we've pretty much been at one or the other branding sites. I guess any routine he wants will start tomorrow."

Another two riders came up and Sara moved to the very fringe of the shade. "Any word from your dad?"

"Nope." Holly had hoped he'd at least call. She checked in with his doctor every few days. Her dad was apparently improving, but not as rapidly as he wanted.

"I can't believe he hasn't contacted you. Did you know Donny left?"

"What? He's been on the ranch for years. Where did he go?"

"Word is he told your father either you return and take over or he'd leave. Your father made some pithy statement and Donny took off. I heard he went to see his daughter. Don't know if he's coming back."

"Who's running the ranch?"

"Hank Palmer."

Holly stared at her friend, almost unable to comprehend what she said. "That lazy bastard? Dad must have rocks for brains. Hank is his most recent hire. All the other men have more experience on the Rocking B."

"Probably none of them wanted the job. Some cowboys like their lives, don't want to be a manager, you know that."

TY LOADED HIS HORSES into the borrowed horse trailer. His next purchase would be one of his own. He'd always used one of his uncle's when in Texas. It was nice of John to let him borrow one of his.

The last of the branding was finished. Next year if he had any calves, they'd be taking a turn at his spread. Would he feel a part of the community by then?

He looked for Holly. They'd ride back to the ranch together. Maria was keeping Billy overnight. He and Brandon had become best friends. They'd both be starting kindergarten in the fall, but wanted to spend as much time together as they could. He was glad his son had found a niche so quickly.

Holly was walking his way. Her face was streaked with dirt and she looked so exhausted he was surprised she didn't drop in her tracks.

A feeling of compassion surprised him. He wanted to pick her up and carry her the rest of the way to the truck. Tell her to sleep on the way to the ranch and then hit the sack.

He looked away. He had no business feeling anything for Holly. He didn't trust her, yet had given her a job at the ranch. He didn't want to get to know her, yet couldn't help picking up on things when working with her. She was a tireless worker—gave her fair share and then some. She was respected by the other men and women in the community. A great friend of Sara Montgomery's. Her riding ability almost equaled his. No wonder people hired her to train stock horses. She was damn good at what she did. The gelding she rode was as smart as they came. And she got every bit of skill out of him.

He was coming to respect her. She'd stood up to her father, which made her almost star material in his eyes. Anyone standing up to old man Bennett deserved more than she'd received.

Would she stay long? Was it only a temporary breach with her father? He didn't know. He only knew that he liked having her around. If things had been different ten years ago—

"Ready to roll?" she asked when she reached the truck.

"Yep. Billy's staying at the Dennises' tonight. I don't have to return the horse trailer until tomorrow." He was tired, but a low anticipation built knowing he and Holly would be alone tonight.

"Flip you for first use of the bathroom," she said, climbing into the truck. She pulled out a quarter and tossed it into the air.

"Heads," Tyler said as he got behind the wheel.

"Tails it is, thank God," she said, leaning back. "I'm so dirty you'll probably gain an extra acre of land when I get it washed off."

"You look as wiped out as I feel."

"It's a disguise, I'm really fresh and ready for another sixteen hours of work," she said, her eyes closed.

"How about we stop off and get something from the diner. That way we don't have to cook."

"I'd much rather have pizza," she murmured. "Get a combination and it has all the basic food groups except chocolate."

"I hadn't heard chocolate was one of the basic food groups," he said, backing the trailer around. He tooted the horn at another rancher in farewell and pulled in line with the others already leaving.

She smiled, but he knew before they reached the highway that she'd fallen asleep.

Ty felt a rightness that surprised him. He was tired, dirty and had years of work ahead of him to build his ranch up to what he wanted it to be. But for this one moment in time, he was content.

When he reached the pizza place, he left Holly sleeping in the truck. Almost thirty minutes later he came out, carrying a large pizza and a six-pack of beer. Holly stood near a small car, chatting with the driver. He recognized the town librarian, Tilly Larson. She didn't look much older than when he'd been borrowing books from the library. Of course to a kid, she'd looked old. Maybe as he aged, she'd just look younger and younger.

"Miss Larson," he said when he joined them.

"Tilly, please, Ty. You still reading those mysteries?"

"I am. Nothing like a good murder to relax by."

She laughed and glanced sharply at Holly and back at Ty. "You two together?"

"I'm working for Ty," Holly said.

Tilly couldn't hide her surprise. "I didn't know. What about your dad?"

"He's still in the convalescent hospital as I said."

"So then who is running his ranch?"

"I have no idea," Holly said. She looked at Ty. "We better get a move on or that pizza will be stone-cold."

CHAPTER EIGHT

"SHE KNEW ABOUT US, didn't she?" Holly said after a while.

"Maybe. Most of the kids in high school knew we were dating. If they thought it important enough, they could have told their parents. We were trying to keep it from your father, not the world."

Ty relived some of the frustration of their senior year. He'd been so taken with pretty Holly Bennett he'd wanted to shout it from the mountains that she had chosen him. He now knew it was important he teach his son what his father had failed to get through to him—if someone wanted something kept quiet, there was probably a damn bad reason for it.

Half an hour later, Ty reheated some of the pizza. He could hear the shower running. Holly was still beneath the cascading water. Try as he might, he couldn't get a picture of her body slick with water out of his mind. They'd gone skinny-dipping once—feeling daring and risqué. He'd seen that lithe body streaming with water in the moonlight. He'd never forgotten.

The dinging of the microwave brought him back to reality. He took the plate out and seated himself at the table. In other circumstances he'd wait for his guest. But this was just his new hand, and he was not going to put more importance to her being here than was warranted.

He'd almost finished his portion of the pizza by the time she came into the kitchen. Her dirty clothes were bundled and held away from her. Her hair was loose, still damp, and flowed over her shoulders like honey.

Ty forced his eyes away, clenching a hand to prevent himself from reaching out to touch that silky mane.

"Did you already eat?" she asked, spotting his plate.

"Yeah, the rest is still in the box. Heat it up when you're ready." With luck, there'd be some hot water left so he could shower and change.

Holly went to the back porch, where the ancient washing machine stood.

The phone rang. He reached for it from his seat.

"Alverez," he answered, hoping it wasn't Maria calling about a problem with Billy.

"Hi, Ty, Sara here. We're putting together an after-branding party tomorrow night. All the work is done and we have to celebrate. Can you and Holly come tomorrow night? We want everyone who participated to be at the party."

"I can't speak for her, but I'll be there. Billy, too?"

"Of course. Is Holly there? I'll ask her myself if you won't."

He looked at the back door just as Holly reentered. "I'll ask her." Ty held the receiver away from his head. "Sara wants to know if you'll attend a party they're having tomorrow night. An after-branding celebration."

She smiled and nodded. "Sure. May I speak to her?" She took the phone and began to talk. He rose and took his plate to the sink, rinsing it and leaving it. Heading for the bathroom, he ignored the chatter behind him. Ty needed to get away from the beguiling woman who dominated his thoughts and now dominated his own home.

After his shower, he went out to the corral to check the horses. A couple came to the fence to visit. He scratched their heads, then moved into the barn. The single light-bulb scarcely drove away the darkness. There were more light fixtures. He'd have to get new bulbs in them one of these days. Now that the branding was finished, he was ready to turn his attention to his own plans. Making friends had been a start. Two men had talked to him about training some horses. With the ones he'd already signed up, the real work around his place would soon begin.

The night was pleasant after the heat of the day, the breeze from the west lowering the temperature. He was tired, but not sleepy. Maybe he'd sit on the front porch for a while and make more plans. There was so much to do.

When he rounded the house, he was surprised to find Holly seated there, her feet resting on the railing. The chairs Wilson had left behind weren't very comfortable. He often sat in that exact same pose.

"Horses okay?" she asked. "I'll check on mine soon."

"No need, they're all fine." He stepped onto the wooden porch, hesitating a moment. Did he want to stay here with Holly?

"If you want to be alone, I can go back inside," she said.

"No." He pulled a chair forward and put it near hers. He tilted it back, gazing out over the dark landscape.

"It's quieter here than at my dad's place," she commented. "No background noise from televisions or radios."

"That'll change when I hire a couple more men."

"Planning to do that soon?"

"This summer. Need to get the bunkhouse habitable first. I appreciate all the work you did."

They sat in silence for a little while.

"Ty…" Holly said tentatively.

His gut tightened. He hadn't heard her soft voice in the darkness in years. It still had the power to make him want.

"What?"

"Would you play the harmonica for me?"

He hadn't expected that.

"It's getting late."

"Just one or two songs."

Why not? It would keep them from talking. He rose and went into the house, returning with one of his harmonicas. He sat in the chair, tilted it back and began to play. His father had loved the fact his son was "musical." Ty remembered his encouraging him to practice when he'd been younger. He'd fill the times when he could with songs his father loved. In memory of the man who meant so much to Ty, he began with a Mexican song his father had loved. Soon he segued into another and then a ballad of the old west.

Holly sat silently beside him staring out into the starlit night.

Finally he played "Across the Wide Missouri." It was the song she'd loved best ten years ago. He never played it without thinking of their nights together on the banks of the river, the plaintive notes filling the darkness. The sadness felt stronger for the cocoon of night. When he finished the last note, he slapped the mouth organ against his thigh to knock the moisture away.

"It's late and I'll be up early tomorrow," Ty said. If he could sleep tonight with the images that plagued his mind.

"Sara said to get to their place around six tomorrow evening. Can I ride with you, or should I drive my own truck?" Holly asked, taking her feet off the railing and standing.

"We might as well ride together. I'll be bringing Billy home with me. He'll think they do nothing but party up here."

"Didn't you have parties in Texas?"

"Family gatherings. I didn't go out much after my wife died. Billy needed me."

He rose and pushed the old chair back against the front of the house. When he turned, he bumped right into Holly. For a moment neither moved. Then, as if in slow motion, Ty lowered his head and kissed her.

Seconds later he pulled back and turned. "That was a stupid thing to do. It won't happen again," he said as he strode away.

Could a man be any more of an idiot than to take up again with the one woman in the world he'd never forgiven?

HOLLY STOOD STOCK-STILL, stunned at her reaction to Ty's kiss. She heard his footsteps crunching on the gravel as he walked away. Her body seemed to hum with excitement. The old yearnings surfaced with a startling impact. She drew in a deep breath. If she were smart, she'd head for her room and lock the door. Was there even a lock on it?

But that was the old Holly. This one wasn't ready to end things. Not like this.

She jumped off the steps and followed the sound of his footsteps.

"Wait a darn minute, Tyler Alverez. I want to know what's going on!"

He stopped.

"You tell me, Holly. Ten years ago you walked away from what we had, in a cruel and mean way. Now I show up again and this time not as some cowboy's son, but the owner of a ranch next door. Are you here to see if what you threw away back then was a mistake? What is it you want?"

"You didn't call me all summer long!"

"That's a lie and you know it. When I finally got through to the ranch, you told me to get lost, to never set foot on the property. That didn't sound to me like some poor victim forcibly kept away from the man who loved her."

"You loved me? Truly?" She had believed that at one time and found it untrue. She stared at him, wishing there was more light, wishing she could see his eyes.

"What is it you want?" he repeated. His voice sent shivers down her spine. He sounded so angry.

"I just want to know the truth—all of it."

"I told you, ask your father." He turned and walked away from her.

Holly still couldn't believe her father would have kept Ty away from her that summer. He knew how much she grieved over the loss of their baby. Over the fact Ty hadn't come to see her. Had it all been false? No! Her father would never have been so callous. Ty was trying to cover up, make the past sound different.

But what if he wasn't? What if her instincts had been sound and he had loved her? She had wasted ten years of her life keeping herself from trusting other men for fear of being hurt again.

Ty had moved on. The mention of his wife tonight had been like a knife to her heart. She had no one special, had never allowed anyone close enough to form a bond. He'd found someone else to love and had fathered an adorable child.

What had she done? Stayed away from anyone who might have brought her happiness because she was too afraid to take a risk. Too concerned someone would be interested in her father's bank account rather than in her.

She crossed her arms over her chest as if she could hold herself together as the ache in her heart grew.

Tomorrow she'd visit her father and demand he tell her the entire truth—no matter how hard it would be to hear.

THE NEXT MORNING HOLLY WOKE early. She skipped breakfast and grabbed a cup of coffee before going out to see to the horses. She had cleaned the stalls and tossed some flakes of hay into the corral before she saw Ty. He was on his way to his truck.

When he saw her, he called out, "I'm going to get Billy."

She acknowledged him and continued working. As soon as she was finished with the chores, she was heading into town to see her father. Ty's words had echoed all night long. She tried to remember details of the months after the accident, but only the sadness over the loss of her baby and the fact Ty never contacted her remained.

Finished her chores, Holly took a quick shower and changed her clothes. She grabbed some toast and more coffee. On impulse, she called her aunt. Betty had stayed with her that summer, summoned by Holly's father to help with his distraught daughter. Holly knew she was planning to come stay with Ryan once he was fit enough to go home. In the meantime, she had a new grandson she was crazy about and spent lots of time with Holly's cousin Carole and the new baby.

"Aunt Betty, it's Holly," she said when her aunt answered the phone.

"Hello, dear. Is Ryan all right? Do you need me there now?"

"He's improving daily, so the doctors say," Holly responded automatically. "But I still don't know when he's coming home. Actually, I'm calling about something else."

"What is it dear?"

"I want you to think back ten years ago to that summer you spent with us."

"I remember it," Betty said quietly.

"Do you remember if Ty Alverez tried to call me?"

Betty was silent for a long time.

Holly's heart sped up. Had he tried? Or had he not and Betty was trying to be gentle in letting her down?

"Why do you want to know?" her aunt asked finally.

"He says he did. I never got a call, a card, a visit, anything, until the day before I left for college. So is he lying?"

"Are you seeing him again?" The surprise sounded over the line.

"Actually, I'm staying at his house," Holly said.

"What?"

Holly quickly explained the situation to her aunt. "So unless Dad relents, I'm not going to bang my head against the wall and try to run the ranch while he countermands every order I give. Ty was hiring. I signed on.

Anyway, he says he tried to reach me that summer, but I never saw any evidence of it."

"Your father did what he thought best," Betty said. "I followed his instructions."

"Oh, my God, Ty did try to call me." Holly sagged against the wall. He'd been telling the truth. Her father had isolated her. She pressed a hand against her heart. Her dad had known how desperately she wanted to see Ty. How could he have added to her pain that summer by keeping him away—and not telling her Ty tried to contact her?

"He called, wrote several letters, came to the ranch more than once, but the men had orders to turn him away. So did I. Honey, your father was so angry that summer. He didn't want you bothered by the boy."

Holly could scarcely believe her ears. She felt a bit sick. How could her family have done that to her?

"Bothered? I wouldn't have been bothered. We'd made a baby together and lost it. I thought he didn't want anything to do with me. I was so mixed-up that summer, but mostly heartsick at Ty's neglect. Now you're telling me he did try to see me. Oh, God, what he must have thought!"

"Ryan took care of things, dear. He did what he figured was best."

Holly thanked her aunt and soon hung up.

No wonder Ty hated her. He believed she hadn't wanted to see him. And her hurtful words that final day sealed the idea forever.

The phone rang. Holly debated answering. What if it were her aunt calling back. Yet it was Ty's phone. She hadn't provided her with that number.

"Alverez ranch," she answered.

"Is Holly Bennett there?"

"This is Holly." She didn't recognize the woman's voice.

"This is Nurse Hopkins at the convalescent hospital. First, everything is going well with your father—I wanted to make that clear up front. But he would like to see you today. Would it be convenient to stop by?"

"I had planned to come today," she said slowly. Now more than ever, she needed to talk to her father.

Holly hung up and headed for her truck. The sooner it was done, the sooner she'd know the full truth. Her heart hurt at the betrayal. She'd blamed the wrong man all these years.

She entered the hospital with her stomach in knots. All her life it had been her and her father. She had adored him when she was younger. Respected him as she matured. Her mother had died so young. Holly had believed her father loved her. How could he have done this to her?

As she walked down the hall, her steps slowed. She was beginning to have second thoughts. Maybe she shouldn't see him today. Maybe waiting would be better, give her a chance to get her chaotic emotions under control.

She paused at the door in indecision. But the need for the truth took precedence. She knocked.

"Come in," his familiar voice called.

"Hi, Dad," she said, stepping inside. Every time, she felt startled to see him looking so frail sitting in the wheel chair. He'd been so strong and robust all her life.

"About time you showed up. I've been calling the ranch all week."

"I haven't been there. I got a job at another ranch. I told you I would." She sat on the chair near his.

"Didn't believe you'd do it," he grumbled.

"Why not? I told you I either had to have full control of the ranch or I was gone."

"Who's running the place?" he asked.

"I thought Donny was, but Sara said he's gone, too. Didn't he speak to you?"

He shifted in the chair. Then looked out the window. "He called. Said he won't stay without you. He told me a couple of days ago." Ryan drummed the fingers of his right hand on the arm of the wheelchair. "Jerry might be going, too."

Holly remained silent. If he wanted her to do something about it, he had to give her full rein. On that she would stand firm. But she wasn't here today to talk about the ranch.

"I'm staying at the Alverez ranch," she said. "Ty's calling it the T-Bar-J."

"What?" He stared at her, his eyes narrowed.

"Ty was hiring, I needed work."

"And you couldn't wait to take back up with him, is that it? How could you let him get to you again? Don't you remember how he left you all those years ago?"

"The thing is, Dad, Ty remembers it differently," she said evenly.

"He would, damn him."

"He says he tried to call me, tried to see me, that summer."

"Liar."

"Aunt Betty said he tried, too, and you told her to refuse the calls."

Ryan stared at her, his expression difficult to read. Then he looked away. "I wanted better for you than him."

"So you did keep him from contacting me. And lied to me about it," she said. Somehow she'd hoped there would be some other explanation.

"I did what I thought was right," Ryan defended himself.

"No matter how much it hurt me."

He turned to her again, pounded the arm of the chair. "I didn't hurt you, that damn cowboy's son did. Got you pregnant. He had no business hanging around you, I told you time and again to stay away from Jose Alverez's kid."

"Yes, well I didn't. I loved Tyler. I wouldn't have slept with him if I hadn't."

"He wasn't worthy of you. You need someone else."

"It's been ten years. Haven't you ever wondered why I haven't found someone else? Fallen in love and gotten married?"

"Hell, yes. I don't understand you at all. If you're still pining for him, you're more of a fool than I'd like to think," Ryan said.

"I haven't been pining for Ty all this time. Though it shook me badly when he vanished. Or seemed to vanish. What I couldn't get beyond was my judgment. I loved him so much, Dad. You can't imagine. But when I thought his love was false, that he'd just been using me—because that's what you told me that summer, over and over—I believed I couldn't trust my own feelings anymore. I had *believed* he loved me. If he'd fooled me, how could I trust myself with anyone else?"

Ryan stared at her. "Holly, honey, he wasn't the man for you."

"Do you understand what I'm saying?"

Why couldn't her dad listen to her? He sounded like a broken record. She needed acknowledgment that her feelings counted.

Slowly he nodded.

"I found out he did try to reach me that summer. Knowing that, maybe I can put things in perspective. Maybe what I felt was true. Maybe his feelings had been true as well. I wasn't wrong in my judgment."

"Teenagers don't fall in love forever. It would have passed. There's no judgment involved, just hormones."

"Maybe you should have let it play out as it would have. He moved on. He married, has an adorable little boy. I'm still stuck in a time warp."

"You stay away from him!"

"I'm a grown woman, not a little girl anymore. I'll see whomever I wish," she said calmly. She felt numb. She had wanted him to say something to mitigate the situation. To explain why he'd taken such a drastic step and broken her heart. To just keep saying Ty wasn't for her was no answer.

"Not if he's married," Ryan said triumphantly.

"His wife died."

"Dammit, girl, stay away from him! He'll break your heart."

"I thought he did once, but now I think it was you who caused my broken heart."

"Holly," he said, holding out his hand.

She just stared at him.

Ryan scowled. "Get away from Tyler Alverez. That family has nothing to do with ours. I need you running the ranch."

"Change your mind?"

"You belong on the Rocking B. Not working for someone else. I'll call the attorney and have him write you up some papers. You get back home and run that ranch!"

She'd hadn't expected him to cave.

"So all my decisions will be final until you return home," she clarified.

He nodded, frowning. Obviously he wasn't happy with the situation, but he apparently disliked the idea of her at Ty's even more.

"I'd fire Hank first thing," she warned.

He opened his mouth as if to say something, then snapped it shut. Shrugging, he said, "Whatever. You'll be in charge—temporarily."

"I'm not buying the Helton bull."

"It's a good move."

"We're skating close to the red zone on finances. I want to build up our reserves before we make any major expenditures. This nursing home isn't cheap and who knows what other expenses might arise. We don't know how long you'll be here." She looked at him closely. "Unless you want me to consider McNab's offer to buy some of the land."

"Never! You're too cautious. I'll be back on my feet soon."

"But until then, I'd be one hundred percent in charge, right?"

Ryan nodded once, abruptly. "You run that ranch like I taught you. But only until I get home. And no selling off any land."

"Understood. Call me when the papers are ready." She got up. "Why did you keep Ty from talking to me that summer?"

"You were eighteen, young, poised for great things—your first year of college, moving beyond Turnbow. I didn't want you tied down to some cowboy who could hardly make ends meet."

She glanced at her faded jeans and scuffed boots. "Well, I sure went far, didn't I?"

Walking out of the room, Holly wondered if he'd really have the attorney draw up a power of attorney. If so, she could go home. Get away from the temptation of Ty Alverez. Make sure she was kept so busy she wouldn't stay awake nights longing for what could never be.

Holly got into her truck but didn't start the engine. Things would have ended up so differently ten years ago if she'd known her father was trying to keep them apart. She would have gone after Ty herself. These days, it was hard to think about how listless she'd felt all summer. As if she'd been in a haze, waiting for the rest of the world to come to her.

She should have known Ty wouldn't have abandoned her.

Why hadn't she even listened to him that last day? The end result could be blamed on no one but her. She could have changed everything and hadn't.

Holly wanted to drive off somewhere and think things through. But she didn't have that luxury. Ty had hired her to help him out. He definitely needed someone working with him around his ranch. She owed him the loyalty he'd asked for.

She wanted to weep for the lost opportunity. For the romance that was stolen from her. For the direction her life had taken as a result.

Dare she reach out to take what she wanted—another chance with Ty.

CHAPTER NINE

HOLLY RETURNED TO Ty's ranch. His truck was parked by the back of the house. She went inside and called, but no one answered. Heading to the barn a minute later, she noticed the pony was missing, as was one of the horses. Ty had taken Billy for a ride.

She could do some work in the barn or see if she could catch up with them. She elected riding. Her best guess was they'd set out for the river. It was going to be warm enough today for a little boy to play in the water. And Holly would like to know if the latest repairs on the fence had held.

Holly's guess was correct. When she crested the small rise separating the river from the field she'd crossed, she saw the horse and pony tied to a tree, dozing in the shade. Looking closely, she spotted Ty and Billy at the water's edge. It looked as if they were skipping stones.

As she drew nearer, they heard her and turned. Ty's hat was pulled down to shade his eyes. She wished she could see them, gauge his reaction to her joining them.

She stopped near the other horses and dismounted, tying her mare to a low limb.

"Hi," she said. "I thought I'd find you two here. Billy going swimming?"

"We didn't bring a towel and I don't want him to have to put on clothes when wet and ride all the way home in them. He'll get plenty of days to go this summer," Ty said. He seemed guarded. "Did you see your father?"

"I did." She walked over to them, smiling at the little boy. "Hey, Billy. Do you like the river?"

"Yep. Daddy said he used to swim in this very river when he was a little boy like me," he said proudly. "Watch, Holly. I can make this rock jump on the water." He let loose with a small stone, but it merely sank.

Billy frowned. "How come it didn't skip, Daddy?"

"You threw it too high. It arced into the water. You want to toss it low so it skims along the top." Ty picked up a flat stone and had it skipping four times before it sank below the surface.

Billy looked at Holly. "Can you do that?"

"Maybe not as good as your daddy." She picked up a smooth rock, remembering suddenly the afternoons she and Ty had sat at the water's edge, idly skipping stones as they made plans for a future together. The forgotten image caught her unaware.

"Something wrong?" Ty asked.

She shook her head. "Just an odd memory," she said, leaning over to skip the stone. It bounced twice before disappearing.

"You used to be better," Ty said.

"I used to practice more." She sat on the ground and smiled at Billy. "I'll just watch you. See how many times you can make it bounce."

Ty sat beside her, not too close, but near enough to talk.

"I talked to both my father and my Aunt Betty," she said when she was sure Billy was too involved to pay attention. "I'm sorry I ever doubted you then. I can only blame it on grief and depression. I knew you loved me, I loved you. I should have demanded to see you. Or gone to town and found you for myself. But I did hardly anything those weeks after I lost the baby."

She didn't need to tell him how her father had deliberately and continually put the idea in her head that Ty had only been amusing himself. She should have stood stronger in her own beliefs.

She turned to him. He watched his son, smiling when Billy made the rock skip.

"So where does that leave us?" she asked, almost holding her breath for his answer.

"Where do you want that to leave us?"

"I don't know." She looked at the river, wishing he'd just come out and say what she wanted him to say. "Maybe we could start over? I mean, we had something back then. I know you found someone else to love, but I never did. I was afraid to trust my feelings.

"Now I know I should have. Maybe see what develops?"

"The basic problem between us hasn't changed, Holly. If your trust and belief in me could be so weak, how can you stand for the long haul?"

"That's not fair. I was young. The circumstances were unique."

"You're older now, true."

"And I know more about life. And about trust. I'm sorry for what happened. I can promise it would never happen again. Believe me, please."

He was silent for a long moment. Then he looked at her. "The thing is I don't know if I want to take the risk."

She blinked at that. "What risk? I'm interested,

you're interested. We might end up where we left off and start planning for the future."

He stared off in the distance, as if reviewing the past, before speaking again.

"Connie was a good woman. She was pretty and lively and loved to dance. We went to a lot of parties when we were first married. She kept an immaculate house."

Holly didn't want to hear about his wife. Why was he talking about her now? As a defense?

"How nice for you," she said, unable to mask the bitterness. It hurt that he'd loved another woman. His son would forever remind her of the baby they'd lost and the love that had ended that fateful night.

Or had it ended? She was drawn to this man like no other. She sensed he felt the pull, too.

"It was hard when she died, on me, on Billy. There are all kinds of risks—this ranch is one."

"I'd be another," she said, knowing where he was going.

"I don't think I'm ready for something like that. And I'm not ready to risk Billy's emotions, either. Maybe you'd stay. Maybe not. He's too young to understand if someone becomes a part of his life and then leaves."

"I wouldn't leave," she said slowly, feeling her heart pound in her chest. He was turning her down.

"I don't want to take the risk," he repeated.

Ty checked his son. Billy was tossing small sticks into the water and watching them drift downstream. He was too preoccupied to listen to the adults talking. Still, he lowered his voice.

"The thing is, Holly, I'm a different man now and you've changed as well. But that trust, that love that we

Get FREE BOOKS and FREE GIFTS when you play the...

LAS VEGAS
GAME

Just scratch off the gold box with a coin. Then check below to see the gifts you get!

YES! I have scratched off the gold box. Please send me my **2 FREE BOOKS** and **2 FREE GIFTS** for which I qualify. I understand that I am under no obligation to purchase any books as explained on the back of this card.

336 HDL ELX2   **135 HDL ELTR**

FIRST NAME   LAST NAME

ADDRESS

APT.#   CITY

STATE/PROV.   ZIP/POSTAL CODE

(H-SR-03/07)

7	7	7	Worth TWO FREE BOOKS plus TWO BONUS Mystery Gifts!
			Worth TWO FREE BOOKS!
			TRY AGAIN!

www.eHarlequin.com

Offer limited to one per household and not valid to current Harlequin Superromance® subscribers. All orders subject to approval.

shared, it's gone. Maybe it wasn't entirely your fault, but it still ended that last day I came to see you. You sent me away. All summer my father had told me to leave you alone, that Bennett would end up winning. I kept trying to see you, kept faith in our love—until you ordered me off the ranch."

"I'm so sorry." Tears filled her eyes, but she resolutely stopped them from falling. Blinking rapidly, she looked away. "When it seemed you'd left me to deal with the baby's loss all by myself, I was angry, hurt beyond belief. I'd lost our baby and I thought I'd lost you."

"Given that, you had a right to be angry. I was, too. But I gave all I had and it wasn't enough. I can't do that again and risk having it thrown back in my face. I'm planning to make something of this ranch. I want my son to grow up in Turnbow, make lifelong friends and know he has a future. I don't want to be at odds with any of my neighbors. It's too much to chance."

She rose. "Thank you for making that clear," she said. She reset her hat and headed for the horses. Her one shot had fallen short of the mark. Ty wasn't interested. Ever since she'd talked to her aunt, she'd held the faint hope that once things were cleared up, he'd sweep her into his arms and say let's start again. It wasn't going to happen. She unlooped the reins and mounted.

"Holly, wait." He came over to her where she sat on her horse.

"Stay."

"Why?"

"Things are going to get hectic. Monday I have a new horse coming in for training. I've also put out more fliers for hiring—I need at least one more hand. We need to finish getting the bunkhouse repaired. You've worked hard these last few days on the branding. Stay here for a while today and relax."

She'd hoped he wanted her to stay for more. But if that was all he was offering, could she take it? Watching him interact with his son, hearing him talk and knowing she didn't know him anymore. He'd had an entire ten years of a different life. He didn't know her, either. But maybe they could become friends if nothing else.

"Okay, for a little while." She felt the tension ease.

"Then we'll all head back and have lunch. Don't want to eat too much, though. Sara seems to put on a fancy spread at the drop of a hat."

Holly nodded, smiling. "She does love to throw parties. Wait until you see what she does at Christmas."

The rest of the day passed in harmony. Holly refused to dwell on the past or on the lack of response from Ty. She focused more on Billy, and found him a delightful child, full of curiosity and enthusiasm. He reminded her of herself when she was little—especially when he began to ask questions about everything. He was insatiable!

Thinking about the morning as she showered in preparation for the barbecue at the Montgomerys', she knew she had missed out on a lot by not trusting any men she'd met over the past few years. Had she subconsciously compared them to Ty and found them wanting?

She sagged against the cool tile, letting the water wash over her. She longed for Ty, wished he'd kiss her again. Wished things could go back ten years. But he'd made it pretty clear he was no longer interested. Time to let go of that dream and find another.

Or work harder on convincing him to give them a chance.

Could she do that? The party would be a good start. There was always a lot of flirting and playfulness. She'd show him she could be counted on to be fun, and not harp on the past. Show him she had changed. He could trust her. If only he'd take that one leap into the unknown.

She finished her shower and donned one of her summer dresses. The spaghetti straps showed off her shoulders to advantage.

Her hair loose, it brushed against the skin of her bare shoulders when she turned her head.

Makeup on, hair done and dress in place, she opened the bathroom door and came to a stop. Ty was slouching against the opposite wall. His eyes widened when he saw her.

"Sorry, did I take too long?" she asked, noting the appreciation in his gaze.

"When a woman comes out looking that good, there's no such thing as 'too long.'"

"Thanks." She smiled, her heart fluttering. He wasn't totally immune.

"Billy's all ready. Keep an eye on him, will you, so he doesn't get into anything before we leave?" Ty said, moving by her, carrying fresh clothes into the bathroom.

"Sure." She wished for more.

Dumping her dirty clothes in her laundry basket, Holly went to the living room to find Billy. He was watching a video and barely glanced away from the television screen when she entered.

She sat and watched the movie with the little boy, almost as fascinated with the animation as he was.

When Ty stopped in the doorway a little later, she

looked over and knew she was in trouble. He looked heart-stoppingly gorgeous. He'd be the sexiest cowboy there. It would be a long evening with every single woman at the barbecue queuing up to dance with Ty. She wanted him focused on her alone.

How could she get him to enough to realize what they once had could be rekindled? She truly believed that but obviously hadn't convinced him.

"Everyone ready?" Ty asked.

"Yes!" Billy jumped up and ran to turn off the television. "Brandon's going to be there, right, Daddy?"

"He wouldn't miss it," Ty confirmed. He winked at her as if they were in this together.

She so wished they were.

TY PUT BILLY IN HIS CAR SEAT in the middle of the truck, and held the door for Holly. Her scent lingered in the still afternoon air, a bit sweet like Holly herself. She'd taken his breath away when he'd first seen her come out of the bathroom. The bodice of that deceptively innocent dress fit her like a second skin; the skirt was short and flirty as it swirled around her legs. Legs that went on forever. He forgot how feminine she was when he saw her day after day in cowboy clothes. Tonight she was all woman.

He'd given her earlier suggestion a lot of thought over the afternoon. He never told her how much he'd been hurt ten years ago. All summer he'd suspected it was Ryan's doing—keeping them apart. But then when she'd ordered him away, all hope had been lost.

Now she was suggesting they start again.

He'd never told a soul that he'd married Connie hoping for the kind of relationship he and Holly had known. They didn't have the same sparks. He'd wanted a family and a home of his own and when Connie had begun flirting with him, he'd thought she could make him happy. He'd tried his best, but he never loved her as he had Holly. Maybe there was something unique about a first love or a love lost.

He'd been the best husband he knew how to be. He had adored Billy, right from the day he was born. And Connie had been a loving mother. Ty would always regret she didn't live to see her son grow up. But the truth was, tonight he was glad it was Holly he was taking to the Montgomerys' place.

He climbed into the truck and they started off. Billy chatted as they drove. Ty wondered what he would have done had Connie lived and he'd brought her to Turnbow. Would seeing Holly again have raised doubts about the strength of his marriage? No, he'd already had those. Seeing her would have brought them to the forefront.

He was a damned coward. The one thing he had wanted forever was Holly Bennett. She had practically offered herself on a plate this afternoon and he'd turned her down. His father had said he analyzed things too much. Maybe his dad had been right.

What if they could recapture the love they'd once known? What if they could build that future together that they'd once dreamed about—wasn't he a fool for turning down the possibility?

What if she broke his heart again? Or Billy's?

"Daddy!" Billy broke into his musings.

"What?"

"I said, can I stay over at Brandon's tonight?"

"No. Not tonight. You were there last night."

"But I don't get to go so much now that we're always at our ranch. I don't get to see him so much."

"Next week you can invite him over to our place to stay the night," Ty said.

"Really. In my own room?"

"Yes."

Holly laughed softly. "You've made his day," she said.

Ty suddenly wished he could make her day.

The drive of the Montgomery ranch was just like it was at the pre-branding party a few weeks before. Trucks and cars were parked everywhere. Lanterns that would be needed later in the night were strung from post to tree. People were dressed up, or not, as they preferred. There was a line at the keg of beer, a smaller one where wine was being poured. And already the aroma of barbecue chicken and beef filled the air.

"I'm helping Sara," Holly said when he parked. "I'll see you two later."

She could hardly wait to escape, he thought as he unbuckled Billy and lifted him up. This time around they knew more people and didn't have to worry about how they would be received. But as he watched Holly wind her way through the crowd, he knew he'd trade it all for a quiet night alone with her.

"Hey, Ty," one of the ranchers called.

Ty waved.

He set Billy on the ground and held his hand. "We'll hunt up Brandon," he said, heading over to where John was wielding the barbecue tongs on the huge grill.

"Seen any kids?" Ty asked.

John smiled at Billy. "I think they're all in the barn. One of the cats had kittens a couple of weeks ago and they're the center of attention today."

"Oh, kittens, can I go see, Daddy?"

"Okay, but come check in with me when you're finished there. If I'm not here, ask someone to find me."

"Okay." He took off at a run for the big barn.

"Children love babies of all kinds. You should get him a puppy or something," John said.

"I'm thinking about it." He looked over at the house. Would Holly be the one bringing out more meat for the grill like the last time?

Hell, he had it bad. He turned back and met John's eyes.

"Need something from the house?" John asked.

"No. Let me get a beer and I'll be back to help."

TY KNEW HE'D OWE MARIA Dennis for the rest of his life. She had taken the kids under her wing and after they'd eaten, brought them to her place to play and allow the parents a night of their own. As soon as everyone had finished eating, Sara had turned on her stereo system, brought outside for the evening, and pointed out a wooden platform where people could dance. The cowboys lined up to ask the women, married or not.

Ty watched from the sidelines, checking on who danced with Holly. Trying to judge her interest level when different men asked her to dance was an exercise in futility. She seemed happy enough with each one. Finally he'd had enough. He put down his beer and stepped out on the platform, heading directly for her. If she was going to dance with anyone who asked, he planned to be next in the lineup.

"Dance?" he asked, just as Sara put on a dreamy, slow-paced song.

She looked flustered, warm from all the activity, but nodded.

He drew her into his arms, feeling her against him for the first time in ten years. If he closed his eyes, he could almost imagine they were at the prom, dancing close, attuned to each other's thoughts and feelings. Her scent intoxicated him, her heat ignited his own. He wanted her as much as he had at eighteen. Her soft curves seemed made for him. When his hand on her back pressed her closer, she seemed to soften and moved with him in unison, body and soul. Slowly they circled the crowded platform.

It was the worst agony Ty had experienced in ages. He wanted her so badly, he wondered if they could slip away behind the trees. He opened his eyes and drew on the small measure of sanity remaining. He'd blown her off that morning. The last thing Holly would be interested in would be getting horizontal with him tonight.

On the other hand, considering the way she clung, maybe the physical attraction was driving her crazy as well. She was single, he was single. There'd be no misunderstandings if they ended up in bed together. No declaration of undying passion.

He almost grinned. Maybe undying passion. It was trust that came hard.

When the song wound down, Ty released her, but kept hold of her hand.

"Dance with me again," he said.

"All right," she said with a smile. Her eyes looked mysterious in the faint lantern light. Her smile was feminine and inscrutable. He wished he knew what she was thinking.

The night was warmer than it had been at the last party. A slight breeze kept it from being stifling, but it would be the height of summer before long. The music went from slow and dreamy to fast and furious. Ty danced every dance after that with Holly. When other men came near, he'd frown at them to keep them away.

She laughed and went willingly back into his arms. It was as if they were magically bound for the evening. Nothing would stop either of them from getting what they wanted—each other.

Finally John announced that the next song would be the last. It was a slow ballad, the familiar tune filling the night as couples gathered for one last dance. Ty pulled Holly in close, inhaling the scent of her, absorbing the feel of her against him, holding her as if she were precious spun glass. He would have liked the night to last forever.

"Stay with me tonight," he whispered against her hair. He wanted to bury his face in those soft tresses and breathe in her special scent all night long.

"I'm already going home with you," she said, pulling back just a bit so she could meet his eyes.

"I mean with me all night long," he said, gazing into hers. The dark blue looked almost black in the dim light. They widened slightly as she understood.

He'd just told her earlier he didn't want to take up where they left off; now less than twelve hours later he was propositioning her. Would she slap him silly—or agree?

"Billy?"

"He'll sleep like a log. He gets up around seven if I don't wake him first, so we'd have until then." He could almost count his heartbeats as she deliberated.

She studied his expression for a long time then asked. "What changed?"

"Nothing. Or maybe everything. It feels like old

times, dancing. I want you. Maybe we could see where things take us. Or maybe we're just two single people who share a night together." He was making no promises. Honesty had to work or he'd do without. But holding her showed him that the sexual attraction was as strong as ever. He wasn't an eighteen-year-old teenager now, ruled by hormones. Yet still he wanted her with a desire that was almost primal in intensity.

She hesitated, then nodded. "Okay."

He didn't want to appear impatient, but he couldn't help willing the song to end. It was one thing to hold her like this when there was nothing else between them, but now that she'd agreed to sleep with him, he was anxious to get home and into bed. It had been a decade of longing for this woman. Would tonight show him he'd held on to a myth all these years? That Holly was merely a woman like any other and only the forbidden aspect had elevated her in his mind?

When the dance was over, Ty went to fetch Billy. The little boy was fast asleep and hardly woke when Ty put him in his car seat. He flopped over, rested his head against Holly's shoulder and was soon asleep again.

"I should have left him with Maria, but he stayed there last night and I don't want to push my luck. She's been a lifesaver for me," Ty said when he got into the truck.

"What did you do with him in Texas?" Holly asked as Ty backed out and joined the line of vehicles departing.

"My Tia Sophia, Dad's sister, watched him if I went out. She loves children and had plenty of time to keep him for me. There's lots of family in Texas."

"I'm surprised you came back to Wyoming," Holly said. "With no family here and all."

"Meaning that I wasn't exactly welcomed here?" he asked.

"Meaning family mostly."

"They'll still be there if we need them. But Wyoming is home. I was raised here and I missed it when I was in Texas." He wouldn't tell her how surprised he'd been when he'd learned of his inheritance. It would always be marred slightly by the fact that his father hadn't returned as a rancher. That had been Jose's dream all his life.

"Besides, it was just your father who made life so miserable here. Most folks were fine with my father being a cowboy on the McKenzie ranch."

"Are you saying my father is a snob?" she asked.

"I'm not out to pick a fight, Holly. Let the past stay how it is. We aren't going to agree on things, so leave it."

"Hard to make love to someone who's fighting with you," she commented.

He laughed. It was that or wring her neck. "We aren't fighting. But if you're having second thoughts, say so. I'm not making you do anything."

"I'm not having second thoughts," she said in a low voice.

He hoped she meant it.

She was silent the rest of the way home. He wondered what she was thinking about. The times they'd made love as teens? Her father's opposition?

He couldn't wait to put Billy to bed. He wanted the rest of the night with Holly.

WHEN THE RANCH HOUSE CAME into sight, Holly almost bounced in her seat with nerves. As the miles had passed, her anticipation rose. She had not been intimate with many men. She'd cautiously dated at college, only to be disappointed when none of the men there measured up to Ty. And feeling her own instincts were unreliable, she'd been careful to guard her heart. But there'd been one or two she'd taken a chance on. Nothing much to remember, except the huge letdown of each episode. She'd soon decided it was better to be celibate than disappointed.

But she'd never regretted a single time with Ty Alverez. He'd set her body and soul on fire. Excitement hummed in her veins. Tonight she'd see if her view of things stemmed from a teenager's ability to exaggerate everything, or if the deep feelings she'd thought she'd known had been real.

Would it make any difference to Ty? She wanted him to want her. To give them a chance together. Would he be more open to trying a relationship if the sex was terrific? Gee, nothing like a little pressure.

Ty quickly unbuckled his sleeping son. Billy's head lolled against his father's shoulder when Ty carried him into the house. Holly followed, closing the door behind them all while Ty continued down the hall to Billy's room.

She slipped into her own room and, putting her purse on the dresser, looked into the mirror. Her eyes revealed both the uncertainty she felt and the burning anticipation. She ran her fingers through her hair and took a breath before leaving the safety of her room. As she walked through the kitchen, she switched off the light. Only the hall light illuminated the way.

Tonight was hers and she planned to make the most of it!

When Ty came out of Billy's room he looked surprised to see her. Holly built up her courage and went straight to him.

"What's up, cowboy?" she asked, walking her fingers up his chest.

He captured her hand, bringing it to his mouth to place a kiss in her palm.

"You look beautiful tonight. I was jealous of all the other men who danced with you."

The compliment swept through her, making her heart beat even faster. Her skin felt too tight, her nerves jangling as she stepped even closer to the danger Ty represented. Tonight would change everything. She just hoped it changed it for the better.

He pulled her into his arms and kissed her. Her head spun, her mind shut down and only her feelings remained to enjoy every nuance of this touch. His mouth was hot and ready for hers; his tongue demanding entry. When he deepened the kiss, she was lost. She clung to him as if she'd be swept away otherwise.

Slowly they revolved down the hall, moving toward the open door to his room. His arms held her tightly against him, she could feel every muscle in his chest and the swelling behind his jeans. A feminine satisfaction settled on her. He wanted her as much as she wanted him.

An endless moment later the light flicked off. She realized he'd found the hall switch. She couldn't see anything, but she didn't want to see, she wanted to sink into the feelings that coursed through her body. Her fingers relearned the texture of his skin, the thickness of his hair, the strength of his muscles. Her mouth remembered the taste of him.

She felt the edge of the bed nudge her legs and almost fell back, but his arms held her up. He unzipped her dress and stepped back, breaking the kiss. She shimmied out of it, letting it slide down her body to lie in a puddle of soft material at her feet. The barely there strapless bra and bikini panties were all that separated her from Ty.

His hands skimmed over her while she reached out to unbutton his shirt. Spreading it, she let her fingertips explore his chest, brushing against his nipples. She smiled to hear the sudden intake of breath.

Her hands drifted down to his belt and unfastened it. He instantly toed off his boots and got rid of his clothes. Holly unfastened her bra and let it drop, reaching for her panties.

"Let me," he said, leaning over to tug the bit of lace down, his fingers trailing fire along their path.

The world spun when he picked her up to place her on the bed and then lay down next to her.

"Are you sure?" he asked, his hand already cupping her breast, his thumb caressing her nipple. The sensations only escalated with his touch.

"Too late to stop."

"If you say the word, I will," he said leaning closer.

"My word is yes, I'm sure." She reached up for his kiss and sank back against the pillows as he followed her, his mouth bringing her pleasure she hadn't known in ten years.

Foreplay was a good thing, Holly thought moments later, but too much didn't make it a better thing. She felt as if she'd explode into a thousand pieces, and still he kept kissing her, caressing her and bringing her to the edge before backing down.

Her nails lightly raked his back and she reveled in the groan of delight he made. "Now," she panted, longing for the connection, for that final release.

He reached into the drawer beside the bed and withdrew a condom. Slowly he rose above her and settled between her thighs. Holly's eyes had adjusted to the faint light of the stars coming through the windows. She could see him as he lowered himself and pushed home. The spiraling heat rose with each thrust and she clung to him, moving with him, his kiss filling her with the excitement that only Ty had ever brought her.

The explosive climax carried her to another realm. She loved this man. She had as a teenager; she had all the long years he'd been gone; she did to this day. She would forever.

"I love you, Ty," she said as he spent himself and slowly eased down to lie beside her, drawing her close.

He'd made no response. She didn't know if he'd heard, but she'd had to say it. Her love bubbled up until she wanted to embrace the entire world with her happiness. Ty Alverez was a man worth waiting for.

Her father had been wrong. Ty had always been the man for her. Now if only she could prove it to both men.

CHAPTER TEN

HOLLY AWOKE THE next morning when she heard Ty stirring around. She sat up, clutching the sheets to her chest.

"Go back to sleep," he said.

He was fully dressed, his boots in hand. Judging by the light streaming in through the windows, it wasn't as early as she thought.

"I'll get Billy up and take him with me to feed the horses," Ty said. He leaned over and kissed her. "Sleep in if you'd like."

"No, I'll get up."

"Wait until we're out of the house," Ty said. He sat on the edge of the bed to pull on his boots, then stood.

She watched as he left, closing the door behind him. Lying back down, she ruefully stared at the closed door. It wasn't the morning after she'd envisioned. She couldn't fault Ty for wanting to protect his son, however. It wasn't just about the two of them anymore.

A minute later she heard Billy racing for the bathroom. She listened to the sounds and wished she had gotten up before the little boy. Now she was stuck until they left. The minutes ticked by slowly.

Her disappointment rose.

There had been no declarations of love from Ty. Nothing had changed in that respect. He was wary and, given what she'd learned from her aunt and father, she didn't blame him a bit. But he could have said something. Given her more than just a perfunctory kiss.

When the house had been silent for several moments, she got up. Her dress and underwear had been placed at the foot of the bed. She slipped into the dress and cautiously opened the door. The house was empty.

She went to her room for her clothes, then headed for the bathroom. Slowly she washed the scent of Ty from her body. Would he want her again or had last night been enough? She blinked back tears. She hadn't wanted a one-night stand. She had hoped it would be a new beginning for them. But he hadn't said a word.

As she went to prepare breakfast, she decided she'd take a cue from Ty's behavior and act accordingly. Pride gave her strength. She'd made her position clear yesterday at the river. He'd made his clear. Despite last night, nothing had really changed.

Yet her heart skipped a beat when he and Billy entered a half hour later. She'd prepared batter for pancakes, cooked up bacon and sausages and had orange juice poured.

"You're just in time for pancakes," she said, avoiding Ty's eyes.

"Yippee, I love pancakes!" Billy said, going for the sink to wash his hands. Ty had to lift him up to reach the water. He washed his hands as well and then poured himself a cup of coffee.

"You didn't have to make such an elaborate breakfast," he said, coming close, crowding her space.

"I thought Billy might like it," she said.

He glanced over her shoulder, then ducked for a quick kiss on her mouth. Before she could even respond, he straightened and moved to the table. "We're ready to eat, aren't we pardner?"

"You betcha," Billy said.

Holly had remembered the pancakes her father used to make when she was a child. She poured three rounds, connecting them so they looked like Mickey Mouse. When the pancake was on Billy's plate, she dotted it with raisins to look like eyes and a smiling mouth. A dollop of whip cream on top for a tuft of hair and she presented the plate. Billy's eyes widened.

"Look, Daddy, it's a face!" Billy exclaimed.

"Do I get one, too?" Ty asked.

"If you like." She smiled as she prepared a second one.

Holly joined them at the table a few moments later. Once the first hunger pangs had been assuaged, Billy piped up to say they were going on a picnic that afternoon.

Holly looked at Ty questioningly.

"We'd like you to join us," he said. "Bring your bathing suit. We can go swimming in the river, if it's not too cold."

"It won't be," Billy said with conviction.

Holly laughed. "You're probably right, but just in case, I reserve the right not to get wet."

"We wouldn't splash her or anything, would we?" Ty teased, his eyes holding hers.

Billy giggled. "Yes, we would."

"At least one man here is honest. No splashing," she said in mock horror.

"Right." Ty winked. "Want more coffee?" He stood and went to get the pot.

Holly enjoyed the family time. It was as she'd always pictured it with Ty. Love and laughter spilling over everything they did. Preparing meals together, doing things with their children.

Only Billy wasn't hers. She looked at the little boy, the old familiar ache behind her breasts. Her own baby had never had a chance.

Breakfast was scarcely over when the phone rang. Ty reached out to pick it up, spoke and then handed it to Holly.

"It's for you."

He rose and cleared his and Billy's plates, running water over them in the sink.

"This is Holly Bennett," she said.

"Nurse Hopkins, Holly. Dr. Apedaile asked me to call you. Your father had an accident. He fell and broke his wrist. The doctor said he'll be fine—we've put it in a cast and he's on pain medications—but it will set back his recovery time. He can't use the walker until it heals. The doctor thought you'd want to come in."

"I'll leave right away," Holly said, standing.

"He's sleeping now from the pain medications. Later in the morning would be better."

"All right, I'll be there." She hung up and looked at Ty.

"My father fell and broke his wrist. I need to go see him."

"Now?"

"Soon. He's sleeping from the medication." She rubbed her forehead. "This complicates everything. He was pushing hard to get out of there, to regain use of his arm and leg. He hates being helpless like that."

Ty didn't say anything. Holly glared at him.

"I know you don't care, but he is my father."

"So go." He turned away and continued washing the dishes.

Holly bit her lip. It would mean skipping the picnic. How could the happiness of just a few minutes ago vanish so quickly? It wasn't that she didn't want to see her father, it was just that she hated giving up her afternoon with Ty and Billy.

"So Holly can't go with us?" Billy asked, looking between the two adults.

"Not this time, pardner. It'll be you and me. When we finish swimming, we'll ride around the ranch."

"Let's go now!" Billy said, jumping down from the table.

"Go brush your teeth and we'll pack our lunch. Then after we finish our chores, we'll head out."

"Got to do chores first," Billy said solemnly. "The animals depend on us."

"That's right."

Holly smiled at the little boy repeating what he'd obviously been told many times. Her heart ached. She could love this motherless boy, given the chance. She wondered if Ty would ever give her that chance.

HOLLY SAW THE TWO OF them off and later that morning left for the convalescent hospital. When she knocked on his door, her father called for her to enter.

"So what have you been up to now?" she asked in a breezy voice, not surprised to see him back in bed. His left arm was encased in a cast.

"Damn hospital. The floors are too slick. I tried to get to the bathroom last night and fell. Landed on my hand and broke several bones. The doctor says it'll be weeks before I can use this hand again. How's a man to use the blasted walker or crutches without a working hand?"

She went over to give him a hug. She knew how impatient he'd been during the recovery from the stroke. This setback had to be awful for him.

"It could have been worse. You could have landed on your head," she said, sitting in the chair next to the bed. Seeing him gave her some measure of relief. Except for the cast, he looked good.

He eyed her suspiciously. "Something's different."

"Yes, I'm sitting in a chair and you're in a bed," she said. She felt the heat rise in her face. Surely he couldn't tell she'd made love with Ty again. He'd never suspected when she'd been in high school.

"Humph," he said, glaring at her. "Jerry came by last night to see me. He's leaving if things don't change on the ranch. Blasted man has been working for me for more than twenty years."

"Did he say why?" she asked.

"Yeah, something about lack of direction from the top. He didn't like Donny's going. The place is short-handed and he isn't interested in staying. And you have a name in the community—my name. I don't want it dragged through the dirt. Ty Alvarez can hire his own cowboys. You get yourself home!"

"Got that power of attorney for me?" she asked.

Her father stared at her. Holly remembered when one of her father's glares sent her running. He'd been a loving father, but didn't let her get away with anything. He'd never used corporal punishment. One of his disapproving looks had been enough to ensure her compliance when she'd been little.

But not now. She was a grown woman, with demands of her own. And a few grudges. If he wanted her on the ranch, he could meet her demands. And stay out of her love life from now on.

"Jerry told me there've been problems. Broken equipment, cut fencing, missing cattle. Do you know anything about that?"

"Some."

"Why didn't you tell me?"

"Because there wasn't anything you could do, Dad. You need to focus on getting well and not worry about the ranch. I have my suspicions about who's responsible. I've discussed them with the sheriff. He hasn't found proof of who's doing it."

"Who do you think it is?"

"Hank."

"Why?"

She shrugged. "Intuition, maybe."

"Dammit. Girly intuition! If you don't have any hard facts, forget it. Besides, he's worked for me for years. I'd suspect Alverez."

"Of course you would. You'd blame Ty for everything you don't like. Did he cause your stroke as well?" she asked pointedly. "Hank's only worked for you for three years. And he's changed since you aren't there. Can't tell why, but he's become surly, disrespectful and insolent."

"He has his eye on you. Probably feels now that I'm not there, it would be a good time to move in. You could do worse."

"Don't start with that. I could do lots better!" she said, thinking of Ty.

Ryan was silent for a moment, then he looked over to the small stand next to the bed.

"Look in the top drawer, Rafferty wrote up the papers for me and I signed them yesterday afternoon. You win, you have full authority on the Rocking B until I'm back."

Holly didn't feel the elation she expected. Her loyalties were now divided. She wanted to take care of her father's ranch, but Ty also needed help to get his going. And she'd much rather be on the new T-Bar-J Ranch than let him move on without her. After last night, she wasn't sure where she stood with Ty, but leaving was probably not the best strategic move.

Still, she owed her father. He'd been her sole parent since she was two, and she knew he loved her. If they could get past his dislike of Ty, his lying to her that fateful summer, she'd recapture the affection she normally had. But right now she was feeling more duty than love.

"All right. I'll take it on," she said.

"Take it on? You've been pushing for this for weeks. Why the reluctance?" he asked. "Dammit, do not tell me you'd even consider staying with Alverez?"

"Actually, he's a good rancher. I've seen his land, heard his plans. He earned the respect of the others around here at the brandings. He didn't have to help, being new and not having cattle of his own, but he pitched in as much as anyone else. I think you're going to have to change your stance or you'll be the lone man out," Holly said, rising to get the papers from the stand. She thumbed through them. Everything seemed to be what she wanted—she had full authority over the Rocking B.

"You better keep me informed," he growled.

"Of course. It's your ranch," she said easily, sitting back in the chair, holding the papers.

"It'll be yours one day," he reminded her.

She wondered what she'd do with a ranch. She loved working with horses, not dealing with cattle. She could manage it until her dad recovered, but the thought of fifty years or so of cattle ranching wasn't as appealing as she thought it should be. Unless, of course, she was keeping it for her children.

Holly went slowly out to her truck some time later. She and her father had discussed the situation at the ranch in some detail. Her first priority was to make sure Donny came back. She needed his expertise and work ethic. Her next item, however, would be to fire Hank Palmer and see about finding a new ranch hand.

She had to swing by Ty's place and get her things. And tell him she was leaving. She'd pick up her horses later.

She wished she could have spent the day with him and Billy. But she had her work cut out, and it didn't include a carefree day by the water.

She knew Ty would be angry with her decision. Would he see this as her not keeping her word? Surely he'd understand her wish to run the Rocking B. To be a boss instead of a hired hand.

Had Ty heard her declaration of love last night? He hadn't said anything then. Maybe she'd said it too softly for him to hear.

Or, as he'd said at the river bank, he simply was not interested.

In fact, he'd been very clear that he didn't trust her at all. So why would one night together change anything? Saying she'd be true forever was different from the reality as he knew it. What would it take to have Ty believe she knew her own mind and wasn't changing it this time regardless?

Probably staying on as a ranch hand working for him. Seeing him day and night for a few months. Or would he keep the barriers up no matter what?

She ached for the lost years.

She'd read a lot about depression after she'd started her first year at college. Because her father had isolated her, her symptoms hadn't abated, but continued until she gradually got better. There were many factors that had made that the summer from hell. And ten years later she continued to live with the consequences.

But no more. Now that she knew the facts, she could act. If Ty thought she would accept his noninterest after last night, he was crazy.

The T-Bar-J was quiet when she drove in. She went to her room and packed her things. Most of the boxes had not been opened, so she just had to put them in the truck for the trek home. Still, it took some time to clear the room. She tossed the sheets in the washer and started it, wanting them finished before she left.

When she was ready, she walked through Ty's home one more time. The house had potential, as real estate agents liked to say. It needed loving care and a family to fill the rooms with the sound of love and laughter. Would she be back?

Only if Ty invited her.

Had last night meant anything to him? Or was it just a walk down memory lane? A one-night stand with someone he already knew. Who would be the next woman to be in his bed? Holly wanted it to be her!

She found paper in the makeshift office and wrote a note to let him know where she was. She'd phone later, but wanted to leave word for him when he and Billy returned.

She placed it in the center of the kitchen table, so it was easily visible upon entering.

Heading for home, Holly tried to forget she was leaving Ty behind and instead focused on the situation she faced at the Rocking B. She couldn't believe her father had finally come to his senses and given her free rein. Was it too late with the hands rebelling? She had several changes she wanted to implement immediately and would have to call on the help of the long-term employees. Surely they'd rally 'round.

Sunday afternoons were typically free time for the men. When she pulled into the homestead, she noted only two vehicles were parked there, the broken truck and Jerry's sports car. Everyone else must have been gone.

She went to the bunkhouse. Jerry was working on one of his innumerable model airplanes. When finished, he'd donate it to the children's ward of the hospital and start another.

"Hey, Holly. Didn't expect to see you," he said when she walked in.

"Where is everyone?" she asked.

"Donny's packed up and moved on. The rest are in town, I think. I wanted to finish this."

"Where's Donny gone?"

"He went to see his daughter. You here for something?"

"Yes, I'm here to run this place until my Dad recovers. And this time, what I say goes."

He smiled. "Got something to back you up?"

"Legal and binding. Can you give me Donny's number? And tell Hank I want to see him when he gets back. And, Jerry, I need you as well."

"Ooo, boy, I smell trouble," Jerry said, laying down his model. "I'll get Donny's number right away. Guess I'll stick around a bit. Seems like it's going to get down right interesting."

"Give me a quick update on what's been going on, would you?"

Two hours later Holly had unpacked her truck, with Jerry's help, and put away her clothes. The rest of her things she'd unpack later.

She went to the office and caught up on the mail. She called Donny's daughter's home and spoke with her, leaving a message for Donny, who was out. And phoned Ty's place twice.

It was after a hasty dinner of soup and salad that she tried Ty again. Leaning against the kitchen counter, she wondered if he and Billy had gone out to dinner or something and missed her note and earlier messages.

"Alverez," Ty answered.

"Ty, it's Holly."

There was a momentary silence. Then he responded, "Forget something?" The cool tone surprised her.

"I'm sorry to leave on such short notice. I tried to explain in my note. My dad needs me here."

"I read it."

"I'd like to see you." She didn't care that she was throwing herself at him.

"You made your choice, Holly. Goodbye." He hung up.

"What? Ty?" She replaced the receiver just as she heard footsteps on the back porch.

Hank sauntered in like he owned the place. "Hey, Holly, Jerry said you were back and wanted me."

"Wanted to see you," she corrected automatically. She

wished she'd thought to meet him at the bunkhouse. They were alone in the house. Not that she expected him to be a problem, exactly. But he wasn't going to be happy with her decision.

He smiled.

She suppressed a shiver. "I have your final check. I'm firing you and this time it'll stick. My father has legally turned over the management of the ranch to me. Talking to him won't change the decision this time."

"You can't do that," he said, growing angry.

"I can and am doing it. Wait here, I'll get your check." She hurried to the office and was annoyed when Hank appeared in the doorway as she was picking up the envelope. She refused to be cowed by this cowboy. But she wished there was someone else close by.

She held out the check.

He ignored it. "You need help running this place. Hell, your old man isn't ever going to be up to taking care of it again. And you won't be, either. You need me. You'll see. You aren't up to running a spread this size alone."

"None of that is true, but if it were, it's no business of yours anymore. Get your things and get off the ranch. I'll give you until tomorrow morning." She was pleased her voice held firm.

"What if I don't leave," he said, leaning against the doorjamb and watching her with a menacing look.

"Then I'll call the sheriff and have you removed." She stood tall. She was not going to be intimidated by this two-bit cowboy. She had more important things to deal with. Like calling Ty back and getting him to listen to her. "And I expect you to stop sabotaging the ranch!"

"What in hell are you talking about? I've never sabotaged anything."

"The fence—"

"You still riled because I didn't fix the blasted fence as fast as you wanted?"

"No, I'm riled because you cut it."

He looked at her like she was crazy. "That's a lie. I never cut a fence anywhere. Cattle could get out. What are you thinking?"

"That a lot of the trouble we're having around here started when my dad got sick. And you started making your push to date me."

"I think you need a man to run a ranch. So shoot me. But I'm not wrecking the place. You can have your ranch and your prissy ways. I'll find me a real woman."

He tore the check from her hand.

"You'll be sorry for this, Miss High-and-Mighty Bennett. You can't run this place alone, and one of these days you'll realize that."

"Get out, Hank. If you don't cause any trouble, I'll give a reference to any ranch who checks. But if you cause me any grief, I won't say a good word. And you know that'll make finding a job tough."

"Bitch!" He turned and left. The slamming of the kitchen door shook the house.

She sat down behind the desk, her knees definitely not able to hold her much longer.

The phone rang. Hoping it was Ty, she snatched it up.

"Holly, it's Donny. I got your message."

"So when are you coming back?" she asked brightly. She clung to the hope he would return. Without Hank and Donny, she'd be down two men. Three if she counted her father. Things could get dicey until she found competent help. "As I told your daughter, I'll be running things here now."

"What about the others?" he asked.

"Same crew as before. Except for Hank. I fired him and he's gone for good this time. Please, Donny, I need your help." She explained about the power of attorney and her firing Hank again with no possibility of her father overturning her decision this time.

"I reckon I'm too old to start over somewhere else," he said slowly. "I'll be back in the morning."

"Thanks. I really appreciate it!" She hung up feeling relieved. She'd also make sure she increased Donny's wages. She needed him too much to let him get away.

Holly leaned back in the desk chair and stared off into space. Today had packed a roller coaster of emotions. From waking up with Ty to talking with her father to dealing with Hank and now getting the assurance that Donny would return. She knew if she was given the chance, she could pull the ranch around without selling acreage to McNab. But it would mean not buying that bull from Helton—and some other belt-tightening strategies.

Sighing softly, she wished she could discuss the situation with someone.

Ty popped into mind. Would he even consider letting her use him as a sounding board?

She picked up the phone and dialed the now-memorized number.

"Alverez."

"Ty, I want to talk to you," she said quickly. "Do not hang up."

"There's nothing to talk about," he said. The frost almost came across the line.

"What would you have me do, work as an employee for you or run my own ranch? What would you do? Remember, as soon as you got that land from your father you left your cousins and came directly here. Is what I'm doing any different?"

The silence lingered. Finally he spoke. "The difference is the entire situation. I'm expanding. My relatives are in this with me, even though they live in Texas. When the chips are down, Holly, you run to Daddy."

"That's not true. I told him I wanted full control or I'd leave. When I left, it convinced him I was serious. So he gave me that control."

"So working for me was just a strategic move on your part to get him to give you what you wanted."

"No. At the time I thought my leaving was for good."

"I never thought it would be for good. I did think, though, you'd stay a little longer. Not forever, but a few more weeks at least."

She clutched the phone tightly, wishing she didn't feel the inevitability of his words. She wanted a second chance. She wanted them to explore what they'd begun last night. She certainly didn't want him to think she'd used him or cut out because of his rejections.

"Look, I've got to go. It's time for Billy's bath," Ty said.

"That's it, you've got to go?"

"That's it. Like you had to go, right? Goodbye, Holly."

She sat with the phone still at her ear until the dial tone resumed. Hanging up, she calmly rose and went to the kitchen. She couldn't believe that after last night Ty could be so unemotional. Hadn't making love meant anything to him?

He'd told her he didn't trust her. Why couldn't she

have taken him at his word, been grateful for his honesty and moved on?

She now had full control of her father's ranch. Why wasn't it nearly enough? Several weeks ago, it would have been. Before Ty returned. Now nothing short of the man himself would ever be enough. Only Ty looked like one thing Holly wasn't going to get.

TY HUNG UP AND HEADED for the bathroom. He was angry Holly called.

He clenched his fists and began to fill the tub. His back ached a little. From last night, he figured. Ignoring it, he called Billy for his bath. He was going to get good at ignoring a lot of things, he knew.

"I brought my toys," Billy said, coming through the door with an armful of plastic toys he liked to play with in the tub. Normally Ty let him keep them in the bathroom, but when Holly had been with them, he'd had his son take them to his room each night. Since she was gone, Billy might as well leave the toys.

Billy looked at him. "Are you sad, Daddy?"

"What? No, I'm fine."

"You look sad," his son said. He sat down and Ty pulled off his small boots.

If even a child could read him, he'd better shape up, Ty thought wryly. He wasn't going to let himself get a reputation of longing after Holly Bennett. Once burned, twice shy. He'd get over her or die trying.

Tomorrow he'd begin looking for ranch hands and start work in earnest. Charles Riley was bringing his horse over, so he'd be back in the saddle with a training regimen starting the next morning. He had enough tasks to do around the barn and house to keep him busy for five years. Too busy to think about a suntanned blonde with a smile that tugged at his heart. Holly had made her choice. He hoped he could live with it.

CHAPTER ELEVEN

TWO DAYS LATER Holly and Sara met for lunch at the café in Turnbow.

"I feel I haven't seen you in ages," Sara said as soon as they'd sat down in the booth at the front. The large window to the side provided a view to Main Street traffic and the comings and goings of locals. The heat wave that had started on the weekend was escalating, with no relief in sight.

"I saw you at the dance Saturday. It's only Tuesday," Holly said, used to her friend's tendency toward exaggeration.

"But we didn't get to talk there. I had to play hostess. Since then I've spent all my time doing laundry and packing. We leave for Kentucky in the morning. I can't wait to see everyone. We haven't been back in ages."

"How long are you going to be gone?"

"Just a week. John doesn't want to be away from the ranch that long. And my mother does wear on a person pretty quickly. But I'll see friends and visit with my grandparents while I'm there."

"Which translates into lots of parties, right?"

"I love giving parties," Sara said with a smile. "I'll have the rancher's deluxe, what are you having?"

Holly didn't have enough of an appetite these days

for the huge hamburger with all the fixings and fries. "I'll have a Reuben." And skip the fries.

Once their orders had been taken, Sara leaned over the table a bit.

"Okay, dish. I want all the facts."

"About taking over for my dad?" Holly said.

"No, about working with Ty Alverez. You didn't tell me you two had such a history."

"As what?" Holly asked warily. Had Sara heard the entire sordid tale?

She ticked each fact off on her fingers: "You two were an item in high school. A car crash almost killed you both. And then you split up. Ty and his father moved away. Your father was fit to be tied. Only now you have a second chance."

Holly looked at her. "Almost killed us? I know I was in the hospital for days, but just found out from Ty that he'd been injured badly enough to require care, too. I didn't even ask him about it."

Sara blinked. "You didn't know? How could you not know? From what I heard, the truck was totaled."

"No one ever told me," Holly said slowly.

"Not even Ty?"

Holly shook her head. "Actually, until I saw him at your place a few weeks ago, we hadn't spoken since the night of the accident." Her ordering him away from her house that summer didn't count.

"I don't get it," Sara said.

Holly fiddled with the silverware on the table, keeping her gaze firmly on the spinning spoon. "I thought Ty had abandoned me. I didn't learn until recently that he hadn't." She quickly told Sara about her dad's deception.

"Oh, Holly." Sara was silent a moment as if taking it all in. "Why didn't you try to contact him? I sure would want to know what the hell was going on if some guy didn't call me after we'd been so close."

"We lost a baby. I was almost four months pregnant when we had the crash. With that and recovering from the accident, I had a major case of depression. I needed him to come to me."

"You poor thing," Sara said with compassion. She reached out and squeezed Holly's hand. "Why did your dad interfere?"

"He didn't like Ty's father. He'd told me before to 'stay away from Alverez's kid.' Only I couldn't. I was so crazy about Ty I dated him secretly. We thought no one knew. After the crash, I expect it all came out. I left for college that September and by the time I returned home at Christmas, it seemed forgotten."

Sara studied her. "That's why you rarely date. You still love Ty."

Holly's eyes flew to meet Sara's. How had she guessed the truth?

Slowly, she nodded. "Even after all the time and heartbreak. I've virtually put my life on hold because of him. But he doesn't want me." She was proud her voice hadn't broken.

"Maybe. He came back to Turnbow."

"He married, has a son. If Connie hadn't died, they'd still be married."

Sara shrugged. "But she *is* dead. What happened when you were at his place? Did you recapture any of the romance?"

Holly felt the heat rise in her face as she thought about their night together. It had been better than before.

Maybe because they were grown, or maybe because it had been so long since she'd felt that level of passion. She couldn't believe she'd been the only one to find it magical. Yet Ty hadn't said a word.

Sara started to say something had stopped when she glanced out the window. "There's Ty talking with Sheriff Johnstone. They both look pretty serious. Do you suppose something is wrong?"

Holly looked. The two men were deep in discussion.

"Wonder what's up," Sara said. "Ohmygosh—does Ty have a black eye? Could he have been in a fight somewhere?" Hardly able to sit still, she leaned closer to the glass.

It did look like Ty had a bruise around his left eye when he turned slightly and she had a better view of his face. "Why don't you go and find out?" Holly said.

"You go," Sara said.

"What?" Holly looked at her in dismay.

"Right now before they finish and he leaves. I'll stay here for when the food arrives. Hurry."

"I can't go there just to be nosy," Holly said, though she longed to do just that.

"Yes, you can. Go. He's your neighbor. If there's some kind of trouble, you need to know about it, too," Sara said.

Hesitating, Holly shook her head then slid out of the booth and headed for the front door. The men turned to look at her as she approached. Ty's gaze was cool, the sheriff's was friendly enough.

"Hi," she said once she'd reached them.

Ty's eye was swollen and the skin discolored.

"Hey, Holly, I was going to go out to your place. This saves me the trip," the sheriff said. Brett Johnstone had been sheriff for a dozen years. He knew all the ranchers and most of the cowboys around Turnbow.

"Going to my place? Why?" Holly asked, flicking a glance at Ty. His rigid stance had started to worry her. Had he been injured elsewhere? Not his back, she hoped.

"Seems there was some trouble last night out at Ty's place. He came in this morning to make a report."

"About what?"

"Looks like some of your cowboys tore up the fence between your place, Hudgins's and Ty's. Scattered cattle through in each direction. Some of his longhorns were driven to Hudgins's and some of yours onto his property. When he discovered what was going on, he tried to intervene. They jumped him. Do you know anything about this?"

"Are you sure? The men who work for me wouldn't have reason to do such a thing," she said, surprised at the charge. "When did this happen?" She turned to Ty. "How did you see them? There's a hill between that section and your house." Had her cowboys gone out to cause trouble last night? Or was it Hank?

"You sure about your men?" the sheriff asked. "It happened long after dark. You might have gone to bed and not heard them leave."

"I can't imagine it," Holly said. "Why would anyone do that anyway?"

"This is the third time that section of fence has been cut," Ty said. "You know that. How else would it get cut if not from your side or mine? The men had to come from somewhere. And they weren't working for me."

"There was more than one man?" she asked.

"There were two. When they were leaving, one mentioned the Rocking B," Ty said.

"I still don't know how you saw them from your place," Holly said, picturing the way Ty's ranch was laid out.

"I didn't, initially. One of my horses was antsy, kept neighing while looking in that direction. He wouldn't settle, so I saddled him up and went to investigate. I thought it might be a cougar or wolf or something. When I crested the hill, I saw cattle where there shouldn't be any. Once I got closer, I saw the men. We had an altercation. You know that area by the trees—it's pitch-black at night. They got away, but the damage had been done. That fence is shredded."

"And because they said something about my ranch you think I'm responsible?"

"I never said that you were responsible," Ty said.

"But you think someone from my ranch is responsible," she pushed, wanting clarity.

"Well, Holly, that's what I'm investigating," Brett said. "Mind if I ride out later and talk with the men? If any are sporting bruises, it might mean he was in the fight he can't explain."

"It reminds me of another summer, when your father sent men to make sure I knew I'd done wrong with his daughter," Ty said softly, his eyes hard as agate.

Holly stared at him. Sometime—sooner rather than later—they needed to sit down and talk about that summer, every detail. She started to tell him that, but now was not the time. So many assumptions made—on both sides—needed to be explained.

"Come to the ranch anytime, sheriff," she said. "Can I fix the fence or should I let it stay that way until after you check it?"

"I'm heading to Ty's now. I'll let you know when

you can repair it. In the meantime, I don't suppose the cattle mingling will hurt anything."

She looked at Ty. "I had nothing to do with this."

"If you say so," he replied, then walked away.

Holly turned to the sheriff. "I saw two of my men this morning. The others were already out when I went to the barn. But neither of them had bruises. You know I've had trouble myself over the past few weeks. I suggest you find Hank Palmer and see what he looks like."

"I'll be hunting him down as well. Let me know if you hear of anything that might help. I'll be out there soon," he said. Touching the brim of his hat, he walked away.

Holly returned to the café. Sara had been avidly watching from the window and almost pounced on her when she sat down. Her Reuben was already cooling at her place when Holly began to tell Sara what she'd learned.

She only held back the hurt she'd felt at Ty's indifference.

Why didn't he understand her family responsibilities? He couldn't blame her for taking charge of her father's ranch in his absence. He'd have done the same. And he certainly couldn't think she had anything to do with last night. Could he?

She ate quickly. "I have to get to the ranch." She knew none of the men working there would have been involved, but she had to see for herself. If anyone had any signs of having been in a fight, he was history at the Rocking B.

HOLLY HAD TALKED TO EVERY man on the ranch by the time the sheriff drove in. None had seen or heard anything last night. None showed signs of involvement in any kind of altercation, and the sheriff said Ty had given as good as he got, so she felt justified in her faith in her men.

The section where the fence had been cut was a long ride from the house, which was why Holly had always felt safe meeting Ty there as a teenager. She'd known the men's schedule each day and had made sure they'd be far from the river before slipping out to see him. No one had lived at the Wilson ranch then, either. Even if it had been occupied, it was unlikely anyone would have been able to hear them from the homestead.

If Ty's horse hadn't been acting spooked last night, he wouldn't have suspected anything was wrong himself.

But who was causing the trouble? And why was it now spilling over to two neighbors' ranches?

Holly ate a quick meal and then showered and dressed in clean jeans and a shirt. She was going to the T-Bar-J to talk with Ty. Sara's words about why she hadn't tried to reach him that summer echoed in her mind. All the excuses in the world didn't change a thing. The fact was she had been at fault in not trying to reach him. Had she thought she'd been the only one damaged by the loss of their baby?

Actually, that was exactly what she'd thought. And her father had fed that notion.

She was not going to let history repeat itself. This time Holly was going after what she wanted and no one was going to get in her way. Cards on the table. If he didn't want what she had to offer, fine. But at least they'd discuss everything and get it all out in the open.

Daylight was fading when she turned into the long

drive to his house. She'd considered calling to make sure he was home, but decided he'd probably tell her not to come, so hadn't risked it. The house was dark when she reached it. The horses snuffled softly in greeting. Two came to the corral fence to check her out.

She brought the truck around to the back. Ty's was parked near the kitchen door. He had to be home, unless he and Billy were out riding somewhere, in which case, she'd just wait.

She got out of her truck and heard the soft sound of a television. She walked to the back door, knocked, waited a minute, then entered. Following the muted voices, she found the two in Ty's bedroom, the small television the only illumination. Stretched out on the bed, both looked settled for the night. Her heart began to beat heavily. In another life, if things had been fair, if dreams came true, she would be coming into her room, the room she shared with this man. And the little child would be theirs. Holly had often imagined what their daughter would have looked like. Probably dark-haired like her daddy—eyes brimming with mischief. She'd seen Ty like that so many times during their senior year. Where had that boy gone?

The heartache surfaced. Made worse by seeing Billy, being reminded Ty hadn't let the past hamper him. He'd made a child with another woman and that hurt a lot.

"Hi, Holly," Billy said spying her. "Did you come to watch TV with us?"

Ty looked over, obviously surprised to see her. He rose easily. His boots off, his sock-covered feet made no noise as he crossed the room to her.

"What are you doing here?" he asked.

"I came to talk."

He studied her for a moment then nodded. Turning back to his son, he said, "I'm going to make some coffee for me and Holly. You watch the show so you can tell me how it ends, okay?"

"'Kay," he said, leaning back on the pillows and shifting his attention back to the television.

Holly felt Ty following only inches behind her as she led the way into the kitchen.

"Did the sheriff turn up anything at your place?" he asked, taking out the coffee.

Holly sat at the table and shook her head. "He saw the fence, tried to figure out where the riders came from. But with the cattle that had tramped through, he couldn't determine that, only that they took off across your land. Why would anyone do that?"

"All your men are fine?"

"Not a scratch on any of them. The sheriff had them all take off their shirts. No bruises or cuts or abrasions. And he looked up Hank, who is staying at the motel out near the highway. He was also fine, no injuries. Are you sure you hit both?"

He flexed his right hand. She could see the bruises on the swollen knuckles from where she sat. He nodded, pouring the water into the coffeemaker and pushing the button. He turned and leaned against the counter. "Now what?"

"I didn't really come about last night." She cleared her throat, hoping she could do this. "I wanted to talk about the accident, recovery, depression and a father who interfered."

"Leave it, Holly. It's done and over."

"Not for me. Sara told me today you'd been badly injured in the crash."

He narrowed his eyes. "*I* told you."

"All I remember about that summer is the tears. I cried enough to flood the river. First for our lost baby, then for our lost love. My only contact to the rest of the world was through my father and Aunt Betty. And now I know how slanted that was. Looking back, I realize none of my friends came to see me once I was out of the hospital. I didn't notice at the time, but now I'm wondering why. I was in a fog most of those months. Going to college helped me get back on track. But I want to know everything you can tell me about that summer."

Ty looked at the floor for so long Holly thought he was going to ignore her until she left. Finally he looked up.

"You still take cream in your coffee?"

"Yes." A small fluttering of hope spiked through her. He'd remembered. It wasn't much, but she'd take any tiny bud she could grasp.

He fixed the coffee, handed hers to her and put his on the table. He pulled out a chair and turned it. Straddling it, he rested his hands on the back.

"We both ended up in the hospital that night. You know the other driver died?"

She nodded. "My aunt told me he had died. And that he'd been drinking and was way over the limit, according to the highway patrol."

"If we'd been a few seconds earlier or later, we wouldn't have been at that intersection when he ploughed through," Ty said.

"I know."

"He hit your side. You took the brunt force. I was knocked out, hit my head on the side window, had cuts and contusions as the doctors said. Nothing like you. For a few hours they didn't know if you'd make it or not."

Holly was surprised by that. "I didn't know. No wonder my dad was so overprotective that summer. Aunt Betty said I scared the living daylights out of him."

"He was furious when he found out about the baby. I was still in the hospital, trying to find out anything I could about you when he came storming into my room. He threatened everything from dismemberment to prosecution for rape."

"Rape? Impossible."

"Statutory rape, since obviously you became pregnant before turning eighteen. I told him we planned to get married and he said over his dead body, or mine."

"I heard nothing about it, except to stay away from you—that all you wanted was to get into my pants and now that there was no baby holding you, you were off on other pursuits."

Ty took a sip of his coffee. "My father heard him when he came to see me. He pulled yours aside and spoke to him for five minutes. Never once did Ryan say a word, but when he left, the threat of prosecution had vanished. I never knew what my father said to him. He wouldn't tell me. But he also urged me to stay away from you."

"Why the feud, do you know?"

"Beats me. My uncle told me there was bad blood between the two and that I had gotten a lucky break not to get tied up with your family. Whatever it was, neither had a good word to say about the other," Ty said.

"So then what happened?"

"I still couldn't see you, but one of the nurses told me about losing the baby, and how dangerously critical you were. I came back several times once I was released, but your father had one of his men at the hospital whenever he couldn't make it. Criminals aren't even guarded so closely."

He rubbed his jaw and took another sip of coffee. "One day before you were home again, when my father and most of the hands at the McKenzie ranch were gone, two of your father's men showed up to teach me a lesson. Direct compliments of Ryan Bennett, they said.

"My father threatened to have them arrested, but it was my word against theirs. Your father swore they never left the ranch that day. Who would believe a cowboy's son against one of the area's most prosperous ranchers?"

"I'm sorry," she said quietly.

"Do you know what sex the baby was?" he asked.

"She was a girl. One of the nurses told me. Now anytime I see a little girl about her age, I wonder what our baby would have been like. I don't go around children a lot. It hurts too much."

His dark eyes held hers in compassion. He took a deep breath. "Wonder what we would have called her."

They fell silent, both remembering the dreams that had turned to dust.

"I tried to see you, I really did. I called, your aunt answered. I wrote you two letters and never heard back from you. I came to the ranch more than once, but there was always some cowboy around to make sure I didn't get far. My father told me to forget you. But I couldn't. I needed to see if you were all right. I needed to see you.

"I was elated that last day when I finally got all the way to the house. I thought nothing could stop me. I worked hard all summer, saving for college, trying to forget how impossible it was to see you. Instead of using that money for college, I bought you an engagement ring. I wanted you and your father to know nothing had changed for me. I loved you, Holly."

"You bought me a ring?" She was stunned.

"I threw it away when you told me to leave and never return." He shook his head wryly. "I should have returned it and gotten my money back."

She stared at him, feeling his pain at that last rejection. How could she have not flown down the stairs and into his arms? She had longed for him all summer. Tried once to call him, only to chicken out in light of his neglect. Only it hadn't been neglect.

"I'm so sorry," she said.

He shrugged. "Water over the dam. Time moves on."

"And you found another woman to love," she said, holding on to her control with all she was worth when she really wanted to weep, rail against him for choosing someone else to have babies with. For forgetting her so quickly when she never forgot him. Never got over him.

"Daddy, it ended," Billy came running into the kitchen. "They made a pack, all of them, even though they are all different."

"Good for them. You about ready for bed?"

"Do I have to?" he whined. He sped over to Holly and held up his arms. "I haven't told Holly about riding Ace."

She picked him up, reveling in the little-boy scent. He snuggled against her as if they'd done so for years. For a split second, she felt grief for the unknown Connie, who would never again be able to pick up her son. Who wouldn't see him grow up, or ever become a grandmother.

"What about Ace?" she asked. Her emotions were

raw after the revelations. She wanted normalcy and time to absorb the truth. She couldn't believe her father had been so cruel, but the facts kept piling up.

"We went to the river and some bad guys cut all the fence. There were cattle everywhere. Ace wasn't even afraid. Some of those horns are even bigger than him, but he just walked along like he was a cow, too."

"That's what you get with longhorns. And you stayed away from them, right?"

"Daddy was there. He could save me if one got ornery."

She laughed at the language. It sounded so mature for a four-year-old. "Good for your daddy. Mine used to let me ride with him. I grew up on the back of a horse, too. And I'll tell you a secret. I like horses better than cattle."

"Me, too. And my Daddy does, too, don't you, Daddy? He takes dumb horses and makes them smart enough to work cattle. Some even win prizes."

"I know." Holly felt another pang. That had been their shared dream. Training cutting horses, stock horses. Working on breeding them. Another area in which Ty had gone on without her.

But she'd learned to deal with things on her own. Her resolve strengthened. She wasn't giving up. He'd made love to her the other night and it had been better than ever. She was clinging to that.

"Okay, pardner, let's get ready for bed," Ty said, rising. He replaced the chair and put his cup in the sink.

Billy slipped down and grinned at Holly. "Good night," he said. "Are you sleeping over again?"

Holly looked at Ty.

For a long moment, his gaze held hers. Her heart

raced as excitement built. Would he want her to stay over? Billy, of course, meant her staying in the room off the kitchen. She wanted to stay over in Ty's bed.

"Not tonight," he said at long last.

Holly didn't move when they left. He hadn't thrown her out. She was going to wait.

She thought about what Ty'd told her. It was at such odds to the way she'd always known her father. He'd always been there for her. From a little girl, lost without her mother, her dad had taken care of her. He shared his love of the land, taught her right from wrong, played dolls with her when she was young.

She'd believed him. Why not, he was her father. She'd never known him to lie to her before. Or since.

What was it about Ty that he couldn't accept?

Especially now. He had turned out fine. He owned a ranch, free and clear, which was more than most ranchers could say.

Ty came back a short time later.

"He was tired. I bet he's asleep already," he said.

Holly smiled against the pain in her heart. "He's a darling little boy. Does he look a lot like his mother?"

"Not a lot. Connie had dark eyes and hair, so Billy picked that up from both of us. I think he looks more like my cousin Pete."

"Did you love her a lot?" The words came without thought. "Never mind, I don't want to know."

"I'm not going to talk about my relationship with Connie with you. Want to sit outside? It's cooled down since the sun set," Ty said, still near the doorway.

"Sure."

When they settled on the old chairs, he stared out into the darkness. The stars appeared so close, sparkling in the clear night sky. The moon was a sliver, bright and silvery. He could make out the barn, hear the horses in the corral. The cocoon of darkness enveloped them both. For a moment he reminisced about those spring nights they'd snuck away and talked until midnight. Her father had never caught her sneaking back in. Ty always knew there'd be hell to pay if he did. But he'd thought it worth it.

He asked her to tell him about that summer as she remembered it. He'd always wondered why she made no effort to contact him—if only to rail against him like her father had.

"Not much to tell. You've heard it all. I was a one-dimensional person that summer. Finally I had to get ready for college. I didn't want to go at that point, but had nothing else planned and my dad wouldn't let me not go, so I got ready."

"You left the day after you ordered me away," he said.

"I was finishing my packing when you showed up. I don't know what hit me, but suddenly I was so furious. I had waited for you all summer and you showed up the day before I was leaving. Part of me wanted to hurt you as much as I'd been hurt."

"Which wasn't necessary. I'd already had a hell of a lot of hurt that summer." Ty remembered, but tried to forget. He'd moved on. Married.

Another sore point. He'd failed his wife. He'd married her still in love with a girl who had spurned him. He'd done his best, but it hadn't been enough. He just hoped Connie had never known.

"Did you hear anything more about last night?" she asked.

"Nothing new. I talked with Hudgins today. He hasn't

had any problems before this. He's going to check his entire boundary, but my guess is this is directed at me, so only the portion that connects to my ranch will be affected," Ty said.

"Why you? The fence was cut before you came. Plus I told you about the other problems, with the windmill and all. I think the vendetta or whatever is against us. My father isn't the easiest man to get along with."

He half smiled in acknowledgment of that. "Anyone with a grudge?"

"No one I can think of who would do something like this, except Hank. Unless it was a former cowboy. Dad fired a man in January. But that was months ago. I started seeing the problems a few weeks before you moved back. Plus you said there were two of them."

"There were two. And ready to fight when I got there. But in the greater scheme of things, no harm was done last night. Except to mix up the cattle. It wasn't like they killed them or rustled any."

"Maybe they *were* planning to steal the cattle. I don't even want to think about what those men could have done. What if they'd hurt you more than they did?" She tried to see him in the starlit night. His outline was clear, his features unreadable.

"I'm not some eighteen-year-old kid anymore. I've been in my share of fights over the years, so I'm better able to defend myself," he said.

"I'm so sorry," she said again, returning her thoughts to the eighteen-year-old who had been taken on by two seasoned cowboys. It was unfair.

"Yeah, me, too."

"My heart was broken that summer, Ty," she said softly.

He reached out for her hand and held it in silence.

"Stay over," he said out of the blue. "Not in the guest room."

He rose and drew her to her feet. Slowly pulling Holly into his arms, he kissed her with the longing that had been building since she first showed up.

With his mouth on hers, she blossomed, opening to his lips, her tongue dancing with his. Warm and welcoming, she returned the fervor of the embrace. The blood pounded in his veins and he wanted to soak in every aspect of the woman in his arms.

"Inside," he mumbled, unsure he could wait that long. He wanted to strip her right here and now and make love to her all night long. But a bed would be better. If he could focus enough to get there.

He turned off lights, checked on Billy one more time, then closed the door to his room, Holly stood near the bed, her boots already off. He moved toward her.

"Shouldn't you turn off the light?" she asked, her eyes alight with happiness.

He shook his head. "Tonight I want to see every inch I touch."

She reached out when he drew closer, and began to unbutton his shirt. He waited until she was done then pulled her T-shirt over her head. The lacy lavender bra was feminine and sexy. He felt his desire ratchet up a notch. She unfastened his jeans. He unsnapped hers. Slowly she moved in a sort of striptease, sliding the jeans down her long legs. The matching lacy panties almost made him swallow his tongue. She was as beautiful as he remembered. He should have kept the lights on the other night.

There were several scars on her side, tangible proof

of the near-death experience of so long ago. He brushed his fingertips lightly against them.

"You almost died," he said, his voice husky with emotion.

"But I didn't," she said, smiling up at him. He could see the love in her eyes. Yet he didn't trust it. They'd been in love before and it had ended badly.

"Come on, cowboy. I'm waiting," she said flirtatiously.

He instantly slipped out of his jeans and shorts, scooped her up and placed her on the bed. Tugging at her jeans where they clung to her feet, he feasted his eyes on her, then joined her and kissed her like there would never be another day.

She was hot and ready, pulling him against her until he felt as if they could meld into one. Her skin was silky soft. He loved caressing her. He wanted to take it slow, make it last. They had all night. Billy would sleep soundly. This time was just for him and Holly.

CHAPTER TWELVE

HOLLY WOKE EARLY the next morning. Male legs were entwined with hers and a heavy arm lay across her stomach. Turning her head slightly, she saw Ty lying so close to her she didn't need a sheet for warmth. The light above still shone. Slowly she smiled in delight. Last night had felt so very special. She couldn't remember a time she'd been so cherished. He'd made sure of her pleasure every time before taking his own.

She moved her hand to brush his hair. It was thick and disheveled from her running her fingers through it during the night. She loved the texture.

His eyes opened and he gazed into hers.

"Good morning," she whispered.

"It is," he said, pulling her closer to kiss her.

"I need to go," she said a minute later. "Billy will be getting up soon."

"Come back tonight," he said, kissing her again.

"I'll have to see."

"See what?"

"What's going on. I can't come over here every night, you know. People will talk."

"Who's to know?"

"Billy for one. And the next time he's at the Dennises he'll be sure to say something."

Ty sat up, putting his feet on the floor. "There is that. I'm not going to tell him to keep quiet. I can't have him grow up thinking I'm hiding anything."

Sitting behind him, she reached out to run her hand down his back, noting the muscles, the tanned skin, the faint scars. "I wouldn't want that, either. So we need to be a bit discreet," she murmured.

"I didn't realize it would be hard dating with him around."

"You haven't dated since Connie died?"

"Not much. And Tia Sophia was always around to watch him. I didn't bring anyone home."

Holly felt a spurt of happiness to hear that.

Reluctantly, he got up and gathered her clothes. "Do I have time for a quick shower?" she asked.

"I think so. He usually gets up around seven, so we have an hour. I'll take one with you," he said, standing.

She took one look at him and shook her head, laughing. "Not today. I need to get in and out and from the size of things, that would not be quick."

"I can make it quick."

She laughed again in pure delight. She loved this man. She could spend the rest of her life with him, if he'd give her the chance. What would that take? He'd cared for her once, loved her. Maybe lightning would strike twice.

"Raincheck? I've got to go. I have a ranch to run." She brushed her lips across his once more, then fled to the bathroom, thankful the little boy slept on. After a quick shower, she put on yesterday's clothes, thinking she'd change as soon as she got home. She hoped none of the ranch hands had been keeping track of her.

Ty had pulled on his jeans but that was all. He met

her with a cup of coffee as she went into the kitchen. "Take it with you," he said, leaning over to kiss her. "Come back tonight," he repeated, his lips still against hers.

"I'll call and let you know," she said. She gave him one last kiss and then took the coffee and left before she was tempted to drag him back into the bedroom and risk Billy waking up.

Holly arrived home just as two of the men on her ranch were saddled up and starting out. She walked over. Donny rode his horse to meet her.

"Randy and I are going to repair the fence. We got the okay from the sheriff last night. He was looking for you," he said, resting his arm on the saddle horn. A carefully wrapped bundle of wiring was fastened behind him.

"Did he say anything?" she asked, ignoring the implied question. It was no one's business but her own where she'd spent the night. But she felt the heat of embarrassment flood her cheeks.

"He said to tell you he's checked hospitals and doctors. There were no reports of anyone with injuries like he's looking for. If they were just bruised, they're probably lying low and that's that. He said he was asking other ranchers about their employees. Doesn't seem there's much to go on," Donny said. He looked toward the south end of the ranch. "Too far to hear anything going on down there. Who'd want to cause trouble like that?"

"I'd suspect Hank if the problem hadn't started before he left," she said. "The sheriff saw him yesterday, but there were no signs of a fight."

Donny sat up, reseated his hat and nodded. "I can't

see Hank doing such a thing. Be back later," he said. Randy joined him and they headed for the breached fence.

Once Holly had changed, she grabbed some toast and went to the office. The light on the phone was flashing. She listened to her messages—one from Sara, one from the sheriff. She called Sara first.

"Can you come over early tomorrow to help out?" her friend asked. "I'm going really casual this time, only sandwiches, veggies and dip and some desserts."

"Good grief, not another party?"

"Yes, didn't you hear? Jesse Williams and Penny McAlheny got engaged. We're throwing a shindig to celebrate."

"I thought you were going to Kentucky."

"We are, but we've postponed it a little. One of my close friends is throwing an engagement party of her own in two weeks, and I'd rather be around for hers than go now and miss it."

"I didn't know you knew Jesse and Penny that well."

"We don't, but John's friends with Penny's dad. Anyway, they want it really casual, so we're doing sandwiches and nibbles. Can you help?"

"What kind of sandwiches?" Holly asked warily. She knew her friend never went casual when it came to parties.

"Wraps and tri-tips, and subs and PBJ for the kids. Easy. You can do the PBJs if you want. Elise and Tilly and Bonnie will be here at three."

"Count on me as well. What can I bring?"

"Just energy and enthusiasm. This is going to be the last party for a while."

"For how long?" Holly asked, amused. A while for Sara was probably two weeks.

"Until the next time to celebrate. The Fourth, I guess. So where were you last night? You could have called me back then to relieve my worrying about the last-minute notice and all."

"You know I'm always glad to help. And where I was is my business."

"Oooo, I like the sound of that. Tell all!"

"Nothing to tell." Except she'd spent the most glorious night of her life with the man she loved. Though no words of love had been spoken this time. She needed Ty to give some indication of his feelings. He'd been as attentive and caring as ever, but the words he'd said often when they'd been teens hadn't been said since. She swallowed. Was he only taking what she so freely offered, without looking to the future?

Had her actions that summer killed any chance of his loving her again?

"With Ty?" Sara prompted.

"I have to go. I'll be there tomorrow at three," Holly said, suddenly not wanting to think about Ty. If he had no plans for a future with her, she'd be hurt all over again. She knew she would survive, but at what cost?

Picking up the phone again, she returned the sheriff's call. He planned to visit her father that morning to see if he could shed any light on the situation. Glad the sheriff was broaching the subject with her dad, she decided she'd wait for the inevitable fallout. She was sure her dad would see the event as evidence she couldn't run his ranch.

She'd argue that point when he brought it up. In the meantime, she had work to do.

As expected, her dad called around two, complaining she wasn't keeping him in the loop and demanding she tell him what was going on. Holly told all she knew and asked who might have a big enough grudge against them to sabotage the ranch.

"No one I know would risk damage to cattle," he said. "We're all ranchers around here."

Obviously *someone* wasn't above a bit of sabotage, cattle or not. She just hoped the sheriff found him— or them—soon.

After dinner, Holly wandered out onto her back porch and sat on the stairs. She could hear the horses in the corral. Hear the sound of canned laughter from the television in the bunkhouse. The lights from the common room were the only ones she saw, other than the stars, which were just coming out as the night sky darkened. With all her being, she wanted to go to Ty's. But had decided not to.

It was one thing to go when she had something to discuss and clear up, but she felt awkward driving over just for another chance at making love. Tomorrow was the engagement dance and she'd see him then. As much as she longed to recapture the feelings they'd shared so long ago, everything had changed. They were grown, had had different life experiences over the years.

Ty more than she. She hadn't left the safety of her father's ranch. She should be out pursuing her life's calling. The horse training she'd done had provided her a nice income, which she usually saved since her father didn't charge her rent. He still hadn't made her a partner or anything, though he told her time and again she'd inherit after his death.

She sighed. For years she'd hated Ty for abandoning her. Now she knew the truth, and the flip side of hate is love—and she had it in spades.

But she didn't know how he felt. Did Ty see her as some pathetic creature depending on her daddy rather than making her own way in life? Could he recapture the feelings for her he'd once had?

Standing, Holly brushed off the seat of her jeans. This pity party was stopping now.

She went inside and called Ty from the kitchen phone.

"Alverez," he answered. The sound of his voice made her knees weak. What a wuss.

"Ty, it's Holly."

"You're not coming," he said flatly.

"Not tonight."

"Fine." He hung up.

Holly couldn't believe it. She quickly redialed.

"What?" he asked.

"What do you mean hanging up on me. I'm not coming tonight, but tomorrow there's another party at Sara's. You know Billy will be with Maria's kids. Stopping by one night to discuss the fence cutting is one thing. Staying over two nights in a row is something else."

"He doesn't know you stayed."

She felt her argument deflate. Maybe she could drop by— No. She'd decided not to and she was sticking to her decision.

"Are you going tomorrow?" she asked.

"Might," he replied. "I knew Jesse when we were all in school."

"Then I'll see you there. Good night, Ty."

"Good night."

Trying to put out of her mind what she *could* be doing now, Holly headed back to the office to read some of the new journals that had arrived recently. Maybe with some luck, she'd be able to ignore the desire that consumed her thinking of Ty.

TY HUNG UP THE PHONE AND hit his head twice against the wall above it. If he lived to be a hundred, he'd never understand Holly Bennett. He'd thought they'd reconnected last night. It was too soon to know for certain, but he sure felt like he'd come home. They'd talked about that summer, both finally learning all that had happened. Now she wouldn't come over. Was it a game for her?

"Daddy?" Billy came into the kitchen.

Ty straightened and turned to smile at his son.

"Yep?"

"Can I have some ice cream?"

"Sure. Let's get some and sit outside. We'll look at the stars." And keep an eye on things, he thought. If his horses started acting up again, he'd know something was going on. The sheriff still had no lead or clues.

Ty suspected the vandalism was tied to his return. But why? If Ryan Bennett had been around, he'd assume it to be the old man's way of trying to run him off.

So who?

He and Billy ate their ice cream and he pointed out the constellations to his son.

His thoughts turned to the daughter he and Holly almost had. A big sister for Billy. If she'd lived, he and Holly would have married and probably had more children. But none would be Billy. Ty looked at him, overwhelmed, as he had been on other occasions, by the miracle that was his son. He wouldn't change a single thing about him.

"Can I sleep over at Brandon's tomorrow?" he asked.

"Tomorrow?" Ty asked absently. Had he missed something?

"After Sara's party. We're going, aren't we?"

"I don't know yet."

"But Brandon wants me to stay over."

"I'll check with his mother. It should be okay." If they went.

He leaned back and tried to see things from Holly's point of view. Her father had lied through his teeth and her impression of that summer had been distorted for years. Had their discussion last night cleared up things? She had never said.

He hadn't offered her the chance, taking her to his bed instead. Did she have any idea how badly he wanted her in every way? Their sharing dinner together during the days she stayed with him were as he'd once imagined their lives would be. Working together, sharing meals, spending the night in each other's arms. It had felt right.

Yet she'd taken off like a shot when her father summoned her. Riding to the rescue of the Rocking B? Or running away again?

HOLLY ARRIVED AT SARA'S PROMPTLY at three. Tilly and Bonnie were already hard at work, and Sara was directing everyone. Elise arrived just after Holly and soon the women were working companionably together in the kitchen, making enough sandwiches to feed an army. Almost elbow deep in cut-up broccoli and cauliflower, Holly glanced out the window to keep an eye on the arrivals. Penny came in to offer her help, but Sara shooed her from the kitchen.

"It's your special day, go enjoy it. And no making

out in front of the children!" she joked to the flustered young woman.

From around four o'clock on, neighbors and friends arrived. Holly noted each new vehicle, then returned to her job.

"He's not coming until after five," Sara said, sidling up to Holly. Her eyes were merry with amusement.

"Who?" Holly feigned.

"Ty," she said and laughed.

Holly shrugged. "Whenever."

"What are you two whispering about?" Tilly asked when she came to stand beside Holly and reached over to wash her hands.

"Holly's beau," Sara teased.

Tilly looked at Holly. "Ty?" she asked.

Holly glared at Sara. "We're just friends," she said primly. "And I worked for him for a little while when my dad was being pigheaded about the ranch."

"You're back home now, right?" Tilly asked.

"Yes. I'm running the Rocking B now. Until Dad recovers."

"Humph." With that, she turned and went back to the sideboard, where she was making sub sandwiches.

"What does that mean?" Sara asked.

"I have no idea. Is this enough?"

"Looks like it. If we need to replenish during the evening, I've got some more in the refrigerator. Oh! Maria is bringing the kids to see the puppies. I've got to get out there."

"What puppies? I thought you had kittens."

"Those, too. One of our cattle dogs whelped the other day. She has five. They're as cute as can be. I feel overrun by babies—calves, too, you know."

"Hardly cute and cuddly."

"I don't know. When they are first born…" Sara said. "Let's finish up here and go see the pups," she suggested.

Holly cleaned up her area, taking platter after platter of veggies and dip and putting them on the various tables already full of food.

"Holly, Holly!" Billy's voice came from behind her and she turned. He was running full out toward her, his face bright with excitement. She smiled, her heart tugging a little. Blinking, she looked beyond him. Ty was walking toward her, sexy as hell with wary eyes and an unsmiling face.

Billy reached her first and launched himself at her. She scooped him up and gave him a quick hug, then placed him back on his feet.

"Howdy," she said, tapping the hat that matched his father's. "You look mighty fine."

"It's for the party. Where's Brandon?"

"He and some others went to the barn to see some new puppies. I was just on my way. Want to go?" She latched on to that excuse to avoid talking with Ty. She felt as flustered as she had that day in the fall of her senior year when he'd leaned against her locker and first flirted with her.

"Can I, Daddy?" Billy asked.

"Sure, we'll both go. You're looking mighty fine yourself, Holly," Ty said.

"Thank you." She'd been careful in the kitchen not to splash anything on the yellow summer dress. It wasn't often she was out of jeans.

"I haven't seen the puppies yet myself," she said as they headed for the barn. "Sara said they're only a few days old. If she lets you pick one up, you have to be very gentle. They're still babies and need a lot of care. The kittens are still in the barn, too. Maybe you can play with them." She was babbling, but she couldn't help it. She darted a quick glance at Ty. He was watching her.

"Can I have a puppy, Daddy?" Billy asked.

Ty shifted his gaze to his son. "We'll see."

When they entered the barn, there was no question where the puppies were. The crowd of children and adults gave it away instantly.

Billy raced over.

The puppies were darling, cuddled together, their eyes closed. They were all black, though the mother had large blotches of white on her fur. Maybe they'd change as they grew older.

Holly knelt beside Billy.

"Want a puppy?" Sara asked from across the enclosure.

"Yes!" Billy said fervently. Everyone laughed.

"Me, too," said two other children.

"I had one dog named Buster. He slept in my room at night." Holly leaned closer to Billy and lowered her voice. "And he slept in my bed, but don't tell my dad—he never knew."

Billy grinned up at her and her heart caught again. He looked so like Ty, it took her breath away. "If I get one, I want him to sleep in my bed, too."

"Not if it's a working dog," Ty said. "He'd have to stay in the barn."

"Then we don't want a working dog, do we Holly?" Billy said, turning back to the puppies.

Sara caught her eye, raising an eyebrow as if in question.

Ty walked with Holly when they left the barn. Maria had once again offered to watch the kids.

"You're going to have to take Brandon for a week sometime to give her a break," Holly said.

"Maybe if I had help. Do you really think your father didn't know about the dog in the bed?"

"Now, I'm sure he did. But back then, I thought it was a big secret. Dad was like that, gruff on the outside, sweet and loving on the inside."

Ty remained silent.

Holly looked at him. "He was."

"If you say so. He never had anything good to say about me or my dad. But I'm not here to talk about your father. Not tonight," he said, reaching out to take her arm. Pulling her to a stop, he leaned over and kissed her.

One of the cowboys whistled.

He broke the kiss and looked down at her as if challenging her.

"You blow hot and cold, Tyler Alverez," she said, feeling dazed he'd claim their relationship so publicly. What relationship? That was what she wanted to know.

He laughed and slung his arm across her shoulders, urging her forward. "That's funny coming from you. Let's go get the eating out of the way. I hear there's going to be dancing later. I can't wait to hold you."

Holly gave up trying to understand the man. The thought of dancing with Ty was exciting. They had gone to only three dances the year they dated—the winter formal, Valentine's Day and their prom. Of course, she'd had to deceive her father, say she was going alone. But once there, the two of them had been inseparable. Would she always find the same magic in his arms?

It was not quite dark when the food was put away and

the makeshift floor set up for dancing. Children still ran around and laughed. The few teenagers there moved to the corral, watching horses and waiting for the older folks to let their attention lapse. The sound system was turned up, the music coming from four different speakers, assuring uniform volume throughout the dance floor.

Holly had to credit Sara, she knew how to throw a party. Penny and Jesse were having a great time. They led off the first dance—in practice for their wedding, Sara announced.

After the first few measures, several other couples moved onto the floor, eager to dance before it got too late. Dawn came early in the summer months.

Holly glanced around. She had left Ty to help Sara clear away the food and he'd joined John and some other ranchers near the keg—drinking beer, swapping stories.

Now that the music started, Holly had expected Ty to come for her. But she didn't see him at all.

"Dance, Holly?" Bud Forrester, a cowboy from the Triple D ranch, asked.

"Love to, Bud." They'd dated a couple of times. But the minute anyone seemed to be getting serious, she backed out. She tried to remain friends with the men she liked—even if she could never see herself falling for them.

He danced well. It was fun. And she resolutely kept her eyes on her partner, and not searching for Ty.

She danced with John for the next song. Then Ben Hudgins.

"Haven't seen much of you lately, Holly," Ben said. "Must be all tied up trying to run that ranch while your father's laid up."

"I've been busy." She never saw the man without feeling annoyed by how persistent he'd been in trying to date her. What kind of life did he live alone on his ranch? He had few hands, fewer friends as far as she could tell. And rumor was he hadn't dated anyone after she'd turned him down six months ago.

She hoped he wasn't still interested in her. She wasn't sure where she stood with Ty and would hate to have anyone experiencing the uncertain same emotions.

"Is your dad getting any better?"

"Seems to be. He hated missing the brandings."

"He might not be up to ranching again once he's home," Ben said.

"I can't see my dad quitting."

Two songs later Ty appeared.

"My turn," he said, holding out his hand. For a moment she hesitated, then put hers into his.

Just then the music really pumped up and everyone lined up for a line dance.

"Just my luck it's not a slow one," he said above the music. She laughed.

"They'll be along soon enough," another cowboy called. The stomping and turning was fun and Holly threw herself into the dance. She, too, wished it had been a slow song. But there would be plenty of those, especially as it got darker.

The next song was a Texas two-step. Ty pulled her into his arms and moved easily around the floor, not bumping into anyone, guiding her to the beat, turning and showing her that his Texas training stood up to Wyoming dances.

Finally, when Holly was beginning to think they'd

have to slip away and find a quiet spot if she was ever to be held against him, the music slowed. The lights dimmed. A cowboy gave a catcall, and couples around the floor moved closer, snuggling into their partners. Holly finally was drawn against Ty's hard body, his head lowering, his hat brushing her hair. He tucked their linked hands into his chest and splayed the hand against her back as if to touch as much of her as he could. They barely moved, shifting slightly in time to the music. She could feel his heart beat. Feel the warmth of his breath on her cheek. Time seemed suspended as they danced to the dreamy rhythm.

"Billy's staying at Maria's tonight," he said softly in her ear. "Come home with me."

How could she say anything but yes? She'd found happiness, true happiness, for the first time in ten years.

"Yes," she said, her heart surely his once more.

THEY WEREN'T THE FIRST TO leave but slipped away as soon as the general exodus began. Holly insisted on driving her own vehicle to Ty's instead of leaving it at the Montgomery ranch, which would stir up curiousity. She didn't want to get the town gossips talking. They'd had enough of a field day with the loss of her baby and the discovery of who the father had been.

Ty led the way and was at the door of her truck when she parked behind his.

He took her into the house. They entered through the kitchen, dimly lit by the light over the stove. He spun her around and kissed her.

Holly laughed in sheer joy and twirled with him as he danced them to the bedroom. The kisses became longer, more erotic as the passion spiked.

By the time Ty had slipped the sundress from her shoulders and shed his own clothes, she felt intoxicated by desire.

CHAPTER THIRTEEN

TY WOKE AT DAWN. He lay in bed, wrapped around Holly, savoring the closeness, the rightness. For a long moment, he drew in the scent of her, his eyes closed, imprinting every nuance on his mind. If this was all they had, he never wanted to forget any of it.

He was reluctant to leave the shared bed, to leave the willing, sensuous woman. But he had horses to feed, chores to do. At eleven he had to pick up Billy and get back by one when the first of the two new hands he'd hired would arrive. His work was cut out for him over the next few days, making the run-down bunkhouse habitable, getting into the thick of his new business, training the new hands to his way of working.

Ty slipped from the bed, leaned over and kissed Holly's cheek. God, she was so pretty. Her hair was fanned across the pillow. Her cheeks were lightly tinted, like the first blush of the sunrise. He covered her with the sheet. She never stirred.

Taking his clothes into the bathroom, he showered and dressed. He stopped long enough in the kitchen to set the coffeemaker to brew before going to check on the animals and start the morning chores. Once he had a few ranch hands around, he'd take Sundays off and sleep in until noon—if Holly was in his bed.

The air was crisp and clear. The cloudless sky announced another warm day. The two new horses he had to train were in their stalls in the barn. Maybe he'd start leaving them out at night with the others since the weather was so mild.

Once the horses had been fed and the few chickens he'd acquired given some grain in exchange for the eggs he found, he returned to the kitchen.

"Good morning," Holly said. She was beautiful in that girly dress she'd worn last night.

"Sleep well?" he asked, walking over to kiss her.

"Ummm," she said, raising her arms to loop around his neck, returning his kiss with enthusiasm.

"Coffee smells good," she said when the kiss ended. She leaned against him slightly as if savoring the feel of his body against hers. Like it hadn't been pressed up against hers most of the night. Not that he was complaining. He loved the feel of her soft curves, the smell of her, the taste of her. He'd never get enough.

Why couldn't he just reach out and grab hold?

"Want breakfast?" he asked.

"I can cook if you'd like." She slowly pulled away, looking sexy and satisfied.

"In that case, I want a big breakfast, eggs, sausage, hash browns, pancakes, waffles."

She laughed. "I'll fix you something but not all that. What do you really want?"

"Eggs, bacon and biscuits. I can make the biscuits," he volunteered.

Soon they were companionably working side by side at the counter and stove.

"Where did you learn to make biscuits?" she asked

as she watched him mix the ingredients and then begin to roll out the dough.

"From my mother, as a matter of fact. One of the few things I remember about her—winter mornings in the warm kitchen, she baked baking-powder biscuits. She never measured, as I remember. But she'd always let me stir and then cut out."

She smiled. "A happy memory. I don't have any memories of my mother."

"You were what, two, when she died?"

"Yes. I can't imagine how you remembered that."

"I remember everything you told me when we were dating," he said. He'd thought about her a lot, with anger, granted, after he and his dad had moved to Texas. Back then he'd thought he'd never see her again. Now look at them.

"Billy won't remember his mother, will he?"

"No. He was younger than two when she died. I have pictures and show him every so often. He has a big one of her in his room. We talk about her."

"Most of what I know about my mother my father told me. I have pictures, too. But it's not the same," Holly said. She looked at him. "But I grew up with a great father, and Billy will, too. It'll be enough."

He focused on the task at hand. He wasn't sure it would be enough. He wanted Holly to join their family, move in with them, have children with him. Would she stay if they married?

The phone rang. Ty answered, spoke for a few moments then hung up.

The biscuits were ready, the eggs just turned and the sausage sizzled.

"Ready to eat," she said, scooping the eggs onto warmed plates as he took the cookie sheet from the oven.

They sat at the table and began breakfast.

"That was Hudgins. He had a couple of his men riding the fence last night during the party, thinking to catch out our vandals. They heard something, but when they rode out to explore, they only smelled dust in the air. Sounds like our guys favor horses. No sound of a vehicle. He wanted to know if I saw anything."

"Hmm. That's a good idea. If we took turns watching, maybe we'd catch them."

"Not you," he said.

She bristled. "Why not me?" She laid down her fork and stared at him. "The Rocking B is the one having the most trouble. We need to protect our property."

"Send Donny or one of the other men," Ty said, not rising to her bait. "Glaring at me isn't going to make me change my mind. These men could be dangerous. If you're planning anything like this, send one of your men."

For a moment, he thought she would argue. But she took a breath and shrugged. "We'll see," was all she said.

"What are you doing today?" Ty asked, letting it go for now.

"Going home and changing before anyone sees me. If I was smart, I'd have stashed a change of clothes in the truck," Holly said. "Then I'll go visit my dad. He'll want to hear about the party. He likes to be kept up to speed on what's going on in the county." She took a bit of bacon. "When are you getting Billy?"

"At eleven. Then I've got a new man starting."

Holly looked surprised. "You've hired someone?"

"Sure. My last hired hand left." He winked. "I still

have a lot of work that needs to be done. And I've got another hand lined up to start on Thursday."

"Getting any more cattle?" she asked.

"Not for a while. I've got two horses to train now and plan on getting more as soon as we settle in and have things in shape."

"You're taking business away from me," she said without heat.

"What're you talking about?"

"I've been training stock horses since I left college after that first year. I make pretty good money around here. Guess that'll dry up. I don't have a fancy award or title or two under my belt."

He looked at her, remembering. Once, they'd planned to open a training facility together. They'd had everything laid out, how the arenas would be, that one would be covered so they could keep working in inclement weather, how they'd structure their programs.

"We could work together," he said softly.

She looked at him, hope blossoming. "Maybe." She stood and took her plate to the sink. "I'd better get going. I have a ranch to run."

"Stay a little longer," he urged. It had seemed so right having her across the table from him.

She ran water over her plate, squirted soap in the big pan she'd used and left it soaking.

"Call me?" she said.

He rose and came to her, taking her into his arms. "I'll call as soon as you get home and invite you back. Will you come riding with me and Billy today?"

"I've got to see my father. Another time, though." She reached up and kissed him, then turned to leave.

"Tomorrow?"

She laughed and kept heading out the door.

Ty listened to the echo of her laughter. He'd have to push the point soon. He couldn't live in limbo. He either trusted her and wanted her in his life or he was going to run scared. He had always wanted her. Would she say yes if he asked?

HOLLY WALKED OUT OF THE sheriff's office just as church was letting out. She'd decided to stop in before going to see her dad to get any updates the sheriff had, but it proved to be fruitless.

Slowly walking along the sidewalk, she tried to think of who might be responsible for the vandalism. She planned to discuss it with Ben Hudgins later and see what his thoughts were. Maybe tonight she'd ride down near the fence and sit out for a little while—watching.

Lunch first, then her father. The café was almost full. More and more families stopped in for lunch after church. She claimed a small table for two near the back and sat. Before she could order, Tilly called her name.

"Mind if I join you, dear?" the librarian asked, coming closer. "It's packed and my friend Ethel is not feeling well. I'm eating alone like you. Unless you're saving this chair for your friend Ty."

"I'm not. Have a seat," Holly said, gesturing to the empty chair. "How was church?"

"That new preacher sure gives a fine sermon. You should start going again, dear."

Holly smiled and made no comment.

After they ordered, Tilly looked around, as if cataloging those present.

"Nice party last night, wasn't it," she asked, turning back to Holly.

"Sara does throw a good party. Penny and Jesse looked blissfully happy."

"You were enjoying yourself with Ty Alverez, I could tell." Tilly was a closet romantic. She presented a stern face to the town in her role of librarian, but Holly knew she loved a good romance as much as the next woman.

"We're friends," Holly said carefully.

"Good for you!" she said with satisfaction.

"Shouldn't we be?"

"I remember how bad things were ten years ago, Holly. Your father sure raised Cain after that accident. Reminded me of when he and Jennifer Alverez got into that bad crash."

Holly stared at her, the noise around her fading. Her focus was entirely on the librarian.

"What are you talking about?"

"I figured you knew the story," Tilly said. "Did I speak out of turn?"

"What story?"

Tilly studied her. "Your mother was a friend of mine. It hurt everyone when she died. She was a wonderful woman and so happy to be pregnant again. She desperately wanted another child. She loved having you. Her aneurysm shocked us all. To lose both her and the baby, it was a blow I wasn't sure your father would ever recover from. He was a man alone, no family, and a two-year-old to deal with. I know having you helped. Having to run that ranch of his, he hired help to watch you during the day."

Holly nodded. She knew all this. There'd been several housekeepers while she was growing up, until she turned sixteen. When Hilda had left to get married, her father said they could manage on their own. Holly had taken on most of the cooking and cleaning with some occasional help for the heavy work.

"One was Jennifer Alverez," Tilly said.

"Ty's mother?" Holly frowned. She tried to remember. Most memories before she started school were hazy.

Tilly nodded.

"I don't remember her."

"You would have been about three or four. She was there almost a year. Her husband was a ranch hand for the McKenzies. He didn't make that much, I expect. She supplemented their income by watching you."

"What happened?" Holly felt a chill of foreboding.

Tilly tilted her head slightly, as if trying to decide how much to say. Finally, slowly, she began, "Your father had been without companionship for a long while. Jennifer was beautiful—a gentle soul from Virginia. She had the sweetest, southern accent. I can still remember how she pronounced *house* and *about*. Anyway, it came out at the hearing about the accident that your father tried to seduce her. She resisted, quit her job on the spot and was fleeing for home when her car crashed. Your father was behind her, trying to catch up, to apologize, he said. Then it was Jose Alverez and his son, Ty, who were heartbroken."

"I never knew," Holly said. Her father chasing after Ty's mother? Impossible.

"Jose went after Ryan when he learned what had happened. There was a fight. Ryan did his best to hush it all up. How would it look, a leading rancher trying to seduce a cowboy's wife? Jose tried to have him charged, but your father got revenge against Jose instead. Got him thrown in jail a few weeks later on a drunk-driving charge. Jennifer had died and Jose was wild with grief.

I don't think anyone blamed him for drinking. Still, rumor was that Ryan caused that crash as well. The animosity simmered all those years. It came to a head again when you and Ty were injured. Jose left right after you went away to college. Ty was at the university, so there was nothing left in Turnbow for him."

Holly was stunned. Her father had tried to seduce another man's wife? Ended up causing her death? Impossible.

"You have the story wrong," she said. She couldn't believe it.

Tilly looked at her with sympathetic eyes. "I'm sorry, Holly. A lot of it was hushed up. Your father was shaken by Jennifer's death. I don't know why Ty doesn't know the story, but I always thought it so romantic that the two of you fell in love, despite the rift in the families. Like it was a way to heal the split."

"You knew about us then?"

"You used to come to the library and slip off to that back carrel where Ty would be waiting. I may have been at the front desk, but I always know what goes on at my library!"

"If it had happened as you said, why wouldn't Jose have told Ty?"

"I don't know. But it's true. If you have doubts, ask your father. Or Donny at the ranch. He was working there at the time. Or Evelyn Stott. There was plenty of gossip for a while, then it cooled down. Nothing was ever proved. And when Jose got out of jail, he avoided anyone from the Rocking B."

Ty mustn't know. They'd have discussed it in the past, if not recently, if he did. He'd be furious if this were true. He already disliked her father. This would give him ample ammunition to strengthen that dislike. What would it do to feelings he might have toward her, the daughter of the man who caused his mother's death?

"I'm seeing my father this afternoon. I will ask him." If she thought her words would cause Tilly to recant, she was mistaken.

The older woman nodded. "I always thought your dad hated Jose because of guilt for what he'd done. And for Jose's being a better man and not filing charges when they might have been warranted," Tilly said gently.

"Ty doesn't know." If he had a clue, he'd never have had anything to do with her.

Unless— Her father had said Ty was out for revenge. She hadn't understood what he meant. Was that why Ty had returned? Could he mean to use her to exact some kind of retribution for her father's part in his mother's death?

No, Ty wouldn't do that.

The waitress delivered their lunches. Holly looked at the salad she'd ordered, feeling sick. "I can't eat." She fished out a few dollars and laid them on the table. "I've got to go. Have them wrap my lunch and take it home if you want," she said to Tilly. Rising, she quickly left and headed for her car.

The father she thought she'd known was fast disappearing. Who was this stranger she was on her way to visit?

HOLLY COULDN'T GET TO THE convalescent home fast enough. Tilly had to have the facts skewed. Her father couldn't have been so dishonorable as to try to steal another man's wife. He'd raised her with integrity and honesty. He had been a loving father, giving her almost everything she wanted.

Except the boy she'd loved above all else.

"He thought he was protecting me," she said, trying to deflect the thoughts that pounded.

He'd been convinced Ty had been exacting revenge. But revenge was only a consideration when great harm had been done.

Not her father.

Ryan Bennett sat near the window of his room. His left arm and wrist were still encased in plaster. His feet in slippers, not the boots Holly was used to seeing. He looked old and tired. Her eyes took in everything. How he gazed out the window. How he seemed so alone. She tried to reconcile this image with that of a man forcing his attentions on a married woman. Chasing her until she crashed her car and died. She couldn't.

"Dad?" she said, stepping inside. For this conversation, she wanted no interruptions. She closed the door.

"Holly." His face brightened seeing her. "You're earlier than I expected. I just finished lunch."

She came over and sat in one of the visitor chairs.

"I had lunch with Tilly," she began.

"How is she? Haven't seen her for a while. No time for reading when there's work to be done. Of course now, maybe now she can send me some new mysteries. So, did the sheriff find those men yet?"

Holly shook her head. "I want to talk to you about something Tilly told me. About Jennifer Alverez."

His expression grew wary. "Jennifer is dead. She died a long time ago." He looked back out the window.

"Tilly said you tried to seduce her. She fought you off, raced for home and you followed her. Her car crashed and she died." *Please tell me Tilly is wrong!*

"What's she trying to do? Stir up trouble? There's

enough of that around with Ty Alverez back in town and men cutting fences and damaging pumps."

It wasn't lost on Holly that he didn't instantly deny the charge. Her hopes plummeted. "Was Jennifer Alverez one of the housekeepers we had?"

"It was a long time ago, Holly. Leave it be."

"I want to know what happened. If you won't tell me, I'll ask around until I find someone who will."

He turned to her then, his eyes narrowed in anger. "Like who?"

"Tilly said to ask Donny."

"Donny works for me!"

"Does that mean he won't answer any questions I ask him?" she asked. "How about newspaper accounts, or were those destroyed? The sheriff should have records."

"Don't get all worked up. And don't be raising a ruckus over something that ended nearly twenty-five years ago. No good will come of it," Ryan almost shouted.

"Then *you* tell me what the truth is. Tell me about Mrs. Alverez."

Ryan silently gazed at his daughter. Finally he spoke.

"She was a beautiful woman. Sweet as could be. She was from Virginia. A true southern belle. And she had the misfortune to get tied up with that no-account cowboy, Alverez." He frowned, glaring at Holly.

"She married him. They had Ty," she said.

"She was too good for him. Lovely as a spring sunrise. She had that skin they call peaches and cream. Couldn't stay in the sun for long or she'd get burned. Light hair, but silky. She was the prettiest thing I ever saw and she was wasted on that cowboy. I offered her everything."

"Dad!" It was true. She'd hoped Tilly had distorted the facts.

"She fit in. You adored her. She was used to finer things in Virginia than she got in Wyoming. Things I could have afforded to give her. I wanted her. But she wanted Alverez."

"Dad, she was married, had a son."

"She should have been *my* wife!" he yelled, pounding the arm of his chair with his good fist.

Holly listened, staggered. She didn't detect a hint of remorse or regret for his actions. Only that Jennifer had chosen her husband over her employer.

"If she'd only listened to me. I could have made her life heaven on earth."

"Dad, what about your morals? How could you try to lure her away from her husband?"

"I thought if she knew what I had to offer, what it was like to be with someone other than that cowboy, she'd want what I wanted." He swore. "But she turned me down and threatened to have the authorities after me. Me, Ryan Bennett, owner of one of the biggest spreads in the county. She didn't know how lucky she was that I was interested in her."

Holly couldn't believe this was her father speaking. This was not the man she remembered from her childhood, the man who taught her right from wrong. Still, she needed to know the full story.

"So she left and you chased after her?"

He looked surprised, then resigned. "No. I *went* after her. She was distraught. It was raining cats and dogs. I wanted to explain. It wasn't just for an afternoon, I wanted her to be my wife, to divorce Alverez and marry me. The closer I got, the faster she drove until she couldn't make the curve out by Helton's place. She ran off the road and crashed into those cottonwoods that line the river. God, I tried to reach her. But by the time I was at her car, blood was everywhere, and she was dead."

He shook his head. "She'd been so beautiful, and then she was gone."

Holly felt sick.

"Tilly said you sent Jennifer's husband to jail."

"Jose Alverez accosted me one night after Jennifer's death. He'd been drinking. Damn fool. I started for home. He came after me, swearing it was my fault Jennifer was dead. I didn't want him following me, so I stopped short. He ran into the back of my truck. He was arrested and sentenced to six months in jail. Should have been longer."

"Sounds like you provoked it," she murmured.

He glared at her. "And then you, taking up with that Tyler Alverez. He used you in high school. You stay away from him!"

"He tried to see me. You stopped him. He loved me. Do you know what that summer cost me?"

"Nothing. You were well shed of that baby. You had a chance at college and a great future. You blew it all."

Holly stared at him, unbelieving. How could he have said she was well rid of her precious baby? She didn't know her father at all.

"You should have made something of yourself. Find a good man, start your own family," Ryan said. "Forget the past and leave the Alverez family behind. I did good by you keeping you away from that boy. If you're smart, you'll stay away from him now."

"I probably won't have a choice once he learns of this. He doesn't know. Why didn't his father tell him?"

Holly asked. She doubted she'd get an answer, but she was curious. The Alverez family was the one wronged—why not tell his son?

"'Hatred is a terrible thing,' Jose said to me that night. I guess he didn't want his son to carry the burden. After he went to jail, he admitted I had more power in this town. He stayed away, which was what I wanted. Then you two were in the crash. When I wanted to prosecute Tyler for statutory rape, his dad showed me a letter Jennifer had written to a friend, about my attentions. He'd received it after her death. That's when he'd pieced together the full story. That's why he was so furious that night he rammed my truck. If I prosecuted Ty, he'd make the letter known. It would have ruined my reputation in Turnbow."

"What did the letter say?" Holly's head began to pound.

He rubbed his eyes with his good hand. "Nag a man to death. It detailed the situation. All right? His threat was enough to have me back off. But there was no way I was going to let my daughter hang out with that man's son."

"The son of the man you wronged. Jose Alverez would have raised the roof if he knew Ty and I were seeing each other. And I don't blame him."

Ryan looked away. "He wouldn't have liked it any more than me. But he only found out because of the accident, same as I did."

"I've loved Ty since my senior year in high school," Holly said steadily. "If things had worked out the way we planned, we would have been married for a while now and probably had a bunch of kids—your grandchildren. A lot of time's passed. I don't want another ten years to drag by without him. If he'll have me." Holly was more confused than ever. No wonder she'd never felt she could trust her instincts. Her world had just turned upside down.

"Oh, he'll have you. You come with the Rocking B in your back pocket. At least he'll think so. Revenge and money, two powerful reasons to marry you."

"So's love. That's what we'll have," she said with far more bravado than she felt.

"Marry him and I won't leave you the ranch," Ryan warned.

Holly stood. Her thoughts were in a jumble. She couldn't believe everything she'd learned. The most difficult to absorb was her father's culpability in it all. He professed to love her but had caused her the greatest heartbreak of all.

CHAPTER FOURTEEN

HOLLY DROVE HOME feeling like the world as she'd known it had shifted. Her father was unrecognizable. While his actions had taken place almost twenty-five years ago, because she'd just learned of them, they were fresh and stark. What would Ty do when he found out?

She considered not telling him. Let their relationship develop however it was destined to. If he found out at some point in the future, she'd deal with it then.

But that was unfair. And too much like sacrificing her own integrity. She didn't want to be that person. She couldn't believe the father she'd spoken to today was the same man she'd always looked up to. The man who had given her a strong work ethic and high morals.

When she reached home, she got a glass of iced tea and went out to her garden. Slipping into the enclosed area was like stepping into another world—one of beauty and fragrance and peace. No ugliness marred this place. She wandered along the paths until she came to her favorite bench. It was in shade this time of day. Gratefully, she sank down. She usually took such joy from the myriad colors and shapes of her flowers. But today she scarcely saw them.

She had to think of a way to tell Ty and yet make sure

he didn't freak out and turn on her. It certainly had nothing to do with them. They'd been small children when it all happened.

Yet she knew he'd be as upset as she was, if not more. The rift between the two families had to be laid directly at her father's feet. He deserved Ty's lack of respect. Ty's hatred.

But could she bear to tell him and risk losing him?

She had to.

She sipped the tea, wishing she could wave a magic wand and be transported back to the day before the prom. Everything had been so wonderful. She'd insist they stay longer at the dance, miss the drunk driver and all the grief that had followed. They could have married, had their baby, gone to college and begun a life together.

Would that life have survived the truth of his mother's death? His father would have probably protested their marriage, even with the baby. She didn't see how there could've been any way out of the quagmire. It had all been set in motion years before.

Long after she finished the beverage, she remained on the bench. Slowly the serenity of the garden filled her. She'd carry on no matter what happened. She'd done it before. If Ty turned on her because of her father, she'd survive it again. But she knew it would be a long time before she'd ever feel truly content and at peace.

Finally she rose and went into the house. Calling from the kitchen phone, she reached out to Tyler Alverez.

"Want to come to dinner?" she asked when he picked up.

"When?"

"Tonight. I could fry up some chicken, make potato

salad and you could make some of your mother's amaz-ing biscuits." Mentioning his mother brought a pang. If not for her father, she could still be alive today. Enjoying her grandson, maybe even making a home for Ty on the ranch his father had managed to acquire.

"Marty Reynolds started today. I need to get him din-ner. Want to come here?"

"No. Have him come and join the ranch hands. I'll let Randy know to add a place. You and Billy can eat with me."

There was a pause on the other end. Then, "Okay. We'll be over around six. You know, I don't think I've ever been inside your house except that day. I barely made it inside the door."

"Did you know your mother used to babysit me? I wonder if she brought you with her, since we're the same age." For the first time, she considered the pos-sibility that she and Ty had played together as four-year-olds. She tried to remember, but nothing came. Where had he been the day his mother crashed?

"What?"

"I learned a few things today. I'll tell you after din-ner," she said, stalling. "See you at six."

The die was cast. The first step to an uncertain future.

She called Sara next. She wanted some advice, or maybe to have someone talk her out of her plan. But she only reached the answering machine. She was on her own on this.

She took a quick shower and put on a nice shirt with her jeans. Fixing her hair gave her something to do and, once ready, she went to the kitchen to begin to prepare dinner. She had the potato salad done and the chicken ready to fry when she heard the truck in the drive.

Donny had asked her who Ty's new hand was and seemed to know the man, so she was glad that would work out. She would feel too awkward with a stranger at the table.

"Holly!"

She heard the running footsteps on the back porch. Did that little boy ever just walk? The door was open, so they came right in.

"Hi, Holly," Billy said, charging straight for her.

She gave him a welcoming hug and looked up at his father. "Hi to both of you. Glad you could come on such short notice."

Ty nodded, glancing around the kitchen. She could tell he was trying to remember if he'd ever been there before. Maybe she shouldn't have started by telling him about the babysitting.

"How's the new guy?" she asked.

"I think he'll work out fine." Ty put his hat on the rack by the door, next to hers. In the spot her father usually took.

"I've got beer, wine or scotch."

"Beer's good."

"Can I see your house?" Billy interrupted.

"Oh, sure. Let's do the tour and maybe find something for you to do while your dad and I finish making dinner."

After a quick tour, Holly took them to her garden. Opening the gate, she stood to one side so they could enter first.

"Wow, Daddy, look at all the flowers." Billy stood in awe, looking at the colorful blooms.

"It's beautiful, isn't it?" Ty said. He glanced at Holly. "I didn't know you grew flowers."

She shrugged. "Something to do when I get done work." She loved her English country garden with the wide variety of colorful flowers, the mixture of fragrances.

"You must use a ton of water."

She laughed. "Trust a rancher to think of that first. We have a good well, and yes I do use a lot of water, but it all returns to the soil, so I think it's filtering back to the aquifer."

"There's a bench and a fountain and everything," Billy exclaimed as he darted along one of the paths.

"He could stay here until supper's ready if that's okay with you. It's fenced, so he couldn't get into trouble," Holly suggested

"Billy, I'm going back inside with Holly. Want to stay here?" Ty called.

"Yeah!"

"Don't pick any flowers," Ty said.

"He can't hurt anything. Flowers can be enjoyed inside as well as out," Holly said.

"Yeah, but he'd probably pull up the entire plant."

They went back into the house. They were hardly in the kitchen before he took her in his arms and kissed her.

"I've been wanting to do that since you left this morning. But not in front of Billy," he said.

She rubbed her thumb along his lips, feeling the dampness from their kiss. "Too soon," she murmured. It wouldn't do to confuse the child. But it made her wonder how Ty viewed their future.

It was fun preparing the meal together. Ty told her about his new employee. They discussed all that was needed to repair the bunkhouse.

"So for now he's staying in the room I did?" she asked.

"Until we get the bunkhouse fixed up, which has to be soon. I told you I have another hand coming on Thursday. So by then I need at least a couple of rooms in the bunkhouse functional. Guess they'll take their meals with me and Billy until I need more hands and can afford a cook."

Ty called Billy when dinner was ready. He had his son wash his hands and sit quietly at the table. The chicken drumsticks were a big hit with the little boy.

When they finished, Ty went to the truck and brought in a couple of DVDs. "I didn't think you'd have anything suitable for a child, so I brought a couple of his favorites. We can sit outside and talk, if that's what you want."

She swallowed and nodded, glad he'd thought about that. She wouldn't have known how to entertain the little boy while she talked to Ty. He had years of experience; she had none.

Five minutes later Billy was settled in front of the television, watching his favorite movie.

"We can sit in the garden. With the windows open, we'll hear him if he needs anything."

"Fine." He grabbed his hat on the way out and followed her to the garden.

"Tell me about my mother watching you," he said as they walked along the path.

"I just learned about it today, along with a bunch of other things. I know now why my father didn't want me to see you when we were in school. Or now, for that matter."

She sat on the edge of the bench, looking at him with every nerve in her body quivering in anxiety. She hoped she could do this right, that he'd say it didn't matter and let the past stay in the past.

But partway into her explanation, she realized he wasn't going to do that.

"So you mean to say, your father tried to rape my mother, chased her until she crashed her car and when that wasn't enough, got my father put in jail?" he asked in disbelief when she finished.

"I didn't say rape. It was never that!" It was so sordid. But surely it hadn't been attempted rape.

"Sounds like a cleaned up version of exactly that. But when it comes down to it he forced his attentions on her. So badly she had to quit and run, right?"

"I—I don't know. Tilly said she fled—"

"Sounds like chasing after her to me. God, Ryan Bennett has some nerve objecting to my seeing his daughter. He should have been sent to prison. Or at the very least, shunned by the community." He stood and paced. "Dammit, Holly, why didn't my father tell me? He must have known the impact it would've had on how I handled things—especially that summer."

"Maybe he thought we were good for each other," she offered tentatively. Her heart raced; fear clogged her throat. She didn't want Ty to react like this. She wanted his reassurance that it changed nothing.

But maybe he was giving her just that. Had she seen a blossoming relationship where none existed?

"I've got to go," he said.

"Go? I thought you would stay a while. We need to talk this through."

"Yeah? I've got news for you. I don't know that we do. After this bombshell, what I need is time to absorb things. Tell me again what Tilly said." He stood on the pathway, feet spread, hands crossed over his chest, glaring at her.

She repeated all she'd learned, not revealing that some of the information had come from her father. Ty's stance never wavered.

"How do you feel about this?" he asked suddenly.

"I feel stunned. I couldn't believe it at first."

"But you obviously do believe it. Enough to tell me. What changed?"

She swallowed, meeting his gaze. "I spoke with my father. He confirmed it. After all the lecturing he did to me about honor and good behavior. I feel sick. I'm so sorry, Ty."

"It's not your fault," he said studying her for a moment. Then he swung away.

"Thanks for dinner. I'll get Billy." With that, he strode through the garden and out the gate.

Holly was so surprised she didn't move right away, then she scrambled to her feet and quickly followed. By the time she caught up with him, he was already explaining to Billy that an emergency had come up and that the little boy could watch the rest of the movie at home.

"Don't go," she said, keeping her voice level so not to alert his son something was seriously wrong.

"I almost called you back to say we couldn't come tonight. I should have trusted my gut," he said, moving to pop the DVD out of the machine and putting it back into its case.

"As I should have trusted mine ten years ago," she said.

"What does that mean?" He flicked her a quick glance.

"I told you I should have stood by my beliefs that

summer. I knew you loved me. I should have acted on that instead of allowing myself to be convinced of the contrary."

"And what do you believe now?"

"What do you mean?"

"Marry me, Holly. Move in with me and let your father's ranch take care of itself. Choose me as you should have ten years ago. Make your loyalties known and stick to them."

She paused, stunned. Then shook her head. "I can't do that, Ty. It's too fast. A few days ago you said you wouldn't take the risk with me. Now this almost sounds like an ultimatum. What's going on?"

"I'm trying to see which way the wind blows with you. You said you love me. Prove it. Marry me."

Billy looked back and forth between them, his eyes wide.

Holly glanced at the boy.

"I can't make any decision right now. This is not the time or place."

Ty nodded, picked up Billy and the DVDs and headed for his car.

"Please, Ty. Don't leave like this."

"I should never have come," he said, walking away without looking back.

Holly stood still, listening to the sounds coming from outside. Ty calling for the hired man. The closing of one truck door, then another. The sound of the engine roaring to life, and then it fading as he drove away.

Had he asked her to marry him? Or simply issued a challenge? He was furious over learning about his mother's last days with her father. Rightly so, but there had been no words of love or commitment, just a sudden demand she marry him. For the revenge her father had cautioned her against?

How could Ty even ask such a thing, especially in light of her father's actions? If nothing else, Ryan was morally responsible for Jennifer's death.

How could Holly have lived her whole life in this town and not have heard that story before?

A testament to the power her father could wield, she was sure. He'd caused Ty's mother's death. He'd been a good father to her. He gave generously to charities.

He'd lied and broken her heart.

Twice.

Ty DROVE CAREFULLY, AWARE of the anger and confusion and hurt. He needed to get himself and his son safely home. Then he could vent. Why hadn't anyone ever told him of the horror behind his mother's death? The entire community must have known at one time, but no one leaked a word. Even during high school years when all secrets seemed to come out of the woodwork. How could his father have let the man get away with it? He should have had the cops on Bennett as soon as he got that damning letter. Why hadn't he?

Ty dropped Marty and Billy at the house, then saddled his horse and rode out. He said he was going to check on the fence, but more important, he needed time alone to think things through.

He barely remembered his mother. As he rode, he tried to think back to when he'd been small. A few scattered memories, like the one of baking biscuits. And of a time when he stayed with Tom and Sally Smith. Had that been when his father was in jail?

He pushed the horse hard, riding at a full gallop

until he was tired, his back ached and it was dark. Worried about injuring his horse, he slowed to a walk and turned for home. First thing in the morning, he'd call his uncle to find out what he knew. If that wasn't enough, surely the Smiths could tell him more.

Marty was still watching television when Ty returned.

"Billy went to bed at eight. He's a good kid," he told Ty.

"I appreciate your watching him. It's not why I hired you."

"So you said. Wasn't like I was going anywhere. No problem."

SHORTLY BEFORE SEVEN THE next morning, Ty called his uncle. He confirmed most of what Holly said.

"Why didn't he tell me?" Ty asked. "He only said mom died in a car crash, not that some bastard tried to rape her and then chased her down."

"It couldn't be proved, Ty. And nothing would bring back your mother," he said. "He was carrying a load of guilt because she had to work at all. You know your mother came from a wealthy family back east. They disowned her when she married your father."

Ty had heard that story a hundred times—whenever he asked about his grandparents. "Sure. But a lot of women work to help their families."

"Not any from our family back then. Doesn't matter how it was, I'm telling you how your father felt. As if some of it was his fault. Stupid. I told him so. She worked. An arrogant man came on to her and she fled. She did the best she could. It was tragic," he said. "What brought all this up? Your mother and father are both dead now. Let them rest in peace."

"I just learned about it. I can't believe he didn't tell me."

"Let it go, son, your father had his reasons or he would have told you," his uncle said.

"I was in love with the daughter of that man," Ty said heavily.

"The daughter didn't kill your mother," he said gently.

"She's devoted to her father."

"Family is important. Just like you are important to us. Why don't you come back to Texas?"

"I can't. I want to make this ranch into something Dad would have been proud of," Ty said. If nothing else, he wanted to make his dad's dream come alive. Maybe show Turnbow, Wyoming, that just because a man starts out a cowboy doesn't mean he can't dream big and succeed.

"He was proud of you," Tomas said. "We all are."

"I hope so. Thanks, Tio Tomas. Can you tell me about his being in jail."

"Now that was a trumped-up charge if I ever heard it. Shows how much power a bigwig rancher has over a mere cowboy. That brought your father up short. His one fear was that Bennett would do something to cause him to lose you. But his hate grew, I think. He never got over Jennifer's death. None of us did. She was an angel, your mother. And she adored you."

Ty hung up after a few moments more of conversation. His anguish didn't subside. How could he have not known how his own mother died, and who had killed her?

The phone rang. It was Holly.

"How are you doing?" she asked.

"Hanging in there."

"I couldn't sleep last night. Ty, I'm so sorry. Maybe

I shouldn't have told you, but you had a right to know. I'm still in shock."

"Apparently all the legal aspects were handled legitimately," he said. "I spoke with my father's brother this morning."

"It sounded to me like my dad forced your father into crashing into his truck. Which really makes that, at least, his fault," she said slowly.

The entire situation was Ryan Bennett's fault, but Ty didn't voice the obvious. "Maybe, but my dad's the one who lost his wife and ended up going to jail." He couldn't help the hard tone of his voice. Anger churned deep inside. He wanted to lash out at the world—or narrow it down to one son of a bitch in Turnbow.

"I've got to go," he said.

"Where are you going?" she asked.

"How does that concern you?" he asked coldly.

He heard her swift intake of breath through the line. He wished he could feel some regret.

"Please, don't shut me out, Ty," she pleaded.

He hung up the phone.

HANGING UP THE PHONE, Holly sat at the kitchen table, her coffee growing cold—as cold as she felt. Her heart ached. Had she been wrong to tell him?

No, he needed to know. She didn't want a relationship with anyone to be based on lies and cover-ups.

But his attitude hurt her. How could he love her and treat her this way?

Only, that was the thing. He hadn't mentioned one word about still loving her since he'd returned. Was she assuming too much?

The day dragged by. She talked with the men about

keeping watch for the vandals. Checked in with the sheriff. Dodged a call from her father. Hoped Ty would call her, but he didn't.

Dinner was a hasty sandwich and some soup. She didn't feel like doing much of anything.

Could she change things by saying yes to Ty's proposal? If he was serious.

Would he care for her, or use her as a weapon against her father? It came down to one question. Did he love her more than he hated her father?

Her instincts told her he wouldn't marry her to get revenge. But she didn't trust her instincts. That habit was hard to break.

The facts and questions they raised echoed over and over. She tried to watch television, but couldn't concentrate. Finally she took a warm bath, washed her hair, and was in bed by nine. She knew it was early, but maybe she could sleep tonight since she hadn't last night.

After tossing and turning for two hours, she gave up. Switching on the light, she picked up the book on her nightstand. It took about an hour to realize she hadn't absorbed half of what she'd read.

Did Ty love her?

She believed he did. Maybe it was time to find out. She'd go over and ask him.

She dressed quickly and slipped out of the house. It was after midnight, the night sky full of stars, the moon a half crescent on the horizon. She moved quietly, hoping the truck starting wouldn't wake the men in the bunkhouse.

Partway there, she realized she'd also have to face the new hired hand. Almost to Ty's drive, she pulled to the side of the road and stopped the truck, switching off her lights. This was a stupid idea. How could she show up at almost one in the morning and tell him she wanted to discuss his offer of marriage?

She leaned back against the seat, taking a deep breath. Nothing that couldn't wait until morning, really. So she'd spend another sleepless night. It wouldn't kill her.

She reached for the key and stopped when she glimpsed movement from the corner of her eye. Straining to see in that direction, she managed to make out two men riding horses along the ridge. They were heading for Ty's place!

Was it Hudgins's men riding the fence line? She thought the boundary was farther to the west. Or had Ty and his new man decided to take a night's watch? But Ty would never leave Billy at home alone if not for an emergency. What was going on?

When the riders dropped below the ridge, she started her engine and slowly pulled away from the side of the road. She flipped on her lights and soon was at Ty's drive. She pushed the truck as fast as it could go on the rutted drive. Ty really needed to get the thing graded!

Cresting the slight rise, she could see the house and barn ahead of her in the light of the moon. There was a curious flickering yellow light near the barn. Fire!

Just then she heard one of the horses neigh loudly. Followed almost immediately by the sound of gunfire. She'd been raised on a ranch. She recognized both sounds instantly. Another two or three shots sounded. She floored the accelerator and shot down the drive. To hell with the tires.

Reaching the clearing, she turned the truck so the headlights illuminated the barn. The fire was inside. Another shot rang, this one shattering one of her head-lights. She grabbed the rifle her father kept in the gun rack and flung herself out of the truck, ducking behind it for some protection.

"Holly, get down," Ty called from the house.

The next shot embedded itself into the wood of Ty's house.

Peering over the edge of the pickup, she saw a man in the barn, silhouetted against the fire. But he was moving and not holding a gun. Where was the shooter?

Another shot. Holly spotted him and stepped to the side, took aim and fired. Almost simultaneously she felt the hot pierce of a bullet against her side, spinning her around. She fell to her knees, still holding the rifle. The pain was amazing, surely as hot as the fire in the barn. Momentarily stunned, she lay there then crawled behind the truck. Touching her side, her hand came away sticky and wet with blood. She couldn't believe she'd been shot.

"Rich?" the man from inside the barn called. "Where are you?"

Holly peeked around the truck. Who was causing all the trouble? She tried to aim, but knew the shot went wild. She was having trouble holding the rifle with both hands.

Though not seeing anyone now, she shot again at the barn to let them know she was still here. After a round of gunfire, she withdrew.

Seconds later, Ty slid into the dirt next to her. "You're a lifesaver," he said, grabbing her to kiss her. "I don't have a gun and neither does Marty. Let me have that rifle."

She relinquished it without a word, pressing her hand against her side. It hurt like crazy. She hoped she wasn't going to bleed to death.

Ty swore then aimed and fired. Two more shots were returned. Ty half rose and fired again.

"I'm going to lose that barn. I hope the bastards let the horses out before they torched the place." He fired again.

Holly took shallow breaths—it was easier. She was getting cold.

"You okay?" he asked.

"Fine. Get them," she said.

He looked at her. "Holly."

In the distance the sound of sirens could be heard. Sound traveled great distances in the night. How far away was the sheriff?

"Rich!" the second man called again. He came out of the burning barn, his hands in the air. "Don't shoot. You got Rich and I don't have a gun." He walked away from the barn as more and more of the structure was engulfed in flames. The horses in the corral were frantic, running up and down along the fence, pushing against it. But Ty had built it solid.

"Turn the horses loose," Ty said, keeping the truck between him and the man, his rifle aimed directly at his chest.

Six horses and a pony raced out into the night, terrified by the fire.

"They'll be okay," Ty said, more to himself than to Holly. His eyes never left the arsonist.

"Go make sure they're not causing any more damage," Holly said, gritting her teeth against the pain, "then come back."

"You okay?"

"I think I'm shot," she said. She began to shiver.

"Marty!" Ty roared.

"Yes, boss." The man came running from the house, keeping low as he ran toward the truck.

"Take the rifle and keep an eye on him. See if you can find the second man. Be careful he's the one with the gun." Ty gave the rifle to Marty and knelt beside Holly.

"God, sweetheart, why didn't you tell me?" As his hand found hers, he realized the blood was seeping between her fingers. He ripped off his shirt, bundled it and pressed it against her side. "Hang on, I called 9-1-1. They dispatched the sheriff and fire department. Paramedics will be here soon."

The sirens grew louder. How long before help arrived? She couldn't think. The pain seemed to be spreading.

"Hold on, love, help's almost here."

The sirens pierced the air as the cars negotiated the drive. Once close, their headlights illuminated the scene. The sheriff was first on the scene, followed by two deputies. Assessing the situation quickly, Brett directed his men to take care of the people near the barn, radioed for an ambulance, then hurried over to Ty and Holly.

"She okay?" he asked, hunkering down.

"Shot. She's bleeding pretty badly," Ty said, pressing against the wound.

"What happened?" the sheriff asked.

Ty explained he'd awoken when the horses started making noise. Looking out, he saw the flickering of a small fire. After dressing as quickly as he could, he woke Marty and started out when a bullet slammed against the door frame, keeping him in the house. He had no idea who it was, or why.

"Marty is holding them at gunpoint. One is shot, I think."

Holly gave her side of the story briefly, holding on

to Ty's wrist, wishing the pain wasn't so sharp. How she'd seen the riders silhouetted against the starry sky when she came to see Ty.

More sirens sounded as two big fire engines roared into the ranch.

Ty looked at the barn, now almost totally engulfed. The heat was intense even as far from it as they were.

"It's gone," he said. "Dammit. I just got a supply of hay in, too."

"Looks like it's a lost cause. The firefighters will have to focus on saving the house and other buildings and let that one go," the sheriff said. "Take care of her." He nodded to Holly. "I'm going to question those men."

The deputies had one man in handcuffs. The other had been dragged away from the fire but lay on the ground.

Ty gathered Holly in his arms, resting her against his chest while his left hand continued to apply pressure to the wounds, entry and exit.

"Stay with me, sweetheart. You're going to be fine."

"You a doctor, now?" she asked grumpily. She didn't feel anywhere close to fine.

"No, but I've come too far to lose you now. I love you, baby. Always have."

"Except for when you loved Connie," she said, beginning to feel light-headed.

He kissed her cheek. "I'll tell you a secret. But never tell Billy. I didn't love Connie, not like I loved you. But I cared for her. I thought we could be content."

"Now?" She was afraid she was losing consciousness. If things came out right, she wouldn't mind being shot—as long as she recovered. Surely she couldn't die at this stage.

Yet Jennifer Alverez had been about Holly's age when she died. Her own mother had died before she was thirty. Life had no guarantees.

"Now I want you to marry me. Make me happy. Just love me, Holly. God knows I love you to death."

"Maybe not a good comparison right now," she murmured.

"Trouble here?" one of the fireman squatted by Holly, medical kit in hand.

"Hold on, sweetheart," Ty said. "I know it hurts like blazes."

"As soon as we get you stabilized we'll have you at the hospital in no time," the paramedic said.

"Quicker if you'd fixed that driveway," she mumbled.

He laughed. "That's my girl. Never say die."

"Ty!"

He smiled down at her, brushing her hair from her face with his free hand. "You're going to be fine, I promise. Now accept my proposal and put me out of my misery. Please, Holly, marry me."

Holly wanted to say yes, but her lips wouldn't seem to move. She closed her eyes and slid into the darkness.

THE PARAMEDICS COULDN'T revive her.

"Daddy?" Billy came running out of the house, still in his pajamas. "The barn's on fire! Where's Ace. Did he burn up?" He came up to Ty, nearly in tears, and saw Holly. "Is Holly hurt?"

"Hey, pardner. It's okay. Your pony is fine. One of those men let the horses out so they wouldn't get burned. They took off for the hills but I expect they'll be back when it quiets down here and they get hungry. If not, we'll go after them."

Billy watched as the paramedic worked on Holly.

"She's bleeding," he said.

"She got shot by one of the men who burned the barn," Ty said, also watching closely.

"Is she going to be okay?" Billy asked, his eyes wide.

"I sure hope so, son." Ty said. He'd tried to be calm for Billy's sake, but he was afraid if the paramedics didn't stop the bleeding she would die.

The firemen pressed some fresh cloths against the wounds. He wrapped a tight bandage around her entire torso.

The ambulance arrived at the ranch moments later. Ty asked Marty to call Maria Dennis to come for Billy, he was going with Holly.

"Can't ride with us," the paramedic said as Holly was loaded into the ambulance.

"The hell I can't," Ty said, climbing in right beside her. "I'm sticking to her like glue. Deal with it."

"Yes, sir," the paramedic said. "Guess we can take you after all."

THE NEXT FEW HOURS WERE the worst Ty had ever spent. Even worse than the summer he hadn't been able to see Holly. Worse than the day she'd told him to leave. Then he'd been angry. Now he was afraid. What if she didn't make it? What if his talk had been hot air and she was so seriously injured she died?

They took her right into surgery and barred him from going with her. He paced the waiting room until a nurse brought him a set of scrubs to replace the bloody jeans he wore. He sponged the blood off his chest and arms in the men's room, then put on the scrubs. She'd given him a plastic bag as well, so he stuffed his jeans in that.

Then went back to pacing the surgery waiting room.

It gave him time to think. Holly had to be all right. And she had to marry him. He realized now that her father was something he'd have to learn to handle. He wasn't going to deny himself, or Holly, the chance at happiness because of the past. They'd lost ten years they might have had together if not for Ryan Bennett. He wasn't letting the man come between them ever again. If Holly wanted to have a relationship with her father, Ty wouldn't stop her. But it would be a long time, if ever, before he'd welcome the man into his home.

He just wanted her to choose to marry him. He wanted her to live. He wasn't sure what he'd do if she died.

Time moved slowly. The sheriff checked in briefly. John and Sara Montgomery came to the hospital to sit with him. They let him know Maria had Billy so Ty was not to worry.

He didn't worry about his son. But he couldn't stop the anxiousness about Holly.

At long last the surgeon came out of the operating room.

"How is she?" Ty asked, jumping up.

"She's going to be fine. It took a couple of units of blood to get her pressure back up. We cleaned and sutured the wounds. She'll be sore for a while, but there'll be no long-lasting damage. The bullet missed every vital organ."

"Thank God," Ty said reverently.

"Amen." Sara hugged Ty, then her brother.

"She'll be in recovery for the next half hour or so. Once she's stable, we'll take her up to a room. You can join her now, if you like."

"As soon as I make some calls. Thank you, doctor," Ty said, shaking the man's hand.

"She'll be fine," the surgeon repeated.

The Montgomerys stayed a bit longer, then left. It was after dawn and work started early in the summer months.

Ty called Maria to make sure it was okay if Billy stayed there for a while and updated her on Holly's condition. Then he called the sheriff's office to find out what he could about the situation. He wanted answers beyond the few reassurances Brett had given him earlier that morning.

HOLLY SLOWLY CAME AWAKE. Her side hurt. She was thirsty. Her head ached. Sighing softly, she opened her eyes. Ty sat beside her bed, watching her.

"How are you feeling?" he said, leaning closer and taking her hand, being careful not to disturb the IV line.

"Awful, actually," she croaked. She glanced around. She was in the hospital, hooked up to some kind of drip, and the high bed was the only one in the room. "A private room. Nice."

"Only the best," he said, squeezing her hand lightly. "Need any meds?"

"What I really need is a big glass of cold water," she said. "I'm so thirsty."

"Okay." He released her to reach for a glass on the tray table. He unwrapped the straw next to it. "It bends so you don't even have to lift your head," he said, positioning for her.

"That's wonderful," she said after drinking her fill.

As he replaced the glass, she asked, "So what's the story. What happened?"

Ty brought her up to speed on the situation at the ranch.

"It was Hank Palmer, right?"

"No. Rich Donner and Brian Afree—both work for Ben Hudgins. I talked to the sheriff once I knew you were going to be all right. Rich's also here. Apparently one of the shots I made nailed him. He's going to be fine, too, not that I'm as happy about that as about your recovery. But it's good to know I didn't kill a man."

"I'm glad of that, too. But it was self-defense. Does anyone know why they torched the barn?"

"You aren't going to like the reason," Ty said slowly, recapturing her hand, threading his fingers through hers.

"What?"

"Ben Hudgins wanted to marry you. He saw you as a means to get his hands on the Rocking B once your dad was incapacitated. Apparently he thought you needed a man around to run the place. He doesn't have much hope Ryan's going to make a full recovery, so he figured he'd make things difficult enough for you that you'd turn to him. Play his cards right and he'd have it all—you and the ranch. Only you weren't turning to him. So he figured he'd make me more interested in my own ranch than helping you—that's when the minor vandalism started. The barn was a backfire. He was only trying to burn some of the hay."

"Is he crazy? We dated only a couple of times. Then I let him know I wasn't interested. I wasn't going to change my mind!"

"I guess that's just another little detail he'd have to take care of," Ty said.

"So he and his cowboys were responsible for the cut

fence, the damaged windmill and the coil of barbed wire on your range?"

"And a broken truck at your ranch you didn't realize was sabotage, some missing cattle and a couple of other things, apparently. Brian couldn't wait to give the sheriff an earful. He wants some protection, claimed he was doing his job."

"Attacking you and your place?" she asked in disbelief.

"Hudgins seemed to think you were forming some sort of attachment to me. He wanted to run me out of town. God, just like a hundred years ago in the west," Ty said, shaking his head. "I don't think he thought things through. A man can be excused for that if he's crazy for some woman."

She gave him a disapproving look. "I can't believe you said that. Did he really think I would come around? He's years older than I am. He's closer to my dad's age than mine. And I already told him I didn't want to date him. Don't people have to get close before discussing marriage?"

"Must have thought you were playing hard-to-get or something. He won't be ranching anywhere for a while. There's a high penalty for arson and shooting people. And his hands ratted him out," Ty said.

"So much for good neighbors," she murmured gazing out the window. "I thought for sure it was Hank."

"You seem to be the most popular woman in Turnbow. Hank wants you, Ben. Me."

She looked at him.

"But they wanted the Rocking B. I want *you*," Ty said. "Only you."

She now remembered every word he said last night, until she'd lost consciousness.

She licked her lips.

"I asked a question before you decided to check out for a while," he said softly.

"I remember."

"When you passed out, I was so afraid I'd lose you. I never want to experience that fear again. Marry me, Holly. Love me and Billy and any kids we have together. We'll do what we planned when we were teenagers, raise cutting horses, train them, and enjoy life on our terms and…"

"Yes," she interrupted.

"That's it?"

"Do you need more?"

"'I love you, Ty,' would be nice," he said.

"I love you, Ty. And I love your son. I would be so proud to be your wife."

He scooped her up, disregarding the IV drip, and kissed her with all the love in him.

The heartache of the last ten years faded as his kiss promised the brightest future of all—a future with the only man she'd ever loved.

Holly was deliriously happy. "I'll have to call Sara and tell the men at the ranch."

"How soon can we get married?"

"Tomorrow would work," she teased.

"I'll take you up on it."

"Just kidding. I do not plan to be married in this hospital bed. How long before I can leave?"

"A couple of days. So plan to come home with me. You can't manage at home alone."

"I'll see if Sara can put me up. She can take care of

me. Or I can call my Aunt Betty. You have a barn to re-build."

"Funny thing, that. The sheriff told me Carl is orga-nizing the ranchers to hold an old-fashioned barn-raising. As soon as the site's cleared by the arson investigator, they plan to order the lumber and set the date."

"That's what friends do—help out friends," she said, touched that the ranchers were rallying around for a rel-ative newcomer. Yet, Ty had been raised in Turnbow and his father had been an honorable man. Some of the old-timers must know the story of her father and Ty's mother. And that Jose chose not to prosecute when he might have had cause.

"Probably because I helped at the brandings," he said.

"Or maybe they recognize one of their own. Accept and be happy."

"And pay forward when the opportunity arises," he said. "You're right, we can't have some small wedding at your hospital bed. We're going to invite the entire town!"

She laughed. "Let's throw a party to outshine Sara's."

EPILOGUE

"CAN I GO SWIMMING now, Mommy?" Billy asked impatiently. He'd helped unload the cart, spread the blanket on the banks of the river and hauled the diaper bag. She settled Jenny Marie on the blanket. The baby kicked her legs and stared up at the leaves of the old cottonwood.

"If Daddy's ready to watch you," Holly said, sitting beside her daughter. The baby was two months old. Holly still couldn't believe this miracle. Ty tethered the horses and pony in some shade and headed their way. This was a special treat. They had settled down after the wedding to build their ranch and business. Ty's expertise and award-winning work was the draw. She was happy to help in basic stock training while he was now branching out into training both horses and cowboys to compete.

Ben Hudgins and his two cowboys had been sentenced to several years in prison. At least Ty and Holly didn't have to worry about any more sabotage these days.

"Can I go swimming, Daddy?" Billy asked, almost jumping up and down in anticipation. The water was low, barely two feet deep in most parts. Soon after the wedding they'd erected a gate on the fence that allowed them easy access to this favorite spot by the river. It had made it easy for Holly to continue to run the Rocking B until her father had been ready to resume the reins. Now they snuck across occasionally. The riverbank on the Bennett side had a much gentler slope into the water.

"Sure. Just stay close until I get there," Ty said. He sat beside Holly and brushed his fingers against Jenny Marie's cheek. "She's good and shaded here," he said.

"I'll move her if the sun shifts," Holly said. "Go get wet."

They heard a horse approaching from the Rocking B. Standing, Ty watched as Ryan Bennett slowly rode up. He dismounted and stood there, gazing at his daughter, granddaughter and son-in-law. He hadn't been mobile enough to attend his daughter's wedding. Holly hadn't waited.

It had been almost Christmas before he'd been able to return home, even with his sister coming to help out for a few months. He now had a live-in housekeeper. He'd never been to Ty's ranch, but often invited Holly over. She had rarely done so, preferring to keep her visits to a minimum so not to upset her husband. She felt torn, longing to regain the affection and respect she'd once had for her father and yet wanting to make it up to both Ty and herself for the long years apart.

"Nice afternoon for a swim," he said.

Billy came to stand near Holly. "Who's that?" he asked.

Holly was surprised to realize Billy had probably never seen her dad before. Ryan rarely attended the parties Sara gave. And he hadn't extended any invitations to Ty or his son.

"That's my father," she said. "Your grandfather," she added deliberately, holding her father's eye.

Ryan looked startled, then thoughtful. He smiled slowly at the little boy, who would be attending first grade in the fall.

"Actually, I came to talk to Ty," Ryan said.

"About?" Ty asked, going on the alert.

"I hope you'll have a bit of understanding about things, now that you have a wife and daughter. I did what I thought best, but am man enough to admit when I'm wrong. I'm sorry that I kept you two apart."

Holly held her breath. That couldn't have been easy for her father to say. And had been a long time coming. Would Ty meet him halfway and accept the apology?

"I know I'm not the man you wanted for her. But I love her and always will," Ty said stiffly.

"Actually, it turns out you're exactly right for her. I've never seen Holly so happy."

He hesitated a moment, his expression bleak. "And I need to apologize for something else. I've grieved for your mother since the day of the crash. What I did was wrong, but I want you to know I only went after her to calm her down. I loved her. I'm so sorry for her death. And I'm sorry I didn't care about what I was trying to take away from you and your father," Ryan said humbly.

"Want to go swimming, Grandpa?" Billy asked oblivious to the tension between the adults.

Holly looked at Ty. Would he order her dad away? Or find it in his heart to forgive. The past couldn't be changed. But the future could. She held her breath as she watched her husband. Then gradually she relaxed. She trusted Ty.

"Not everyone likes the water like you do, Billy," he said easily. He looked at Ryan, his expression hardening for a second. Then the anger seemed to dissipate some. "But maybe your grandfather would like to sit near the river and watch you while you swim," he said.

Ryan nodded, tied his horse and smiled gratefully at Holly. "And then I'd like a chance to hold that precious little girl of yours. She reminds me of you when you were a baby."

He walked to the river's edge and sat on the ground as Billy stripped down to his bathing suit and joyfully splashed in the slow-moving water.

Ty sat beside Holly.

"Thank you," she said softly.

"He's right. Now that I have you and Jenny Marie, I can understand him better. I'd chase after you with all I had if you turned away. He was wrong to try to seduce my mother, but I know he didn't intend for the crash to happen." He put his finger to his daughter's tiny palm and watched as she gripped it. "And I can see how a father would want only the best for his baby girl. I was thinking we shouldn't let her date until she's thirty."

Holly laughed, knowing everything would be all right. Ty had a heart as big as Texas. "We'll talk more about that as she approaches her teens. But for today, I'm happy to let you go on thinking that, sweetheart. Could any woman ask for more? I have you, my children and now I have my father back."

"Yeah, life is good." Ty leaned over to kiss the woman he'd always loved.

* * * * *

Turn the page for a sneak preview of
IF I'D NEVER KNOWN YOUR LOVE
by
Georgia Bockoven

From the brand-new series
Harlequin Everlasting Love
Every great love has a story to tell.

One year, five months and four days missing

There's no way for you to know this, Evan, but I haven't written to you for a few months. Actually, it's been almost a year. I had a hard time picking up a pen once more after we paid the second ransom and then received a letter saying it wasn't enough. I was so sure you were coming home that I took the kids along to Bogotá so they could fly home with you and me, something I swore I'd never do. I've fallen in love with Colombia and the people who've opened their hearts to me. But fear is a constant companion when I'm there. I won't ever expose our children to that kind of danger again.

I'm at a loss over what to do anymore, Evan. I've begged and pleaded and thrown temper tantrums with every official I can corner both here and at home. They've been incredibly tolerant and understanding, but in the end as ineffectual as the rest of us.

I try to imagine what your life is like now, what you do every day, what you're wearing, what you eat. I want to believe that the people who have you are misguided yet kind, that they treat you well. It's how I survive day to day. To think of you being mistreated hurts too much. If I picture you locked away somewhere and suffering, a weight descends on me that makes it almost impossible to get out of bed in the morning.

Your captors surely know you by now. They have to recognize what a good man you are. I imagine you working with their children, telling them that you have children, too, showing them the pictures you carry in your wallet. Can't the men who have you understand how much your children miss you? How can it not matter to them?

How can they keep you away from us all this time? Over and over, we've done what they asked. Are they oblivious to the depth of their cruelty? What kind of people are they that they don't care?

I used to keep a calendar beside our bed next to the peach rose you picked for me before you left. Every night I marked another day, counting how many you'd been gone. I don't do that any longer. I don't want to be reminded of all the days we'll never get back.

When I can't sleep at night, I tell you about my day. I imagine you hearing me and smiling over the details that make up my life now. I never tell you how defeated I feel at moments or how hard I work to hide it from everyone for fear they will see it as a reason to stop believing you are coming home to us.

And I couldn't tell you about the lump I found in my breast and how difficult it was going through all the tests without you here to lean on. The lump was benign—the process reaching that diagnosis utterly terrifying. I couldn't stop thinking about what would happen to Shelly and Jason if something happened to me.

We need you to come home.

I'm worn down with missing you.

I'm going to read this tomorrow and will probably tear it up or burn it in the fireplace. I don't want you to get the idea I ever doubted what I was doing to free you or thought the work a burden. I would gladly spend the rest of my life at it, even if, in the end, we only had one day together.

You are my life, Evan.

I will love you forever.

* * * * *

Don't miss this deeply moving Harlequin Everlasting Love story about a woman's struggle to bring back her kidnapped husband from Colombia and her turmoil over whether to let go, finally, and welcome another man into her life.

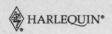

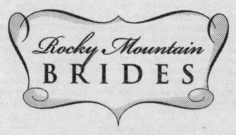

REQUEST YOUR FREE BOOKS!
2 FREE NOVELS PLUS 2 FREE GIFTS!

COMING NEXT MONTH

#1410 ALL-AMERICAN FATHER • Anna DeStefano
Singles…with Kids
What's a single father to do when his twelve-year-old daughter is caught shoplifting a box of *expired* condoms? Derrick Cavennaugh sure doesn't know. He turns to Bailey Greenwood for help, but she's got troubles of her own....

#1411 EVERYTHING BUT THE BABY • Kathleen O'Brien
Having your fiancé do a runner is not the way any bride wants to spend her wedding day. Learning it's not the first time he's done it can give a woman a taste for revenge. And when a handsome man gives her the opportunity to do just that, who wouldn't take him up on it? Especially when it means spending more time with him.

#1412 REAL COWBOYS • Roz Denny Fox
Home on the Ranch
Kate Steele accepts a teaching job at a tiny school in rural Idaho. The widow of a rodeo star, she's determined to get her young son away from Texas and the influence of cowboys. Then she meets Ben Trueblood. He's the single father of one of her pupils— and a man she's determined to resist, no matter how attractive he is. Because he might call himself a buckaroo, but a cowboy by any other name…

#1413 RETURN TO TEXAS • Jean Brashear
Going Back
Once a half-wild boy fending for himself, Eli Wolverton is alive because Gabriela Navarro saved his life. They fell in love, yet Eli sent her away. Now she has returned to bury her father. He, like Eli's mother, died mysteriously in a fire—and Eli is accused of setting both. When Gaby and Eli meet again in the small Texas town they grew up in, one question is uppermost in her mind: is the boy she adored now the man she should fear…or the only man she will ever love?

#1414 MARRIED BY MISTAKE • Abby Gaines
Imagine being jilted on live TV in front of millions of people…. Well, that's not going to happen to this particular bride at Adam's TV station—not if he can help it by stepping into the runaway groom's shoes to save Casey Greene from public humiliation. Besides, it's not as if it's a real wedding. Right?

#1415 THE BABY WAIT • Cynthia Reese
Suddenly a Parent
Sarah Tennyson has it all planned out. In two months she'll travel to China to adopt her beautiful baby girl. But that's before everything goes awry. Apparently what they say is true…life *is* what happens when you're busy making plans.

HSRCNM0307